D1084564

AUNTY HIGH OVER THE BARLEY MOW

Dennis T. Patrick SEARS

AUNTY HIGH OVER THE BARLEY MOW

McCLELLAND & STEWART

The Canadian Publishers
McClelland and Stewart Limited
25 Hollinger Road, Toronto M4B 3G2

Printed and bound in Canada

With gratitude to
Robert and Frances Van Pelt,
and Dale and Stanley Pietak.

Canadian Cataloguing in Publication Data

Sears, Dennis T. Patrick, 1925-1976.
  Aunty high over the barley mow

ISBN: 0-7710-8026-3

I. Title.

PS8587.E27A95   C813'.5'4   C77-001344-9
PR9199.3.S43A95

Dedicated to the memory of my long dead aunts: Rosie, Minnie, and Theresa Aileen, all of whom died in the twenty-second year of their lives. May their shades be now eternally at rest.

And when the grey cocks crow and flap,
And winds are in the sky,
"Maurya, Maurya, are ye dead?"
You'll hear Patch Shaneen cry.

Joseph Campbell

At first there was me and
Bride–Bride being my sister, you see, only that
was short for Brigid–there being women of that
name in the family of my father. Mother fought
hard against naming my baby sister "Brigid."
She said it was a name for housemaids and vaudeville jokes, but my father was stern, so Brigid it
was. And I was young and Bride younger still,
and there was the two of us against the whole
world because our parents didn't count and all
adults were foreigners. And so we ran and leaped
and laughed and the blue earth spun . . . Now
Bride is gone and there's only me–and O God,
I do be growing old. . . .

I

For I was ten and Bride barely eight when our father got the letter from his brother down east in Ontario saying grandfather was dead at eighty. Dead and laid away among the other departed Fallons in the cemetery on the sand hill where the green-black pines whispered day and night around and over the bones of Carden's departed.

In that summer of nineteen and thirty-three our family was at the dinner table eating side pork and fried potatoes when John James, the next neighbour south but one, came back from the Saskatchewan hamlet of Carmine with a week's mail for us. Father was chewing a rind and looking out the window where the locusts were munching away the wheat as far as the eye could rove. The grasshoppers munched and the drought dried and the rust rusted. The crops were all gone and hope was all gone and courage after it.

Father opened the letter, and when he'd read it he tossed it before my mother with a hard swallow deep in his throat. Mother burst into easy tears that dried on the vine as she read on to where Uncle Miles said grandfather willed the Carden place—five hundred acres, buildings, three steers, and a lame horse to father and what did father intend to do about it.

It took two months. Two months to sell the cows and the implements and turn the horses loose on the prairie to run as they chose. And when that was over and done, my parents and Bride and me all got on the train and fled like the swallows to a green place called Carden where father had been born and where, he said, real apples grew on flowering trees and all you had to do was reach up and pull one down and bite into it until the juice ran.

We were the best of three days getting there. When Bride and I were not sleeping, stretched out on the hard black seats with a coat over us, we ranged up and down the aisles staring at people as poor as ourselves or hanging around the smoker where men played poker for a nickel ante.

Uncle Miles met us at Dalton Station and drove us to our new home. Uncle Miles was a tall, lean man like my father; bitter-eyed and arms heavy with muscle.

When we trooped off the train, father carrying a suitcase in either hand with a third tucked under his arm, Uncle Miles approached slowly—almost reluctantly. Father set down the luggage on the slivered boardwalk and the brothers shook hands, briefly. Neither smiled. Except for a curt nod Uncle Miles ignored mother. Bride and I hung tightly to each other's hands, staring up at the grave, unsmiling uncle of ours. He looked down at us and a little quiver like a flick of light ran across his lips.

"I'm not strong on remembering names," Uncle Miles said to father, inclining his head at Bride and me.

"Patch and Bride," he let the names trickle around his tongue when father told him. "I would have thought the girl would have favoured mother." Uncle Miles seemed disappointed. "She looks like you, Ward; you and the old man."

Uncle Miles led us in the direction of his automobile without offering to help carry our luggage. The car was elderly–a touring model, with a wreck of a canvas top supported, more or less, by folding metal braces. The car had a pungent, though not unpleasant, odour of cow manure. Uncle Miles smelled of cow manure, too; there were dried flecks of it on the welts and sides of his high-topped, laced boots over which his pants were rolled.

Father sat in the passenger's side beside Uncle Miles; mother, Bride and I crowded in with the suitcases in the rear. Miles drove too fast for the gravel roads; the car jounced and thudded into and across mudholes. For the first few miles no one spoke.

"You're a wealthy man now, Ward." Uncle Miles was dry-voiced. "You always were the old man's fair-haired lad. The oldest son. 'Ward's going to be like me when he grows up,' " he mimicked.

"I never asked him for a thin dime." Father's voice was cold and even. "You were the one that lived the nearest."

"Absence makes the heart grow fonder," Uncle Miles snickered into his dark red moustache.

· "For somebody else." Father kept his eyes ahead of him on the road.

"What with you and the whores he kept in stock the old man hadn't enough fondness or money for anyone else."

"Were you not there for his last illness?"

Uncle Miles laughed–a short, jarring sound. "What illness? He was as sound as a horse and went out like a light. Heart, I suppose," he added.

"I understand the mortgage is big enough to cover the place," father said.

Uncle Miles shrugged. No one spoke until we reached Grandfather Matt's place.

When we drove into the yard we saw a house of raw red brick looking back at us out of two dead windows, each

11

flanking a door, under the sagging roof of a verandah pulled down like an eyebrow that gave the house a frown.

The first thing we kids did when we boiled out of the car was to run some stretch back into our legs. It was September time and the morning sun was glowing across the pasture fields and the crown of hills beyond. We ran and ran to where a running flame seemed to be raging about the foot of a high hill, and when we came to the place of the fire we found it but a band of dwarfed trees with leaves like banners all turned scarlet by autumn.

"Sumacs," said Uncle Miles dryly, when we returned boasting and filled with beauty. "Just sumacs."

And then we knew Uncle Miles was like all the others who in their years grew old and walked in fog and heard no bird sing nor saw a flower dance.

The dead hand of grandfather lay heavily over the inside of the house. He was a man who ran to medicines rather than doctors, and there were elixirs and nostrums and dried brown pills stuffed and crannied into every nook and niche the house afforded, although separately or in combination they were unable to kill the old gentleman. He died sitting up at the kitchen table in the midst of composing a love letter to a woman in Pittsburgh. Uncle Miles said his heart got fed up and quit on him and so he died. Medicaments and books. Books were piled on tops of bureaus and scattered through cupboards. Worms got into them and mice wrecked the pages so that when you picked up a book the pages came fluttering out in nibble-sized pieces. There were encyclopaedias and books on taming the horse; books about Greek gods and Christian devils and alien religions and heathen worship. There were books of verse, books of prose, and books that were neither. I guess there must have been a thousand.

The whole house save cellar and attic was cut up into rooms and warrens that the sun could not get at to warm them up or clean them out. If the sun could have got past the two gloomy firs that sulked on either side, the dull green blinds yanked down over each dead-flyed window would have been too much for it. Above the upright organ in the parlour the ghost of my grandmother looked out from a great oval frame, while ranged above her like the moons of Jupiter were each and every one of her three dead daughters—my aunts—slain by tuberculosis in the bloom of life, and all in their twenty-second year. Grandmother died in the year of '05 of the same wasting consumption, turning on her bed of death to point to the east, croaking deep in a swollen throat, "Fire! fire! fire!"

"She's crazy," the watchers murmured. "It's the delirium on her." But that night before the flush of dawn, a nearer, redder flush was seen and that was the house and barns of Michael Touhy going up in smoke and the work of a lifetime with them.

When his wife died a string was cut inside my grandfather. He turned to drink and riot and women with ostrich feathers in their hats and clock-worked stockings. They came from all over, these women: from Montana and Sydney, Nova Scotia and Portland, Maine and Port Arthur, Ontario. He sent for them and they came and grandfather paid their way, and when they grew tired of his eternal lusting and bad manners they flew back the way they came. The way grandfather got them was he put advertisements in papers saying here was a gentleman-born in need of a housekeeper and only those sound of wind, limb, and morals need apply. And when they'd come grandfather would leer at them and offer them whiskey until they'd fright and run and lock the bedroom door against the jars and knocks from grandfather laughing and raging without like a buck rat frantic to be mounting his doe. Uncle Miles, who never married or felt a woman's thigh and was therefore pure, denounced the shame of it all as did his aunt Kate who went to confession every week and rattled off all her sins bar one because on the death of her man—old Con Carrigrew—she shared her bed with a hired man named Darmody for any number of years until one night he packed his turkey and disappeared in the direction of the main line.

If the house was surly the barn was not. The barn was a great, grand, vaulted place with lightning rods of porcelain balls beneath spear points and wires from each grounding into the turf beside the foundation stones. When Bride and I tipped the iron latch of the man-door set in one of the huge doors leading to the threshing floor and stepped inside we found a cathedral of golden sheaves rearing toward the roof beams, with very seaman-like ladders running up either mow. I remember Bride skinning up a ladder like a cat.

"Look, Patch," she gusted, then leaped down into the stacked barley sheaves in the mow below.

There was forever a music within and around that barn. Inside it was the sighing of wind through gable and crack, the flutter and coo of tenant pigeons, the chatter and fuss of wee brown sparrows. Age had tinted and hued every beam and board the colour of pipe tobacco. Under the V of the roof ran a track of iron for the unloading of hay, and along this track I swung hand over hand, a breathtaking swat away from the floor below, until I could reach an aperture in the roof that was one of the ventilators. The ventilator was a bit of a wooden house with slatted sides making an open grill through which stagnant airs from inside might escape. The vent had a metal vane that told the direction of the winds: a prancing horse pawing toward the four corners of the universe, unmindful of weathers, come rain, come hail, come sleet, come snow, come lightning and thunder.

We'd always been close, Bride and I: out on the Saskatchewan prairie we'd gone gathering the wild sweet-briar roses, climbing the girlish aspens to raid a crow's nest, making a tepee by the tying together of the tops of buffalo-berry in which to play the game of "wild Indian." We were close, but different. From the perspective of forty and more years I believe now that Bride's was the greater courage. I've seen her blue eyes grow round and large with terror until they were almost black set against the paleness of her face, but always Bride would hold her ground or advance as bravely as the long-dead scarlet-coated British who marched at the double-quick up Bunker's famous hill.

No Fallon that walked was a physical coward, but inside me I never possessed the strength of my sister. Hard of fist and harder of head I could rage and fight, but when the emotional pressure rode me like Lugan's Black Mare my guts crumbled and became curds–my blood whey.

Of course we fought. Bride would often retire into a little play-world of her own where I could not follow. She'd get hold of an old Eaton's or Simpson's mail-order catalogue and sing out of them. It was comical at the time to hear her; I haven't smiled at the memory for many a year gone by. Bride would have the door to her bedroom shut and I'd hover jealously outside, ear to the keyhole, listening as she piped in some ungodly melody of her own devising:

"Ladies' patent leather pumps
Three dollars and twenty-five cents,
Good quality rubber douches with vulcanite nozzle–
Only sixty-nine cents or two for a dollar and a quarter . . . "

Then I'd snort with suppressed laughter and mime Bride's voice and ask her to be sure and let me know when she got down to the underwear. There'd be a terrible silence during which I could visualize the flames leaping up to Bride's face. Then the door would open with a rush and out she'd come and be on to me and we'd roll and fight like the gingham dog and the calico cat. Once I yanked hard, several times, on Bride's thick black hair. She looked at me for a moment, then her face crumpled and she fled, leaving a trail of jerking sobs in the air behind her. She shut herself in the outdoor toilet, being so quiet I grew afraid.

"Bride!" I called contritely, digging a bare toe into the earth by the privy door. "Bride! Are you there? Are you all right?"

No answer.

I called several times before she told me to go away and that she hoped I'd be bitten by a garter snake and die slowly and in horrible pain.

The most potent threat of all came next.

"I'm going to tell daddy when he comes in from the fields."

Then the bravado would run out of me like sand through an egg-timer. If father ever caught me playing the bully with Bride, retribution was swift and terrible. Once when my sister and I were at war and I had her down in the yard, me astride her, plastering mud and clay all over her face and neck, father came up all unbeknownst to me and I was caught in a grip of steel and thrown two yards away. This was followed up by father gripping my overalls bib with one hand while he slammed the flat of the other again and again across my face and head until the blood spurted from my nostrils and I couldn't see for the grey haze of pain. Bride, muddied face and all, clung to father's leg, imploring him to stop; she cried we were only playing, but father's rock-hard palm smashed across my face until mother came running from the house.

"Ward!" she screamed. "Stop! For the love of God you'll kill the boy."

Father flung me aside. "By the bleeding Jesus if I ever catch him at his sister again I *will* kill the young bastard." And he strode away, his back taut and square with the rage that was upon him.

Accustomed to the flat roll of the prairie, Bride and I were awed by trees and hills. East of the great barn was strung a limestone ridge and below that a ten-acre basin of balsam and osier the old ones called "The Balsam Swamp." Out of a cleft in the cliff flowed a spring of water tumbling with a gush down the face of the limerock, then sweeping away beneath tag alder and balsam thicket. Bride and myself were tempted to explore the swamp by tracing out the run of the brook in the way the great Champlain poked his head and his French ways into the rivers and streams of Canada. We put a fright on each other by recounting in actual numbers the bear, wolf, and wild-cat population we'd find prowling and savaging the baby

16

wilderness. In did we go, step over step; me to the fore like your own bold huntsman, and Bride close onto my heels, eyes flaring with fear and ears eager for the sounds she didn't wish to hear at all. We ducked under boughs of fir and stepped over downed, dead cedar, following every curve and twist of the brook running black and hard, singing a water song as it raced toward river and sea. And then in the dark, cool stillness where one bird alone struck a fretful note a fearsome monster emerged from a thicket and set himself for the attack.

"Run, Bride!" I screamed. "Run for your life, for it's onto us!"

And run we did, Bride's bare heels scampering before and I lunging behind, and not until we came to where father and Uncle Miles were knocking apart pine stumps for the winter's kindling did we rally. When we blurted our tale father looked quizzically at Uncle Miles.

"There were bears around when we were boys; do you run across the odd one yet?"

Uncle Miles laid his fingers to the side of his nose and blew a jet from his nostril.

"Nah, they don't come down this far anymore. You'd have to go to Minden to see a bear these days. What did you say it looked like, again?"

By common adult consent the monster was judged to be a porcupine, so the old ones went back to knocking splinters of orange-coloured pine from the stumps whilst Bride and I, freed from terror yet sadly chastened, went to look at an empty crow's nest in a great pine hard by the barn but bearing south.

I was a full and manly
sixteen and was taking Lila Kennedy to the
Orange Hall to see a performance of the Swiss
Bell Ringers. Bride was pressing my pants with
the old sad irons, heating them on the cook stove,
one by one, then knifing an edge to the crease of
the trousers to my best suit. I see her now through
the mists of time, slender arms struggling with
the heated irons and her admonishing me to not
be so liberal with the brilliantine, and did I have
a clean handkerchief. And Bride knotting my tie
and stepping back to admire her work. Then as I
left, she stood in the door, blinking back tears;
and she waved a little wave. "Have fun," she
cried. But she knew, and I knew, the world had
turned and things would never at all be the same
again.

2

The farm we'd inherited lay in the Township of Clifden hard against the Carden line. Carden was given over to the wild Irish held in check by the parish priest and a lack of money to spend on drink. Clifden was held in tenure by the Anglo-Saxons, kind, amiable, fundamentalist of religion, prurient of thought and careful of action. The separate school for Catholics, as we were, was four miles distant in the village of Kilmore, but that of Protestant Clifden was a mere hop and skip of a mile and a half east.

The first day Bride and I were to attend the Clifden public school, I awakened to face pure terror.

"I'm feelin' terrible sick, this morning," I complained at the breakfast table. "I'm most unwell: I was awake with the coughing half the night . . . "

Bride snorted over her oatmeal; I shot her a baneful look.

Mother, slouching at the end of the table across from father, her bulbous breasts half crawling out of her nightdress around which was a carelessly slung negligée, put out a wan hand and tested the heat of my forehead.

"You don't seem feverish, Patch," she said in her thin voice. "But you may be coming down with the flu. I hear there's something going around."

Father spooned a dabble of scum from his teacup, frowning. "Do you ever rinse the teapot? I think I just ran into a spider web.

"The only thing that's going around," he added, "are the balance wheels in Patch's head. He's no more sick than Max Baer. He just doesn't want to go to school." Father looked blandly at me. "He's scared he's going to take a licking from some of the proddy-dogs. Keep him at home, Iris; keep him safe and warm in bed and bring him soup on the hour; and if any of the Clifden lads come looking for him—hide him in the root cellar."

Bride burst into laughter. I was savage.

"I'm going," I said furiously. "I didn't plan on staying home. And I ain't no ways scairt of them Clifden fellas."

Bride and I washed and combed and brushed our hair while mother wafted dreamily about the kitchen, rummaging for materials to make our lunches.

There was something hollow and vacant about mother. Her eyes—so light as to appear grey—seemed perpetually out of focus. Thinking back I cannot remember seeing my mother angry. Petulant, certainly, and often vaguely sulky; but I never saw mother light up in a flare of anger. Old Timothy Connolly, whom we were to meet later, declared, "It's a poor piece of steel that has no temper to it." There was little if any steel in mother: a bit of silver, maybe; that and a coating of dross. She reminded me of a useless substance bred in some alchemist's crucible as he sought to turn base metals into gold.

So it was that Bride and I, each with new shoes and ears scrubbed raw, plodded fearfully down the gravel road under tall, cool elms toward the four-square brick edifice holding unknown and therefore awesome qualities.

"I'll not talk to the girls until they talk to me," declared Bride. I clenched my fisted hand around the ring of the honey-pail that held my brown-sugar sandwiches and inwardly vowed to protect my sister even if the boys at Clifden were as big as Max Baer himself.

We were first there–ahead of the teacher. She came at the half-eight, a thin, puling woman of thirty plus. Miss Guildforth had the thin, starved get to her of a neglected horse. She threw up her head at the sight of us and looked down the side of her nose out of spectacled brown eyes as though she was getting set to rear and kick the whipple-tree. I opened my mouth like a gaffed trout but nothing emerged, so Bride came to the fore and saved us.

"I'm Brigid Maeve Fallon," she piped bravely, "and this here's my brother Padraic, but you can call him 'Patch' if you'd rather, for we all do."

So Miss Guildforth took us inside and logged us down in a mighty register book, enquiring of us what grades Bride and I were in.

When we were signed in, documented, and allotted our seats it was time for the nine o'clock bell, the rope of which hung down from a hole in the ceiling behind the teacher's desk. The kids who had been playing and rollicking around outside in the yard filed into the one-roomed school house, some shy, some self-conscious, some indifferent, all of them foreigners to Bride and me. All grades were taught in Clifden School, but as there were only about eighteen pupils it was no great hardship on Miss Guildforth. I had to sit two rows of seats over from Bride, and when we stood to sing the anthem I looked over to give Bride strength and let her know I was there. She was peaky-faced and white and staring straight ahead at the blackboard, her fist a little white knot closed on the edge of her desk.

We sang "The Maple Leaf Forever"–that one where Wolfe the dauntless hero came and planted firm Britannia's flag on Canada's fair domain. There was a picture above the blackboard on the wall behind the teacher showing old General Wolfe in his red coat swooning away in death in the arms of other men in red coats. I looked at Bride again and she was singing out strongly although I knew certain she no more knew the words to the song than I did because out in Saskatchewan we always sang "O Canada" instead.

We sat down then, and everybody bowed their heads while the teacher commenced the Lord's Prayer. I mumbled along with the others until Miss Guildforth swung into the "for thine is the kingdom, the power and the glory" part. I'd never heard the Lord's Prayer decorated with that kind of thing before, so I closed my mouth tight until white ripples showed at the corners of my lips. A big fellow, the next desk over from me, who was watching me pretty close, gave me the tip of his elbow but I stared straight down at the top of my desk. When the prayer was finished the big boy raised his hand and snapped his fingers for attention.

"Miss Guildforth,"–he was an eager weasel–"the new boy didn't say the Lord's Prayer."

The teacher peered over the arch of her nose at me.

"Is that true, Padraic?" she said my name as though it were as difficult of pronouncement as a Greek proverb.

I stared stubbornly at my desk and she repeated the question.

"I never heard that prayer," I blurted. "That's a queer prayer you're all saying–an heretical prayer was you to ask me."

"I'm sorry; I forgot you and your sister are Catholics." Hers was a gracious smile for all of her big nose. "You needn't repeat the words if you'd rather not."

At the ten o'clock recess as we streamed out and into the yard, the big tattler boy caught me roughly by the arm, jerking me sideways.

"What do you mean by saying ours is an heretical prayer? I'm no heretic."

"You are, too–you Protestant bastard!" And I tied into him.

The way my father and Uncle Miles fought was to strike

24

great, loose, swinging blows with arms like mallets and fists like sledges. This boy was too long in the reach for any such tactics: I dug into him like a badger into a sheep dog; like a circular saw into an elm knot. I clung and I bit, I kicked and I hammered. I tore the shirt of him in shreds and reached into his mop of hair with hands like claws, tearing and wrenching.

And there was Bride dancing attendance all around us in a ring. "Kill him, Patch!" she raved. "Kill the dirty christer! Murder him! Chew him up and spit him out!"

But while the element of surprise was with me and I battered my opponent silly he got over the shock and laid his weight into me and so brought me to the ground and sat on me while I wept with fury. I got up at last, dusty and ruffled like a worsted rooster, and Bride helped me over to the pump and washed my face with her handkerchief.

It was a day or two before the other kids could accept Bride and me as anything but outlanders and barbarians, and, thinking back upon it, I can't blame them at all. But time passes swiftly before the minds of children, and it was soon learned that I could hit a long ball and Bride was a dandy shortstop. The turbulence was over and the decks cleared for fresh storms ahead.

I in my sailor suit and being carried off to war, and the train pulling out and I staring from the window with marbles in my throat and eyes burning with tears. And there was Bride, awkward in her first high-heels, running and tripping along the wooden platform, waving her hankie, and the moisture from her eyes making a wreck of her new-made face brave in rouge and powder. And Bride blowing a kiss to me and the sound of her last cry buried in the long, low wail of the locomotive taking me away from home and Bride and the green stretch of Carden, perhaps forever. . . .

3

I heard my parents talking about it far into the night. What little money had been brought from the west was gone and a year's taxes stood unpaid on the place grandfather left to us.

"You'll have to go see the township," said mother in that matter-of-fact way of hers as if everything could be settled by going to see someone.

"Them!" said my father in a quarrelsome manner he had when some fear was astride his back. "You don't know these Anglo-Saxons the way I do; I was born here, don't forget, and raised among them. They stick close together; the Fallons belong on the other side of the line, if they belong anyplace; I can't see me crawling to the council for relief."

"We can't just starve," argued mother. "I haven't a stitch of winter clothes to put on Bride and Patch, and they have to go to school."

Father was silent, but I could sense his exasperation. My parents' bedroom was next to Bride's and across the landing

29

from mine. They had left their door open and most of the conversation was audible.

"I did think, Ward, when we left the prairie, things would be better. You weren't a success in Saskatchewan, either," mother laboured on in her whine. "I was never so ashamed in my life—having to apply for relief and lining up to get mouldy old vegetables people sent out by freight from the east. When I lived at the coast and daddy was alive we never heard of the word 'debt.'"

"There was lots you didn't hear from 'daddy' and there was lots about you your old man didn't know."

"There you go—flinging everything back in my face just because you can't support your family like other men."

"Great Lord Jesus, woman! Don't you know there's a depression? Sure, your old dad was so goddamn tight when he walked his arse squeaked. He wouldn't have paid a nickel to see Christ swim the Atlantic. And where did all of his great stocks and investments go after the Crash? And him dead and your mother dying in the old folks' home in Vancouver because all of what your father left went up in smoke the same as many another tightwad bastards'!"

"I had a good chance—I had lots of good chances to marry well," mother dug away at him.

"It's a living wonder you didn't jump at one of your great 'chances.'"

"I thought you had character . . . I thought you would make something of yourself."

"I did. I made a damn fool of myself when I married you."

"Oh, Wardie." Mother called father "Wardie" when she turned to wheedling.

Father yelled. When he yelled I knew he was at the end of his tether. "All right, goddamn it, I'll go! I'll go."

And the next day he went—and it being a Saturday I went too—to the general store of Abel Coventry. That store was in the hamlet of Mavely, and was half the industry of that place, the other half being a gas station and auto and bicycle repair shop. An oval sign over the single gas pump said IMPERIAL ESSO; the sign squealed with the rust every time the wind sighed. Inside the grocery store smelled of leather, coffee, new denim, and storage oranges. Abel Coventry was a lean string of sixty-five, slumped into a salt-and-pepper suit with a string tie knotted in a bunch at the place on his throat where his Adam's apple protruded and gigged up and down every time he swallowed or gathered a mouthful of cut plug to spit into the cracker box of dry sand over near the great heater. He wore his reading glasses up on his forehead where a little vein jumped and wriggled when Abel was studying hard on something–especially money.

Right now the vein was throbbing, although its owner was leaning over the counter studying the swing of the Esso sign across the road.

"Your father was a wonderful man," he mused. "A wonderful man was Matt."

"I wish he'd been less wonderful and more solvent. I need five hundred dollars, Abel."

Abel came around the end of the counter and walked over to the box and spat a great spit.

"We all need five hundred dollars. Ever try the bank?"

"The one in Woodville?" My father's laugh was harsh and dry. "They hold the mortgage and I can't see how I can scrape up the interest."

The storekeeper rammed his hands in his side pockets while he looked out the window. "I mind when you and Miles was young 'uns," he remarked for no good reason. "I had Miles take me round the place just after old Matt died. That maple bush is worth something. Now was you to . . . "

"I'll not sell the bush. That was my mother's favoured place."

"Your mother," said Abel, not ungently, "is dead and buried these thirty-odd years."

"Twenty-eight." My father caught and pinned Abel down with his stone-cold gaze.

31

The grocer threw up his hands.

"I'll see you through the winter on credit, Ward. I'll see you through the winter. You could trim out some of that hardwood that's taking over your south pasture. Swamp it out where a truck can get at her and she'll fetch maybe five dollars a cord."

We went home, father carrying two gunny-sacks—one to a shoulder—filled with canned stuff and flour and sugar. I trotted after with a gallon can of coal-oil.

The farm that had been my grandfather's was not a farm at all. Little of the land was planted and reaped and the crops stacked. The ground was sour and shallow, the skin of it stretched tightly over the chalky bones of limerock protruding here and there among the prickly-ash and black haw like the ribs of a starved mule. This was grazing land and those who lived upon it were graziers—raisers of beef cattle. These cattle were, in addition to scrubs, stout, roundy Herefords with lamb-curly wool in the middle of their broad foreheads, and polled Angus—midnight black and thick-backed. My father bought a black bull for near-to-next to nothing, it being seven years old and designed to ride by truck into Toronto and be carved into bologna.

"There's a calf or two in the black bastard yet," said my father after the bull was home and circling darkly the inner pole corral that was a milking pen. Bride and I stared at the shambling creature, trying hard to see the calves that were said to be inside him, but all we saw were heaving flanks and two liquid black eyes in back of which was reflected a red glare: the mighty minotaur itself, treading the labyrinth, impatiently waiting the annual sacrifice of seven maidens sent from Athens.

There was the house. Out behind—rearward of the summer kitchen and woodshed hanging onto that—were the remains of an ambitious orchard old Mathias set out when he arrived from Ireland, the gleam of land in his eye, and the silver pounds secure in his breeches. Now an orchard is a domestic idea and like all domestic ideas it requires the hand—and a caresome hand at that—of an attentive man: a hand that prunes and grafts; a hand that sprays; a hand that cultivates. Grandfather's hands were ripping, rending, smashing hands; they could heave and lift and slap silly. These are not the hands needed in a Canadian orchard.

I doubt me greatly was there a dozen fruit trees with sap in their veins left in that autumn of 1933. A few old pensioners, boughs hoary with lichen and riddled with woodpecker peckings, sported gnarled, worm-poddled apples with strips and stripes of tiger-red running down the cream of their cheeks. Could you find a space in the flesh between worm holes to set your teeth you had a great munchful, the cidery juice cold with the frosts of October and sweet with the suns of last summer. Uncle Miles, who had been a soldier and was at the Front and was, by this reason, accustomed to anything, advised Bride and me to grab an apple and eat it fast with our eyes shut.

A handful of plum bushes scrawled along the falling board fence at the rear of the orchard separating its acre from the cow pasture and the plot where Mathias planted his corn and potatoes. The plums and one dainty cherry tree with limbs as round and shapely as the thighs of a grown woman were all, save the apple trees, that was left of grandfather's ambition.

South of the barn were the rolling pastures and tamarack swamps, with here and there a dot of maple or a clump of hornbeam. Far to the back where ran the thread of the river Talbert was the maple bush and a patch of second-growth ash, birch, and beech. Beyond that lay Crown land that was all flat bog and blueberry heath—a place of dread where lay the Bottomless Hole that led straight down to China and in which, generations agone, a man and a team of oxen plunged with never a sight of hide nor hooves of the lot of them again, ever. A high ledge of limestone east of the barn looked over the tamarack and balsam swamp. From the face of the ledge roared a spring of water as frothy as new-run beer; this spring meandered and dandled through the swamp, out the other side, waded a patch of marsh-marigold, flung itself under a rail fence and was off to join the Talbert in its dash to the sea. This, father said, was the Sally Brook, so called for the "sallows" the Irish called willows lining its course.

Father would not cut down the great-boled trees of the maple bush that reared straight to the sky without putting out so much as a limb for seventy feet. He was stubborn about that bush, even if it meant cash in his pocket instead of his unco-signed note in the iron safe of Abel Coventry. Over flapjacks Bride and I heard him telling mother how he intended to cut cordwood out of the deciduous grove over next to the Talbert.

Mother was a very indifferent cook; her bread was sour, her cakes fallen and her pancakes flat as elm boards. I think when they were first married my parents quarreled about this; after a while father stopped complaining and much of the time threw his own vittles into the skillet, eating them half-fried, washed down with coffin-nail tea brewed in a cracked brown pot.

"I remember the old man logging that stretch when I was a kid." Father hacked at a pancake. "Damn it to hell, Iris, these flapjacks are like cast-iron."

"Will Miles help you?" Mother half-lolled in her chair, the bulbs of her breasts breaking out over the top of her night-gown.

Father said that Miles had his own work to do; that he was going to hire Timothy Connolly to cut timber at two dollars the cord.

"Isn't he some kind of a drunk or something?" Mother's gaze crawled languidly around the kitchen window where a potted geranium hovered between life and death.

"He's a kind of a something," father agreed. He rose and emptied the remainder of his breakfast into the slop bucket beneath the washstand.

"You should have saved that for the dog," mother complained.

"The dog," growled my father, "wouldn't eat it." And he

34

stomped out with a slam of the door that set the chimes to jangling on the Westminster clock on its shelf above the wainscotting.

The next day after school let out, Bride and I tore home and ran to the far wood where we could hear Timothy Connolly going chop-chop with his axe. Connolly was a squat, barrel-shaped man of sixty who, according to Uncle Miles, had seen the elephant and had been wondering about it ever since. We watched as he worked with a quick swing of his shoulder, driving the narrow blade of his saw into the plumpness of a downed tree trunk.

"What kind of a tree is that?" I asked, stroking the smoothness of the handle to Connolly's Black Diamond axe.

"It might be a son-of-a-beech, or it might be a son-of-a-birch; on the other hand it might be just a good piece of ash. Get away from that axe before it jumps up and takes nick out of you!"

The brush was piled in a neat windrow; the wood, cut in four-foot lengths and split where large enough, was stacked straight between the stems of two hornbeam. As we watched Connolly notched a kerf a foot above the root of a skin-grey beech that was a foot thick. He notched it, then went down on one knee and sliced from the back through to the notch with his bow saw. When almost through the poor tree gave a wailful crack, then with a rush and roar it fell headlong, taking with it its grand crown of autumn leaves dried the golden colour of pipe tobacco, leaves that subsided into a dying rustle as the tree sank to the earth. I felt a wave of sorrow; it had, that tree, stood so proud and beautiful, lifting its arms to the high heavens, letting the wind breathe prayers through them, letting the birds rest there for the space of a song. The wood-cutter caught my regret.

"Everything that has a time to live," he said, lopping a limb from the trunk, "has a time to die. Me, you, this here tree. Do you know what Shakespeare said about dying? No? I'll tell you; he said death was a debt owed that if paid today we

35

didn't owe tomorrow—or something like that."

I thought of my own death and lying cold and still on the brown earth among brown leaves with my limbs chopped off and I wished heartily I didn't owe anybody the debt of death for the little of life I'd had.

"Come on, Bride," I muttered. "They'll be wantin' us at supper."

4

In late November time a great rain set in; the rain rained for three days until the grey-brown drops went running along the underside of fence rails as fast as a squirrel might gallop. The elderly eavestroughing, long gone to rust and holes, spilled out tiny torrents of wet into the weedy patches beside the house where in years a-gone Grandma Hannah grew her dahlias, phlox and bachelor-buttons. Grandma Hannah was in her grave this twenty-eight years and the same rain that fell upon her neglected beds of flowers fell five miles away on her equally neglected final bed on this earth.

My bedroom was across from Bride's up under the whistly attic where the steady drum-beat of the rain thrummed all night through. I had a ghostly feeling that grandfather was hiding up in the spooky attic, hiding and waiting for a chance to come down in the dark of midnight and pounce on me and Bride. "Are you awake, Bride?" I'd call out in a tiny tremble of a voice—not wanting her to lie alone and frightened. There was never an answer, for Bride, unlike myself, was dead in her slumber the instant her prayers were rattled and her face to the pillow.

When the skies had wept for three days and nights and we

thought it'd go on for forty I awakened on the fourth morning to see a pall of snow stretching from my window to the top of the Fallow Hill and as far as the fancy wandered. I was into my blue denim bibbed-overalls and down into the kitchen where father was poking at a sour fire of green elm.

"I should have cut hornbeam," he was muttering. "I remember hearing the old man say hornbeam would burn green or dry."

I thought for surely that long, bitter winter would never end, nor the earth grow green, nor the sun warm. The white blizzards marched like armies out of the north, swirling and sweeping across the red roll of the Longford Rocks that was called "Shield Country." The great brick house with its wide, draughty rooms and high ceilings kept two box-heaters and the kitchen range roaring all the day and glowing with red embers all night, yet the winter drifts and draughts crept in like white mice through crack and crevice so that mother made and ate breakfast with her Sunday coat—the one with the red fox collar—worn over her nightgown that went all the way down to her slapping slippers. Father took Timothy Connolly away from his growing piles of cordwood and got him to help cut ironwood poles for firewood because ironwood, or hornbeam as some called it, would burn slow and hot come green or cut dry. On Saturdays Bride and I would run after the bob-sleigh and the team when the sleigh was loaded to the tops of the bunker posts with long slender lengths of ironwood fastened hard with chains and a binding pole. The slim ends of the ironwood trailed in the snow of the trail between the tracks made by the runners. After supper and far into the dark when the stable chores were done and the stock tended, father would, by the light of the kerosene lantern, cut the ironwood into stove lengths with a web saw that Timothy Connolly called a Swede saw. Once I asked Connolly why he called a plain old web saw a Swede saw.

"Because," he replied, "only a goddamn fool like a Swede would invent the son-of-a-bitch of a thing."

38

What, I wanted to know, would an Irishman invent?

"Damn fool kids, all mouth and questions," said Connolly.

One cold, raw Saturday Uncle Miles snowshoed the mile and a half from his farm to help father saw up a pile of poles. Uncle Miles had been drinking; father said so.

"Here comes Miles and a bottle," he smiled a tight little smile.

"How do you know, daddy?" asked Bride who, despite the cold, was making sawdust pies beside the saw-horse.

Father went on sawing. "Because Miles has a slight cant to the left when he's been into the jar. And he wouldn't walk all the way up here without enough fuel to get him back home."

When he came closer we could see that Uncle Miles had a lopsided grin on the right side of his face that balanced his cant to the left. Always when he and father met they exchanged few words, but looked at one another as if they were searching out some hold they could grab the other with.

"Got another saw?" Uncle Miles' grin crept further into his cheek.

"There's a buck-saw of the old man's hanging in the woodshed." Father ducked his head toward the shed.

"I could cut faster with my jack-knife. Want a little snort?"

Father continued to cut through the pole he was working on, then he hung the web saw over the saw-horse.

"What you got?"

"Maiden-piss," said Uncle Miles enigmatically.

Father reached out a mittened hand and Uncle Miles handed him a pint sealer he had stowed away in his mackinaw pocket. Father unscrewed the glass and tin top and took a couple of swallows.

"It's piss, all right, but where did you find the maiden?" Father spat into the snow.

Uncle Miles sat on the saw-horse and took a hefty belt out of the sealer jar. He looked critically around. "Where's the rest of the family—or are you and the kids doing all the work? As usual."

"You walk all the way here to give me a hand or stick your nose in my business?" Father's eyes were as cold and bleak as the overhead sky.

Uncle Miles seemed not to notice father's look. He drank out of the sealer. "What'd you marry her for, Ward? If she's as slow in bed as she is around the kitchen . . . "

"Miles! The kids are listening." Father took off his mitts and shoved them in his coat pockets. His fixed stare never left Uncle Miles' face. Miles shrugged.

"When was the last time me and you had a fight, Ward?" he asked almost benevolently.

"You ought to remember better than me–you got the worst of it."

It seems that the Irish haven't the knack of going into a fight cold; they have to talk around it and over it and about it until they've a proper edge on their temper.

"Now that's a point that might just be in dispute," Uncle Miles said agreeably. "Tell you what–let's save it for another day; I went a mite far."

Father nodded shortly, pulled on his mitts and brushed his head at Uncle Miles to move him off the saw-horse. Miles got up and sat on the pole pile and drank clear liquor out of the sealer jar, watching father as he sliced length after length from the ironwood with the web saw. Bride and I carried the cut pieces in and piled them inside the shed, with the knotty and large ends out the way father showed us so the wood pile tended to lean in against the wall instead of tipping out where it could fall over.

Uncle Miles grinned at me and Bride, but we couldn't see anything funny. He took another swig from the jar:

"For I'm a rolling toper
And I'm very seldom sober."

Father looked round at his brother. "How long you been on this tear, Miles?" He sounded concerned.

"Coupla 'r three days." He looked father squarely on.

40

"How long's it been, Miles? Fifteen years—twenty? You're here and she's there and that's the way it is 'n neither you, me, or God up a telephone pole are going to change it or make it different."

Uncle Miles' face kind of crumpled; he drained the jar and tossed it away to be buried in the snow. He started to sing again:

"And so I can't forget her
No matter how I try . . . "

Uncle Miles looked up at father, then looked away. Moisture clung to the corners of his eyes. Bride and I kept our eyes on our rubber boots which we scuffled with the toes in the snow and fresh sawdust.

"You got it all, didn't you?" Uncle Miles' lips pulled back in neither a smile nor a grimace but a quantity of both. "A woman, a family, and now all this." His hand cut a circle.

"Jesus Christ! I had nothing to do with the drawing up of the old man's will. Nobody could have dictated terms to him and damned well do you know it."

"Funny, isn't it?" Miles went on as if he hadn't heard his brother. "I spent three years in the trenches to save the world—for you."

Father shrugged. He began a new cut on an ash pole.

"What did the British ever do for us or our kind?" he demanded. "Who twisted your arm to don the khaki?"

Uncle Miles remained mute.

"Or was it your heart twisted your head?"

"Did you ever love anyone, Ward?" Uncle Miles looked up. "You know, I even loved our old man—until I was old enough to know better. He sure as hell never cared much for me. You were the fair-haired boy until the girls came along. When they died you were all the old man cared about—outside of his fool women he kept about the place.

"You know I came up the day before he died—to see how he was. He'd bought a red rooster from the Clancys. Threw it in

41

with the barred rock rooster and they were going at it fist and tooth. 'Go to it, ye divils,' and him laughing all the while. 'Like you and Ward when youse was calves,' he said. 'Ward was the red one.' He said that because the red rooster had the grey one by the comb and was putting the spurs right to it. Father always knew where the knife would cut the deepest."

Father cut through the pole. He picked up the sawed end and examined the fresh cut.

"This ash was thirty-four years old," he said to no one in particular. He pulled the pole through the saw-horse and started another cut.

"Ed Burke found him dead the next day and came and got me. I got hold of old Carry-me-cross, the undertaker, and while I was waiting for him I looked around to see about the stock. The red rooster was as dead as a pope's pecker: the grey had went at him again during the night and cleaned his plate for him."

Father carefully pulled the saw blade out of the cut and hung the frame over a corner of the saw-horse.

"Get onto your feet and we'll see which rooster is which. I've enough of you for one day."

Uncle Miles shook his head. "Not today, Ward. Not today." He clambered to his feet and latched on his snowshoes.

"Where you off to?" father called to Miles' retreating back.

"Over to Dirty John's. I'm all out of drinkin' whiskey," Miles replied without looking back.

"Miles!" father made as if to follow and bring him back, but Miles never looked round and father went back to his sawing.

That winter was so bad I don't want to remember it, leave be talk about it. There was cold and snow and hunger and mother in her fur coat and raggedy-bottomed nightgown stirring lumpy porridge or burning sour pancakes over the kitchen range. Come to think of it I didn't like my mother much; no more did Bride. But when you're young (and I but reached my eleventh birthday that same winter) you need

42

something—somebody—soft and comforting to cling to—someone in whose lap you can bury your face and cry away the little, biting horrors and spites that hang around schools and the children of those who have more money. Mother, Bride and I learned early, was soft of lap, but there was no comfort to her: she'd pat our heads absently, humming something tuneless and her eyes fixed non-seeing like the eyes of a cow being milked.

Except for the school, where we got bags of oranges and nuts, Bride and I got nothing at Christmas time. After New Year's Uncle Miles, who had been away in Lindsay—the county town—drunk all through the Yule season, came up with a doll that had real hair for Bride and a genuine XL knife for me that I have to this day, and Bride's doll, play-worn though it be, is packed away in the trunk with her other things I no longer take out and look at because I always cry.

But as Timothy Connolly was fond of saying: nothing lasts forever except death and a woman's hatred. One morning in the tail of March, Bride and I were walking the sleigh trail to school; we noticed the snow, still deep and cold-looking, was granulating like white sugar; and there were a trillion and a half tiny fleabugs that hopped and skippered over the surface of the snow. As we bent to watch we heard the long, dark caw of a crow from the beechy wood growing all up the side of Dillon's Mountain—which wasn't a real mountain at all, but a high-rise kind of hill they call a drumlin.

"A crow, Bride!" I cried. "The crows are back! It's spring, Bride, it's spring!"

And we joined hands and capered about in a wild, Maenad dance, and the great warm sun shoved the clouds away from his face and filled the air with warmth and bird-songs.

5

We had kept, that winter, in the great gambrel-roofed barn, several head of yearlings, the milk cow and the dark, sullen bull that, whenever we went near the stall in which he was chained, threw up his massive head and glowered at us from his dark, red, rolling eyes. Also, running free in and out of a foxhole beneath the barn was a small flock of sheep, some with rascally black faces, some with long, white faces, and some with curls growing down their foreheads. The boss of the flock was a thick-set ram, short on temper and long on speed. Bride and I stayed clear of that ram because Timothy Connolly said that rams lived only for the day when they could get a clear shot at some kid's arse and bunt him (or her) clean across the Sally Brook.

The ewes were lambing now, out on the naked, brown hummocks of the pasture south of the barn. In the hollows between the hummocks the melt water had gathered in pools, but the new-born lambs lay on the sun-warmed earth beside their mothers whilst the killdeer birds spun and lamented all across the pastures. The cordwood Connolly had cut had been hauled out to the road, and big red trucks driven by burly men came and hauled it away as far as Lindsay and Cannington and Woodville and all over creation wherever wood was burned.

We did so hate to be trapped in school amid a snarl of sums and grammar, did Bride and me. Trapped and tethered while outside the brooks ran full tilt to catch the river before it reached the lake and got away from them. The crows were as noisy as hens and already starting to build in the pines back of Dillon's Mountain. I stared out of the school window and watched the clover leaping to life under the touch of the sun, seeing a red-tailed hawk fanning his wide tail feathers as he curved and tilted in the high blue air.

"Padraic!"

And the roar of the teacher brought me back to earth and away from the hawk and the crows and the brown brooks running lightly across the meadows.

There was a creek called the Perch curving out from some place behind Dillon's Mountain to glide past the schoolhouse and set the boys mad with longing to be out trying for the suckers and dace in summer or riding the slabs of ice down the road of the current when the fingers of the sun got at them and pried them loose from their hold on the shore and sent them barging away with the melt waters.

We had to cross the Perch on our way to school. There was a wooden bridge of squared cedar and a railing on either side, also of cedar. In times of thaw the Perch ran as swift as a swallow, and on our way home from school Bride and I liked to lean against the railing watching the current bearing away the riff and raff of a winter's gather.

One day after the close of school, I, devilled with the spirit of adventure, walked up the rise of the railings and crossed the horizontal top piece and down the slope of the far side.

"Show-off!" Bride tossed her head.

"Bet you're scairt to try it."

"I'm not scared. I'm not scared. I can do anything you can do, smarty."

"Then le'ssee you do it if you aren't scairt. You can't. You

45

can't. An' you know why? Because girls aren't as good as boys, that's why," I egged at her.

Bride gave me a level look. She set her lunch pail on the planking and slowly began to walk up the 4″ x 4″ rise that was tied into the top rail at a 45° angle. She teetered a little, her arms wide for balance and lifting and dipping like the finger feathers of a turkey vulture feeling for the thermal up-draughts. Bride gained the top bar and pivoted to leer at me in triumph. There was a slip of her foot and a scream and Bride was down in the flood below.

I ran to peer over: Bride must have struck her head on a stone because she was lying in five feet of roiling water, the current tugging at her clothing and a chain of bubbles striving to break clear and being carried off by the rage of the water.

I was around and down the bank as quickly as the wag of a duck's tail; I crashed into the stream, my feet slipping on the stones, the water dragging at me frenziedly. I burrowed down through the foam and caught the scruff of Bride's coat, and with the dead weight of her I went careening to the further bank and sprawled her on the mud, myself beside her half-sobbing with terror and exertion.

She fluttered her eyelids, opened them and looked blankly at me. "Am I drowned altogether, Patch?" she whispered. "Am I in heaven with you?"

So relieved I was I cackled helplessly with laughter. "In heaven, me arse," I told her. "You're on the banks of the Perch and that's as far from heaven as you're likely to get."

Bride clambered to her feet, wet as a musk-rat. Her eyes were on fire.

"Goddamn you to hell, Padraic Fallon!" she screamed (she called me by my full name only when she was in a rage at me).

Bride flung herself up the road toward home. I picked up her lunch pail and followed, wheedling at her to be mollified, but she turned not her head or lent an ear until she was home and in the house.

So preoccupied we were neither Bride nor I paid attention

to a panel truck driven and parked discreetly behind the house beneath the great Spy apple tree. It was a small van of the Pacific Tea Company whose salesman came door-to-door once a month peddling tea, coffee and cocoa.

Bride, wet and muddy, burst in the back door and me on her heels lest she turn informer and blab about me daring her to walk the bridge rail. Mother appeared from the parlour, followed uneasily by a smirk of a man, lath-thin and with a sneering moustache riding his upper lip. Mother stroked faintly with a wan hand at the disruption of her hair; with the fingers of the other she pushed and patted at her skirt.

"Why are you so wet, dear?" she asked Bride who was glaring at the man standing in the doorway between the kitchen and parlour.

"I fell in the creek coming home. Patch pulled me out or I'd have drowned, certain."

I scuffled my feet in relief.

"Well . . . " that vague, unreflective voice of mother's pretended concern. "You'd best go up and put on some dry things . . . " Her voice trailed off uncertainly, but she turned and gave the stranger a soft smile.

"Kids will be kids," the man said, looking at the ceiling, his hands in his pockets jingling coins or keys.

Bride shot him a bitter look, then stamped toward the stairs, trailing branch water. I saw the man raise a questioning eyebrow and mother nod in reply. He flipped a hand at her and went out. The truck rattled down the rutted lane and the sound became lost in the balm-of-gileads.

Later, when Bride had changed into a woolly nightie and we were playing rap-rummy on her bed, I asked her what that tea salesman had been doing in the parlour with mother.

"I hate his guts!" she gritted. I looked at Bride and was surprised to see two tears crawling down her face.

Looking back from the height of over forty years I find I cannot, distinctly, remember the face of my mother. In the dead

47

of night I look at the ceiling while lightning flickers across, driving the shadows into corners from which they spring out again until the next sheet of flame shears through the clouds. On the ceiling I try to find and focus on mother, but she slips away as the lightning-driven shadows retreat to the corners, and I cannot get the grasp of an eye on her. She was like that in life, was mother: evasive, impermanent to the point of vacuity. I realize now mother was possessed of a small store of affection–that there was not enough to go round after she had drained the pool of it for her own benefit. I remember trying to kiss her goodbye when I started school in Saskatchewan; she sort of slid her face sideways so that I but brushed her soft cheek with my lips. I remember the jerking sobs that racked me when I went out of the door, my lunch of brown sugar sandwiches in one hand, and struck out alone and lonely for the distant school and the imagined terrors that stalked within it. I was crying because mother did not kiss me goodbye; no more did she kiss me hello when I returned that afternoon, jaunty with my great success and bearing cardboard cut-outs of animals given me by the teacher. I rushed into the frame farmhouse, waving my treasures, but mother staved me off with a pearl-coloured hand, her light, mild eyes looking out of the kitchen window across the prairie.

"Don't be so boisterous, Patch, please!" She passed her other hand across her eyes as though to clear them of some vision she found distasteful.

Bride fared no better. Worse, in fact. But she gave it up and turned her back quicker than I, did Bride. I kept trying, following after mother like a bunty calf after the cow's gone dry. Bride and I had a string of fights over that. "Mummy's boy," she'd taunt me. I'd counter with, "Daddy's pet," because father was forever bouncing her on his lap or tickling her knees or throwing her up to the ceiling, catching her as deftly as he'd catch an apple on the way down.

Nor can I remember my parents exchanging an embrace or a kiss. They must have made some kind of sexual love; if so I was either too young or too dumb to know about it. At night the door of their bedroom was shut as tightly as Pharaoh's stone tomb, save an occasional time in the heat of summer when it was left on the jar to let the muggy air waver through. I'd either be long asleep by the time father and mother went to bed or else I'd waken to the sounds of them quarreling: mother's voice a whine without edge or hope to it; father's a hard, honed baritone cutting through mother's laments.

I will remember always the spring of '34—not for the near-drowning of Bride in the Perch—but that was the time and year when our mother ran away. It was April running into May and Bride and I were coming from school with a mean sleet spiting our faces, and our hands rough-red from the cold because we were too proud to wear mittens as late as the tail of April. We scrambled over the five-barred gate and ran for the back-kitchen door and the warmth of the great range-stove. Bride had gone in the house before me, as I'd run to the out-house first. Bride came out of the back kitchen, her face set and cold the way it got when her temper was upon her or when the pig ate the blue riband she'd won in school for the hundred-yard dash.

"Mom's gone and the stove is out." Bride's voice, like her face, was tight and cold.

In some ways I've always been as dense as a June fog. "Dad and her likely went to Foxford to get something." I stuck the lifter into a stove lid and stared at the dead ashes.

"On a Tuesday? And would she have left a letter?" Bride tucked her head sidewise at the table—still where the breakfast articles—the greasy plates, and muckery-brown coffee mugs sulked while an early house fly buzzed in solitary happiness about the open mouth of a catsup bottle.

"And besides," Bride went on, "daddy and Uncle Miles went to Islay to buy young cattle, today."

I examined the letter. It was not sealed. I turned it over. Mother's neat, clever hand had written steadily without a quaver marring a loop: *To Ward.*

49

"We'd better not open it," I said, itching to get at it and see what mother had written.

"We'll open it, and if there's any blame it can be on me." Bride always had a way of making a person feel boneless and supine; it was the only thing I ever disliked in her.

She slipped the note paper out of the envelope, reading through it quickly. Then Bride read more slowly, enunciating the words aloud as if I were a tot too young to read for myself: *"Ward—I have gone away and won't ever come back. Don't try to follow me or get me back because I won't come. I have met someone I can finally love; you know I never loved you. As for the kids—they will be better off; they always liked you better than they did me, anyway. Goodbye forever. Iris."*

Bride and I looked at each other across the dish-littered table, listening to the complaining of the fly on the catsup bottle. A streak of moisture ran down from each corner of Bride's eyes.

"Wha'—what yu-you cryin' for?" I couldn't keep the sobs back.

"I'm *not* crying for *her*! She was just a bitch! A hoor and a bitch! I'm crying for daddy."

I wasn't too sure what a whore or a bitch was, although one time in Foxford I heard Fighting Bill Doherty call another man a son-of-a-whore and then there was a fight right out on the street and the other man pitched all bloody and beaten into the dust and made terrible sounds the way a man does when his body and pride have been beaten.

While we stood and looked at each other Uncle Miles' old "490" Chev' puttered up to the front gate with the five crossbars and stopped with a rusty screech of brake bands. Bride gave me a deliberate look and, taking the letter, walked quickly out the back door and went to meet our father who was drinking a bottle of beer with Uncle Miles. When men go to buy or sell cattle they drink a lot of beer. They did that, so said Timothy Connolly, because you could slide a lot farther on bullshit than you could on sawdust.

Father may have been a little drunk because he reached out one iron hand and lifted Bride clear up by the pinafore and gave her a great kiss on the forehead. I hung back a little. I guess I didn't have Bride's courage. I guess I haven't got it yet.

Noting the set whiteness to Bride's face father shook her gently; then catching sight of the envelope in her hand he laughed with a beery gust of breath and cigarette tobacco.

"Oh – ho! My little Brigid's been a bad girl in school today and her teacher wants me to straighten her out with a martingale . . . "

Uncle Miles' eyes narrowed. "Maybe you better read what she's got, Waddie." "Waddie" was the name Miles and his mother called father when they were small and dogging it in homemade knee-pants. Now Uncle Miles only used "Waddie" when he was half-lit and full of affection or when some man-made storm was muttering in the distance.

Father settled Bride on his lap and took the paper out of the envelope. He read the words fast, then once more – slowly, slowly – while the angry blood climbed up his neck to his face through a hard growth of red whiskers. All of the Fallon men had jet black hair on their heads, but their whiskers were as red as a Persian cat's.

Father started up as though to get out of the auto, then settled back and passed the note to Miles. Uncle Miles shook his head. "I know what it says; or damn close to it."

"What d'ye mean – you know? Tell me, goddamn you! Tell me how much you know and how you came to know it."

Miles spat a stub of a cigarette out of the car which had no side-curtains, just a canvas top held up by metal braces that folded in if it was a fine day and the driver wished to take the country airs.

"Oh, hell, Ward! Didn't you know? Didn't you guess? No, you didn't; you wouldn't."

"Who'd she go with, Miles? Who was the son of a bitch?"

Uncle Miles looked helplessly into the furious burning of father's eyes. He cleared his throat. "That asshole that goes

51

around selling door-to-door for the Pacific Tea Company."

"Not that weasel-arsed pimp with the moustache?"

"That was him."

"Well I'll be dipped in shit!" Father reached behind the front seat and pulled a fresh bottle of beer out of the case. When he opened it on a device screwed to the dash-board the beer foamed up and bubbled down the bottle. Father shoved the top into his mouth and drank with long, chugging gurgles.

"We're better off without her, Miles."

"No denyin' it, but what about the kids?"

"Have to get some kind of a housekeeper, I guess. I don't know whether I can afford one, though; not until we sell the cattle in the fall."

"Aunt Kate'd come."

Father scratched the back of his head, tilting his beat-up old fedora comically down on his nose.

"D'ye think she'd come? Christ! I'd hate to inflict her on the kids."

"She'd come, all right. She never liked Iris since the day she met her when you brought Iris down east for your honeymoon."

The honeymoon's been over for a long time," father remarked to no one in particular.

Bride made the supper that night while I chopped kindling to get the cold stove going. Bride burned the biscuits only a little and Uncle Miles, who had stopped over for the meal, swore he doted on raw carrots that had been rolled in sour milk. Bride wore an apron around her middle and a flush on her face. She poured out the tea and father put his arm around her and Uncle Miles gave her a whole two-bits.

Later, when we had all gone to bed and the restless wind probed with cold fingers around the eaves of the house, Bride crept to my bedroom door and whispered in.

"Do you miss her, Patch? I do just a little."

"Me too, Bride," I spoke back softly. "Just a little."

6

Aunt Kate had been a Fallon before she married Con Carri-grew. She was a sister, some years younger, to Grandfather Mathias. There had been another sister–the oldest of all–but she never lived long enough to get named: the midwife–old Mag Sutherland–was ginned to the hair roots when the child was born; Mag hacked the umbilical cord in two with a butcher's knife and took the wailing wee mite out behind the house where a water-barrel stood underneath a downspout of the guttering. Mag held onto the babe's heels while she plunged it in and out of the rain barrel that was home to sev-eral thousand things that swam and killed and ate. The midwife lost her grips and our great-aunt who was never named went head-first to the bottom of the barrel and so died before she had the privilege of taking a hundred breaths.

Aunt Kate lived in a small, but neat, shack in a bit of a town called Kearney which was 'way up in the north of On-tario near Huntsville. She lived on the old age pension and a bit made from writing letters for the illiterate for which she charged ten cents a page. Aunt Kate had a marvellous love and talent for the law. She gave free legal advice, much of which was wrong, but her neighbours thought her a near-genius because she knew the difference between a tort and a replevin. Rather than drive the few miles into Huntsville to consult an attorney, the inhabitants of Kearney went to Aunt Kate to enquire how much they could legally soak a neighbour whose cow had made a hash of the kitchen garden.

As we had yet no automobile, father borrowed Uncle Miles' Chevy and drove to Kilmore where the Toronto & Nipissing intended to unload Aunt Kate, two steamer trunks, and a caged, cranky-looking bird Aunt Kate called her "familiar." When they arrived, Bride and I, faces washed and hair curried, stood side by side in the newly sprouted cinquefoil bordering the lane to meet this unknown quantity under whose thumb we might be made to squirm. Aunt Kate sat in the passenger's seat beside father, straight as a thistle and topped with a hat thirty years of age. Her dress and coat were plain, unfrilled black; her hard blue eyes cut holes out of everything they settled upon.

"Well, there they are." Father got out of the car and waved a hand at Bride and me.

Aunt Kate swivelled her frosty eyes from me to Bride and from Bride back to me. We stared back. Aunt Kate looked like a tall, dignified crow.

"What grade are you in?" she barked, and I jumped back.

"Senior Third," I said huskily.

"Hmmmmm. Who was Thomas à Becket?"

I looked down at the ground and dug the toe of my boot into a crow-foot root.

Seeing she was on barren ground Aunt Kate turned on Bride. "Can you sew? knit? bake a pie? Eh—eh?"

"If she could manage all that we'd hardly need you around," said father. Aunt Kate ignored him.

"There's been great changes since my day," she said testily. "I want that room with the south window; I suppose it hasn't been cleaned since . . . "

"Since the old man used to park his girlfriends there," father laughed. "You are probably right; Iris wasn't the world's greatest housekeeper."

"*That* woman!" the words spat. "I'm just surprised you haven't gone crawling after her begging her come back."

"You'd better learn not to surprise so easily." There was a rim of ice on the edge of father's voice.

Aunt Kate gathered her skirts and hustled toward the house. "Bring my cases to the south bedroom," she ordered, not bothering to look back.

Father dropped a wink at Bride and me. "Don't let her ride you too hard. She's as tough as a hickory knot, but she might be worse. If things get too rough I'll have a chat with her."

That was father's way of letting us know his big right arm was between us and the pouncing things that lived out there in the world. Bride and I ran to hold the house door open while father shouldered and dragged the steamer trunks in and up the stairs to the south bedroom.

As father was dragging the trunks up the stairs Aunt Kate strode into the south bedroom, her eagle eye and hawk's nose remindful of a Norman baron entering a town he has just sacked. She went over to the bed with its ancient walnut headboard and poked a suspicious finger into the bedding. Little spurts of dust arose at each poke. She swiftly uncovered one corner of the felt mattress and, lifting the edge, was happy to discover that several small, brown things scuttled away to escape the daylight.

"I thought so," she said in sour triumph.

"This bed is crawling with bugs, Ward. I want water brought in and heated and I want coal-oil to destroy these bedbugs. Were I to sleep a night here I'd be found in the morning—a skeleton in my shift."

For several days Aunt Kate went on a rampage of cleaning, washing, scrubbing, while still finding time to cook three meals a day. But hers was the mentality of the slave-driver, of a bully-mate on a tea-clipper: "Padraic!" She never called me "Patch." "Down to the spring with you and fetch two pails of water. And be sure they're filled; I don't want a bit of moisture sloshing around in the bottoms. Brigid! Have you cleaned the pantry yet? Well, why not, pray? The Blessed Virgin knows when I was your age I was in the fields and I was in the barns, and I was in the house, and I'd still time to acquire the grand education from the sisters."

Grandfather Mathias and his sister Kate were educated in Ireland, although grandfather very seldom stayed in the schoolhouse when the sun was shining warm on the gorse up on the side of the mountain that was called Slieve Car. Slieve Car was in the wilds of deep Mayo where there wasn't hut nor cabin for miles about, only the roll of the brown mountains with a handful of lean sheep pecking at the yellow broom or drinking from the mountainy streams that leaped and flashed in the sun. Grandfather was a few years the elder of his sister; there were other children in the family, too, but some died and one went to Australia and might just as well have died, and I think one got crippled up in the Boer War and lived long enough to draw a tiny pension before he succumbed to his wounds and saved the government of Edward VII all that expense.

Grandfather emigrated first—when he was in his twenties. Sometime in the 1870's he packed his turkey and sailed ho for Philadelphia where he found a land depressed from the post-Civil War boom. Nor were Irishmen welcome, especially Irishmen who had not fought for the Union. He wandered into the north woods of Maine where he cut logs; he went mining for copper in the Keweenaw country which is that bit of land stuck out like a thumb into Lake Superior. From there he crossed over to Canada and to the county of Victoria which isn't nearly as nice a place as the name might indicate. Grandfather went to work logging for the Carrigrew Lumber Company. Old Con Carrigrew was, according to what I heard Uncle Miles say, "as tight as bark to a piss-elm stump." And this may have been true. Some years before, Carrigrew had buried his wife, ordering his own carpenters to knock together the burial box. Of that marriage there was no issue. The saying was that Carrigrew had screwed his wife once–found out she liked it–and quit right there so as not to encourage her.

What happened next, I'm not certain; I know Uncle Miles and father talked little of it and when you needled at them with a question they got gruff and changed the topic. What did happen was Aunt Kate (who was a striking-looking woman in her youth) came to Victoria County and there were two ceremonies: one was the marriage of Aunt Kate to a man forty years her senior; the second was Grandfather Mathias becoming the new foreman of Carrigrew's lumbering operations up on the Red Rock River.

Old Carrigrew was as tough as a keg full of thumb-screws, but Aunt Kate was his match. The first time he attempted to bully her she laid him out with an iron skillet full of fried potatoes. Still, old Con had the last laugh: when he died, about five or six years after marrying Aunt Kate, his affairs were bankrupt and in the hands of the receivers. Aunt Kate was left without dot nor tittle.

She hung on: she taught school, worked as a seamstress in a sweat-shop; did practical nursing and killed no more patients than did the doctors of the period. Sometimes, after grandfather's wife died, Aunt Kate came down to keep house for her brother. It was no good. They fought great fights and when grandfather would import one of his fancy women from Toronto, Aunt Kate would haul her trunks downstairs and hire a livery to drive her to the railroad depot and back to Kearney where she taught school for a time. It was in Kearney she met Phil Darmody, a kind of roustabout without trade or skill. Although Aunt Kate swore to the day of her demise that she and Darmody occupied separate rooms, no one believed her–least of all Uncle Miles and our father. For some reason, no doubt an odd one, grandfather hated Phil Darmody. When old Bill Teague asked grandfather if there was any truth to the gossip about Darmody and Aunt Kate sharing the same bed, grandfather replied, "Not a damn bit of truth to it. He's too

damned ignorant–he fucks her in the sheep pen." And with
that he put the flat of his hand hard against old Teague's face
and sent him ass-over-backwards into the streets of Kilmore.
Some of the young Teagues who were supposed to be scrappers
muttered and looked black, but Matt Fallon was a fighting
man as were his sons after him.

Bride and I did not like Aunt Kate. She, no doubt, had virtues galore, but they were not of the kind we could admire. A
streak of prudery the width of a binder canvas encircled the
woman's mind as a shroud hides the dead. On laundry days
she would not hang her underthings or those of Bride's on the
outside line that ran from the back kitchen to an old apple
tree where a pair of bluebirds lived in a hole high up on the
trunk. The female underwear was hung on a line in the cellar
where the must of decay and the dry odour of cobwebs could
get into the material so the wearer had the impression she'd
spent the day in the potato bin.

"Dirty men–and boys," Aunt Kate reminded me when I
enquired why she put some of the laundry in the basement instead of out in the clear, blue air of God, "are always thinking
dirty thoughts when they see ladies' undergarments. I see no
reason to encourage them."

True, I knew little of sex and cared less at that age, yet I
wondered how any man (or boy) could get steamed up over
Aunt Kate's knee-length bloomers and them a dirty-grey colour; the hue of the monks' habits who used to live in stone huts
on an island just off Ireland called Skellig Michael.

From Aunt Kate, Bride and I learned of all the races of man
the Irish were by far the superior. And of these superior Irish
the family of Fallon topped the lot. True, there had been an
Irish blackguard or two, but even an Irish blackguard was
head and hames over an Englishman; anything that lived east
of the Danube River were, according to Aunt Kate, slaves and
serfs who were too ignorant to achieve heaven and yet too innocent to be sent to hell. The slaves and serfs, according to her
theology, would, upon their hour of death, find shelter in the

kingdom of limbo where a just and merciful God had provided a plot of land for each where they could labour out eternity in much the same fashion as they had lived their short span on earth.

Bride and I discovered early that the only way to keep Aunt Kate from prescribing chores was to get her talking. As she talked her mind left this earth and floated off to another that never existed except in the rat-holes of her imagination.

"Now we Fallons were the nobility of County Roscommon. We are descended from the great chief who held the Barony of Athlone. The Fallons were grand warriors; they fought the Danes and Normans stark-naked, carrying only a spear."

"Wouldn't the Danes and Normans be able to cut their tails off if they were naked?" Bride always had an eye for detail.

Aunt Kate gave her a look that was pure ice. "I can see there's considerable more of your mother in you than anything Fallon."

Bride's chin went up and her blue eyes turned to fire. "I'm as much of a Fallon as you, 'Missis Darmody.' " And the flash of battle flared.

I don't know what would have happened had father not come in at that time from the fields where he was sowing alsike and alfalfa for the summer hay. He ordered Bride and me out of the house where we lingered by an open window. We could hear Aunt Kate's voice rise to a shriek before it was cut in half by father's cold, measured tones. After that Aunt Kate wouldn't speak to Bride for several days, although she turned on me with flattery and honey, calling me "her big boy Padraic."

It was at least a couple of weeks before Aunt Kate's pride surfaced sufficiently for her to go on with her account of the Great Fallons who passed on before: priests, soldiers, martyrs, and men-folk whose gallantry toward the fairer sex did not allow them a sneaking peek above the knees of woman-kind. Bride and I reminded Aunt Kate of the stories of grandfather's escapades and the trunks full of frippery and finery we discovered when we came from Saskatchewan.

"That was a trait that came through our mother," grandfather's sister said sharply. "She was a Crowley. Not that anything save innocent words passed her saintly lips, not to mention deeds. But mother, may she be basking in the benevolent warmth of the heavenly sun, had a terrible cross to bear just from being a Crowley. If there was a dive or den of infamy in West Ireland you'd sure enough find a Crowley within it—indeed, if he didn't own it!"

"What about grandfather's wife?" we wanted to know.

"A Dorgan. Hannah Dorgan. She's been dead for nearly thirty years and took her three daughters with her. The consumption got them all. Hannah's parents—old Fergus and Gussy took the consumption as did Hannah's sisters—Maryann and Jenovah. They all died and your grandmother took their clothes home here to make over into dresses for your aunts. Of course, everything was full of consumption; Hannah might just as well have taken a gun to those girls. She went first, mercifully, not knowing she brought death into this house."

Aunt Kate took a sip of tea from a cup that had great rambling roses twined around it. She once said that cup and the matching saucer were a wedding gift from Mr. Carrigrew. Aunt Kate always referred to her late husband as "Mr. Carrigrew."

"You've seen the photographs of the three girls, your aunts. They all died in their twenty-second year of life. There was Brigid, for whom you're named, although your aunt was a real lady; there was Hannah next, named for her mother; and the last to go was Rosie. They're all in heaven now, with the angels; up there with the angels and watching all the mean, dirty things you two are up to down here."

7

Spring had turned the corner to go dancing across the rolling plains of Carden, turning the grass green with a touch; dressing up the hawthorn and Canada plum with blossoms like whipped cream. Going to school one morning Bride and I noticed, as we passed over the hill that was called Killylick Mountain, a cloud of white stars spattered and scattered under and around the boles of the yet leafless maple and beech. We slid through the rail fence separating the wood lot from the road and picked a few of the largest; there were, also, a few flowers, seemingly of the same kind, but instead of waxy white, the three petals showed a dark, blood red–the kind of red, I recalled, with hindsight, our mother's lips were painted those times she expected the Pacific Tea Company man to call. We left those and carried our bouquet to Miss Guildforth, walking triumphantly up to her desk and laying them, still dew-fresh, on the day's geography lesson. The teacher thanked us very much, said we were sweet to bring her flowers, and gave Bride and me a glow that lasted until the first recess.

"Oh my! Thank you very much, little Fallons," gibed Mickey Malloy. "Thank you *very* much–little brown-nosers. You

61

wait and see—she'll use them to wipe her arse and then you can have them back to take home to your mother."

It was a speech containing several insults any one of which called for a fight: "Just holds without fists, or anything goes?" I peeled off my sweater.

"Anything goes," Mickey grunted, kicking me hard in the belly while my head was yet tangled in my sweater. I might have been in for a lacing save that Bride took the handle from the pump (it was ever loose) and raised it like a tomahawk.

"You'll fight fair, Mickey Malloy, or you'll wear two heads home with you."

The Malloys were a family of renegade Irish Catholics living in Shugan's Swamp. They went to no church, apparently never worked, and the old ones were rarely known to be sober. There was an iron feeling between us Fallons and the Malloys because long before we moved to Carden Uncle Miles had slapped old Barnsey Malloy so hard across the face he staggered back ten feet and fell over, preferring to remain where he fell rather than risk a second wallop.

Mickey was thick through the chest with short, powerful arms. I had a barrel chest and a long reach. Every time Mickey tried to close with me I'd step back and powder him one in the eye, on the nose, on his ears—wherever I could set my ten good knuckles. But if men are made to fight wars women are around to see a stop put to them: one of the Gordon girls ran inside and fetched Miss Guildforth. She came quickly and she came shrieking, but Mickey and I were tired and ready to quit, anyway. Mickey's face was a study in red and blue-yellow and I had a very sore place where my opponent's bootheel had connected.

Now ordinarily this would have been the end of things; Mickey would have had to put up with being teased about his licking and in three days all would have been forgotten. The Malloys were an ugly crew; like the Stuart kings of England they learned nothing and remembered everything. The next Friday afternoon as Bride and I were homing it from school we met a quartet of very ugly Malloys at the Log Corners where, if you turned left, you'd reach Shugan's Swamp and the tamarack den where the Malloys lived, fought, drank, and did all manner of things that sort of reptile indulges in.

There was old Barnsey, two of his sons–Gully and Len–and the long-memoried Mickey.

"Head through the fence, Bride," I cautioned, "and go 'round them and scoot for home."

"I'll stay," she said shakily.

As we closed the gap 'twixt us and the Malloys, old Barnsey, who was leaning on a skinned hickory cudgel, smiled the smile of the devil's own ape. "This is the one, is it," he said to Mickey, "who kicked you whiles you was down and t'rew a big rock at yer?"

Mickey gave a great lying nod.

"Well," said the old man, "I never seen the Fallon I couldn't cudgel yet, and this limb off a dirty branch is overdue for his skinnin', I'd say," and he looked around at the leerful faces of his sons for approval.

I stopped several yards in front of the Malloys. I could feel the darts of fear pinging inside my stomach, and Bride's hand clutched my arm fiercely.

"You go away and leave us alone," she cried. "You go away or I'll get daddy and he'll beat you up."

Even from as far away as we were we could smell the sour reek of homemade moonshine.

"Yes, you go and tell your daddy his squirt of a kid got a lacin'." The tribe advanced on us. Gully and Len were too old for school or had been expelled for hellery; I doubt the oldest–Gully–was yet twenty. Brave, now, Mickey squared his fists and stalked alongside his father.

"Afternoon, gents." I leaped like a hare, for the deep, barrel-deep, voice seemed to come out of nowhere.

A man put his hand to the top rail and hurtled his huge body across the fence; evidently he had been crossing Lee's pasture field to reach the Log Corners. I recognized him as the one they called Fighting Bill Doherty. Other than denim work pants and a grey cotton shirt, Doherty wore run-over work boots and a slouch of a fedora hat. His shirt sleeves were rolled well above his elbows and I don't believe I've seen larger, better-muscled arms on a man since. He had a long, heavy torso, but it was his eyes which seemed most peculiar: they were blue and deep-marbled like the eyes you see in some horses which appear broken and tamed until all of a sudden the wildness comes a-leap out of them and they try to kick the owner to death or run away and smash whatever rig they've been hitched to. He looked my father's age or a little over.

"You'd be Patch Fallon," Doherty said, ignoring the Malloys. "I'm glad I met you. I was on my way to see your dad, so we might just as well walk together. And this pretty little girl is –lemme see–Jean? Irene? No? Ah, yes–Bride; that's it. Bride for Brigid. And a nice name it is, too." He turned to the Malloys who stood where they'd stopped. "There was somethin' you wanted to talk to me about? Got any messages you want to send on to Ward Fallon?"

Old Barnsey hunched over and spit on the gravel of the road, circling the moisture with the point of his stick.

"This'n here," indicating me, "has been pickin' on my little boy here; been pickin' on him in school and t'rowin' rocks and what have you. We wasn't goin' to hurt him or nothin'; you know that, Bill. We Malloys allus fights fair."

"Yeah, Barnsey. Would you figure it was fair if you and me was to have a round or two? You could even get those two oldest thieves of yours, there, to give you a hand in case the sleddin' got tough."

Old Malloy put on the best face possible. "Well, lads," he said to his sons, "time we was gettin' home; the ol' wumman'll have the spuds on. See yuh agin, Bill." And the four turned and walked fairly rapidly in the direction of Shugan's Swamp.

Doherty, Bride, and I walked toward Killylick Mountain and home which was just the other side and southerly. The big man grew taciturn almost at once, when Bride or I spoke to

64

him or pointed out where we'd found the trilliums blooming, he just turned his deep-blue, marbled stare on us and said nothing.

When we reached home Doherty went on to the barn where father and Timothy Connolly were working at the mowing equipment against the cutting of the summer's hay. Aunt Kate stood in the door of the back kitchen and watched sourly as the big man walked toward the sound of a grindstone sharpening mower blades.

"Did that dirty man walk with you? Did he touch your sister? You want to watch out for dirty men like him."

For once I spoke out before Bride. "He chased that Malloy bunch away and them about to hit me with a big stick. He's a real nice man and he didn't say or do anything dirty to me or to Bride. Maybe it's you who thinks everything's dirty all the time."

"Get the wood-box filled before supper or I'll box your ears good." The old woman turned and hustled inside the house.

8

It is a strange boy who has no hero he admires beyond all men, sometimes carrying with him into manhood and old age a vivid memory of that hero although the latter be long dead and dust or faded into the obscurity of some refuge for the aged. The object of this worship becomes, for the boy, a demi-god; he can do no wrong, and long after their trails separate to link no more, the hero lives on, never growing old in a capsule of memory where time has stopped and no clock exists to mark the passage of hours. Such was Bill Doherty to me.

There was about the man a trailing mystery. I doubt if any-one knew his full story; he gave out little and that grudgingly unless he was in liquor and hearkening back to some passage at a construction camp or a sawmill. He spoke with a whisper of brogue only a fine ear for dialect could catch. I heard my father, who probably in all the district knew Doherty best, re-mark that Bill was born in the County of Galway–a place of stone and mountain fronting on the Atlantic Ocean. Father believed Doherty came to Canada as a boy with his father, Pe-ter Doherty–the mother having passed away with the "con," as consumption was known in Ireland at the time. That was back in the 1880's; from there on the story of Bill Doherty branches; it's a matter of choice and credibility which branch one chooses.

In the year of '34 Doherty was, I'd guess, at least fifty. His thick, grizzled hair was forever tousled and matted from his never taking his slouch of a hat off, even when he went to bed. He never saw a barber: Doherty had his hair cut at "Old Mother" Cooley's, a crone of vast age who lived in a log cabin around at the tether end of Dillon's Mountain where the slope coasted gradually down to the limerock plain. Mother Cooley was believed to have married and buried three husbands; of this I do not know. In my time she was on the old age pension supplemented by trimming hair, reading teacups, and mixing up hell-brews to "cure" agues, fevers, the trots, and seizures. I was in her cabin but once and that was when Aunt Kate sent me over to buy a pint of something for the curing of what Aunt Kate called "the women's complaint." The log shack slumped beneath two great elms, one on either side the house, leaning toward each other and embracing at the top-most boughs. One tree had a great scar winding and twisting down its trunk where a ball of lightning had leaped on it and dove into the ground, shredding the bark as it blazed. There must have been two dozen cats, mauling and mewling and yowling about and in the dwelling. The cabin stunk to high hell of old woman and catshit. I paid over the money, grabbed the pint sealer of liquid, and lined out straight across the mountain for home.

As I mentioned earlier, Doherty was a big man. Not giant-big like some circus freak; just big. He was well over six feet and must have weighed 240 pounds and little of it fat. His great muscles were slabs welded to his limbs and torso. As far as father knew, Pete Doherty, Bill's father, went to work as a gandy-dancer on the Canadian Pacific Railway, working his way up to section boss by virtue of a heavy hand that kept the mixture of Bulgarians, Scots, shanty-Irish, Poles, and devil-knows-what-else in line and bent over their spike mauls.

The young Doherty had never known a woman's love or a father's affection. Some old hedge schoolmaster living near the site of where one branch line was building took hold of the boy and taught him to read a bit and cipher, but by the time he was thirteen Bill was as big and strong as three-quarters of the men whom his father drove on the right-of-way. The father yanked Bill away from his times-tables and his "cat ate the rat" lessons and put him out on the gang where old Pete collected a man's wages for his son's work. Occasionally, when old Pete was drunk, he'd grow large of heart and toss Bill a dime for candy, only Bill didn't buy candy. He'd go down to the tar-paper shebeens that followed after the work crews like shrews after a cricket, and buy a tumblerful of raw, brown whiskey in which was mixed red pepper to give it snap.

When he was fifteen or so Doherty grew tired of being cuffed, kicked and rewarded with thin dimes of his own earnings. A quarrel of defiance arose; father and son went at it in the bunk car while the other occupants stood around whooping and yelling in excitement. It was touch and go, for Peter, though nearing his sixtieth year, was an oak of brawn and knotted muscle. In the end he went down and rolled under a bunk, battered and crying. His reign was over. Within the month a young German challenged him and the old man turned away. He was licked. The boss of the division called him in and handed him his quittance. He was heard of no more.

Father and Uncle Miles heard most of this from Grandfather Matt who seemed to have knowledge of it from men around Kilmore who had been with the section gang. Aside from that the only things people knew about Bill Doherty were what he chose to tell. There was a story that he killed a man in a fist fight at a lumber camp owned by a fellow named Manasney, up in the Longford township. Beat him to death with his bare hands. As far as I know it remains just a story.

Doherty's appearance and continuance in the Carden area was, like the man himself, unclear. Ask a native and the answer was uncertain. I heard several stories any one of which may have been right; again, all may have been wrong. He had nothing to do with women. Doherty was polite, hat-raising, but he never looked at a woman with longing; his only conversation with women centred around the weather. He was one of those men whom I was to meet later in life who are neither homosexual nor heterosexual, but rather a-sexual. Alcohol may have played a significant part in keeping Doherty single –or at least uninterested. If a man marries the bottle early enough, there is little room within him to nurture affection for anyone or anything else.

What appeared singular to me was, while Doherty was extremely skilful with his great hands, he was content to labour manually for a negligible amount of food and shelter and for the raw, rough whiskey from which he seemed to draw comfort and vitality. He cut cordwood or logs in winter, hayed and harvested in season with farm owners, castrated and dehorned beeves for the ranchers.

Many a young, strong man, brave on moonshine and anxious for glory, had laid down a challenge which was unavoidable and which Doherty with reluctance accepted. No man in the county or those surrounding could fell the giant or stand against the blows of his massive arms and fists. Doherty's reputation grew; Carden was proud of him. When country men went drinking in Lindsay of a Saturday they listened to outlander's talk about the mighty men in Cavan, in Haliburton, in Lakefield. "Ah," the men from Carden would smile into their beer, "yez haven't met the Fighting Doherty yet."

In older, more glorious days, the men of Kilmore, Foxford, and Carden fought tremendous battles with Orangemen who came to Lindsay for fight and frolic. They clashed head-on with the thick-wristed Scots from the Scotch Line. On the days long ago when Foxford had an annual fair the Irish fought among themselves, hot with whiskey, quarrelsome, and ready to round upon any and all who trod on their coattails. Not that they, these up-county Irish, were forever victorious as the tales of old men leaning on sticks would declare with a spit in the dust and wave of their blackthorn. On one 12th of July in

Lindsay when the Orange parade, with ear-bending whaps of drums, barged up Kent Street, two Cardenites, staggering out of a saloon to hear the noise, pulled the "King Billy" from his white horse. They were quickly discouraged and when more Irish streamed out of the bars the conflict became general. But the men from North Victoria were trounced and wherried out of town amid shouts of, "To hell with yer goddamn pope!" And, "No fucking surrender to papish bastards."

In Doherty's hey-days the faction fights between Catholic, Orange, and Scots were well over. The First Great War intervened, killing or crippling many a young Orangemen or Scot, leaving those who returned quiet and robbed, somehow, of further youthful combativeness. Few Irish Catholics joined the Canadian Expeditionary Force. The Rising in Dublin of 1916, its inevitable stamping out, and the execution of the leaders–one of whom, shot through both legs, had to be carried out and propped on a chair to face the firing squad–left the Irish bitter and cold. Uncle Miles was, as far as I know, the only "Dogan" of the district to enlist, and he was trying to commit suicide.

There were still brawls at dance halls, in beverage rooms, and an occasional grudge fight: someone's cousin had made unwanted advances to the sister of someone else's cousin and the sword would be drawn. The Irish have to whip themselves into a royal rage to ready themselves for battle. A fist fight between two new or old enemies was preceded by a general formality: the combatants might even drink together, their tongues unusually civil and polite until with the spurring of alcohol the conversation turned severe and deepened: "I hear yez think you're a pretty good man," and the beverage room or dance floor would hush and listen.

"I don't know about that," would come the reply. "I guess I'm good enough to take the likes of you."

And battle flared.

Unlike most others of his race in the district, Doherty did not rage, storm, or grind his teeth when the combativeness was on him: other than a low, growling curse, he fought silently, his peculiar eyes riveted on his opponent. He was pitiless; no man ever sought to fight him a second time. I have always believed that Doherty hated fighting; hated it as he must have hated battering down his father in the bunk car years before. By crippling a challenger both in body and spirit Doherty was like a giant grizzly standing high on hind legs to scratch with iron claws a foot higher on a bear tree than any of his kind. I don't think Doherty cared a damn about being the king-bear; he merely wished to be left alone. Being Fighting Bill Doherty, this was not possible. Some man, young or middle-aged, somewhere, knowing Doherty's fighting reputation, "stumped him out" as the Carden idiom had it, and sought to bring him down. On these Doherty had no compassion.

From the time he saved me being striped by the Malloys I was fascinated by Bill Doherty. I longed to emulate him; I affected his slouching walk, the way his great hands swung at his sides as he strode. I attempted to deepen the treble of my voice which was on the change and came out hoarse or squeaky without warning. Once I filled a grain sack with hay and tied it to the pole rafters of the old log sheep-pen. I stripped to my waist and whammed furiously at the swinging bag. "Take that, you son of a bitch!" and I'd bury a fist in the gut of the bag, making believe it was Andy Perry who once stood up to Doherty for ten minutes before toppling like a white pine from a lumberman's axe.

So intent was I upon slaughter I did not detect Bride's presence until I heard her giggle. I turned in fury; Bride was peeking through a big chink in the logs where the mud daub had long fallen away.

"Take that! Take that! Take that, you son of a bitch!" she mimicked. I ran out of the sheep-pen and after her, but she spurted away on brown, twinkling legs and gained the safety of the barn where father was repairing a stall. I stilted away, furious with embarrassment; and also resentment: father, it seemed to me, forever preferred Bride. I cannot recall a time when he ever raised a hand to her. A lash of the edge of his

71

tongue, surely, but he never spanked her. It was me that got the crash of a hard palm across my ear, or a well-aimed boot in the rear end. Twice, at least, father whipped off his heavy leather harness belt and whaled me until I screamed in agony with Bride standing off a way biting her fingers and with tears welling up in her eyes with sympathy although she may have been the cause of my hiding.

9

Jupiter was the old, lame horse that came willed along with grandfather's property. Jupiter was deaf, too; or pretended to be. He never paid attention to words like "Giddy-up," but he could hear the oat bucket rattle a half-mile away.

"How old is that bugger of a horse, Miles?" father asked one day.

My uncle studied a minute. "Let's see. You went west when —in 1910?"

Father said it was 1911 and he remembered because he was twenty-three at the time.

"Nineteen eleven," mused Miles. "Well, I'd say it was 1912 or maybe '13. There was a gang of gypsies came along in a covered wagon and chousing a string of horses. You remember how those gypsies used to go around the country? Well, the old man got talking trade and making eyes at the gypsy girls inside the wagon. He traded an old .38-40 and seven dollars for that horse. Then he tried to get at one of the girls in the wagon. She said she was going to tell his fortune and bless his money. Anyway, the old man gets her skirts up and she hollers like a stuck pig. One of the young bloods–maybe her husband, I don't know–came at the old man with a knife. The old man swatted him one across the mouth, twisted his arm up behind his back and took away the knife. 'Now,' he says, 'I'm not going to bless your money but I'll goddamn soon tell this bastard's fortune for you: he's going to be slit from arse-hole to linch-pin if the whole fucking mob of you isn't gone and down the road inside of three seconds.' "

Father grinned. "Sounds like the old man. Did he ever work the horse?"

"Work? That piece of coyote-bait! He's done nothing but eat and sleep for over twenty years. And Christ only knows how old the son of a bitch was when the old man got him."

But Bride and I liked Jupiter. Once we got a halter on him we could lead him beneath a maple near the barn, then shinny up the maple and out along a branch from where we could get on the horse's back. Aunt Kate told father it was a terrible danger, but he only said that Jupiter was too lazy to buck, too old to run, and too stupid to think of anything else.

But just getting aboard Jupiter didn't mean we were going to get any locomotion out of the sly old bay gelding. On days when he felt lively Jupiter would amble, Bride and I on his back, down the limerock path, which was steep and treacherously arranged, to where the Sally Brook flowed from many interstices in the wall of the ledge. May had floated away on a haze of chokeberry blossoms and a mist of new-born grass; the Sally no longer gushed and geysered from its source; the water appeared sedately, fingering its way carefully over pebbles beneath the shade of the great sugar-maples towering above and on either side–maples whose leaves, come fall time, showered down in flurries of scarlet and gold so thickly as to almost throttle the Sally which did not flood again until the autumn rains, crossing over the bare, red rocks of Longford, turned everything wet and brown while the loft pigeons ducked into the ventilator fixed to the ridge of the barn where they took shelter from the drive of wind and wet beneath the pawing iron horse, the head of which, bravely faced square-on to the grey nor'east.

So Bride and I could jolly the old nag to amble and stumble down-ledge to the brook for a drink. We could get him to the brook and then we could turn his old hammer of a head toward the south pasture where the salt lick was. The lick was no more than a bit of a trough with a gable roof made from ancient boards held together with cut-nails. Father said a German priest invented round nails and, while their holding power was not as good as the old-fashioned kind, they didn't rust as easily or snap off when clinched.

There was no doubt in the world that Bride and I could have walked to the south pasture three times quicker than Jupiter stumbled his way, dropping his ungainly head without warning to nip the head of a timothy stalk with teeth worn as flat as shale rock. But it's a fine thing to be young and be on the back of an Arabian paladin's steed with the red, round sun of June quartering toward the west. At least we thought Jupiter an Arabian steed in spite of Uncle Miles' comment that the horse was an off-breed Clydesdale bastard.

It was about this time we discovered Aunt Kate was corresponding with a "friend." She used purple ink on violet-coloured note-paper that stank of being cooped up for too many years in steamer trunks and the drawers of walnut bureaus. Aunt Kate wrote, sitting bolt-upright, at the cherry-wood dining table in the parlour where the windows looked out between two gloomy firs and from where you could see the dusty road with soldier-rows of shivering aspen on either side. She had two pairs of spectacles: one to see past the edge of her nose, the other to scan close up—newspapers and, in this case, a letter to a gentleman, as she put it, "of quality and degree."

"A saintly man," she said with the reverence of hypocrisy sneaking into her voice. "He was to have been a priest, you know; he heard the call. He'd of been a cardinal by now. It was his mother—a feeble person. She exhausted his time and energies for years, what with him feeding her like a babe and carrying out her bed-chambers. 'Twould have been the Lord's mercy if He'd of taken the woman to His bosom years before He did."

A damp spot blotted into the violet letter-paper, but whether it was a tear or a bead of sweat we couldn't tell for the day was monstrously hot and Aunt Kate had every window battened down and sealed.

"Did he want you to get married, Aunt Kate?"

She threw up her hands with the shrivelled skin and blue knots on the backs. "Married! That man would have carried me off to Rome or Naples or Swift Current and treated me like a princess royal. 'Katherine,' he'd say to me, 'as soon as the old one dies I'll have the gold band of eternal bliss on your finger and a CPR ticket to North Bay or any other honeymooner's garden.'"

"When did his mother die?"

"Die! her die! Hanging on like a stubborn mule and her ninety-four if she's a minute. Even the doctors don't know what's keeping her hanging together, but I know: it's pure spite. Spite and envy because Rodney and I are still in our youth and prime and we can't marry as long as that old devil isn't bedded down in the gravel."

After we had heard the eulogies of Rodney, arranged by Aunt Kate in alphabetical and chronological order, the old lady commenced on our mother of whom, in actuality, no one talked since her departure; nor did she seem to be missed:

"I never knew her, of course," Aunt Kate said with sleet in her voice. "Oh, I met her when your father brought her east on their marriage trip, but 'twas a mere shake of the hand and a nod. I saw nothing in Iris then and the times have proved me right." She was patching a hole in one of her lisle stockings and she bit the end of the thread off savagely.

Miss Guildforth became ill in mid-June nearly two weeks before the school year was up for the summer holidays. I do not, to this day, know what her problem was. Aunt Kate said, when I asked, frostily that the teacher was having "female trouble." When Uncle Miles asked me if I knew what was wrong with Miss Guildforth I told him the female trouble story.

"Well, I figured she hadn't slipped and sprained her balls," he said testily.

So there we were, Bride and I, with two whole weeks of June with its tall timothy and waving banks of red clover and bobolinks hanging onto sweet-clover stems singing a bobolink sound until you thought the whole meadow was afire with bird whistling.

We must have had 150 acres sown down to hay. Hay and ten acres of oats to put flesh and pep on the work team, old Jupiter being well beyond either. Uncle Miles, whose smaller beef farm was a mile away as flies the raven, was too busy with his own hay to help father so a kind of haying crew was made up of father, Bill Doherty, and Bride and me.

Doherty refused to sleep in the house. He made a bunk of sweet hay in an empty manger and slept there; the only time he came inside the house was for his meals. Aunt Kate tackled him immediately.

"Why do you sleep in an old manger?"

"If it was good enough for Jesus Christ it's good enough for Bill Doherty," he replied, shovelling citron preserves over his mashed potatoes. Aunt Kate had to know about that, too.

Bill forked the mixture into his mouth that contained but a handful of teeth, the others having been lost forever in fracas and combat. "It's like this Miz Carrigrew—your potatoes are too sour and the preserves too sweet. Mix the two and they come out jake-a-loo."

Doherty had great muscular hands that were surprisingly deft. One evening after work when the horses were cropping noisily in the barn pasture and the last cow to be milked had swayed her way down to the Sally for an icy drink, the big man sat on an up-turned oil can (in those days oil often came in square five-gallon containers) and whittled at a piece of white cedar. Bride and I watched him intently. Before the night sucked the daylight from under the hawthorn trees Doherty handed over a beautiful (although we didn't know it then) two-masted brig with slatting sails, a taff-rail, keel and all.

"Take her down to the crick and see how she sails." Doherty closed the blade of his knife, turned into the barn and shut the door decisively.

Forty years later as I walked, bemused, along the Sally Brook I found a bit of greying wood shaped, despite years of rot, like a ship's hull and with a stump of a foremast in it. I held it in my hand and the years dissolved, but I tossed it from me and hurried away.

IO

The hay meadows rolled out, uphill and down, away to the south from the barn and the pasture enclosure. The timothy field, when ready to mow, was a shadow-changing spread of greeny-blue through which the winds waved and curried and great cottony cumulus clouds played with their shadows far below as they crossed from sou'-west to nor'-east as stately as any galleon bringing Peruvian gold to Spanish Cadiz. There, the bobolinks flew up in alarm as the horses, pulling the mower, scattered the little birds crying and bubbling in affected anger for their young had hatched and been on the wing for a week before.

The red clover and alfalfa meadows were a paisley pattern of pink-red and blue. Though not as high as the timothy, the clover had heavy, thick stalks which sagged to the ground with the weight of blossoms and the cast of winds. A million bumble bees and sweet-seeking wasps made the entire field a-buzz.

Father operated the mower. It was a slow, cumbersome rig in some ways, but interesting in the way old farm machines were in the days before everything got rubber-tired and motorized. Ours was a machine bought some years before by grandfather Fallon. It was made by the John Deere Company, and had wheels with yellow iron spokes and rims. Most of the rest was green. The mower had a cutter bar that could be raised almost vertically or let down flat by means of a hand lever. Bride and I loved to follow the mower around the perimeter of the cut, watching the proud stalks fall easily back over the cutter-bar as the shuttling blade mercilessly sliced through even the thickest stands of clover or timothy. Bride and I could follow the mower in our bare feet in the timothy field, but when father started in on the red clover and alfalfa the shaved stubble was too thick and tough and we had to slip on canvas running shoes.

The cut hay was allowed one day to lie curing in the sun; then Bill Doherty began raking it into rolls with the one-horse hay rake. He was the only person, my father said, who could get something close to a day's work out of Jupiter. Doherty never struck Jupiter with a whip or whacked him with the end of the lines. After the horse was hitched and Doherty settled in the seat of the rake he simply flapped the reins loosely across Jupiter's breeching and said, "Get up, there, and don't stop until I tell you."

"That Doherty can talk 'horse,' " father remarked to Aunt Kate, once.

She sniffed. "All he can talk is whiskey. I'd hate to be the woman that married that one."

"I'd rather be that than the man that married you," father said sharply.

"Ah, you didn't know Carrigrew. Poor, dear Con Carrigrew," and Aunt Kate's eyes misted with artificial tears.

"Oh, yeah, Uncle Saint Carrigrew; I missed him. But what about this one you're keeping the post office in business with now? Do you think he's the blessed treasure old Con was?"

Aunt Kate gave a straightener to her spine and spun back into the house.

When the coils of hay dried they were forked into little stacks called haycocks where they could be gathered and forked up on the wagon racks. Bride was too young, but I had the job of driving the team from stack to stack, then tramping down and "building" the load until it mounted up over the front and back boards of the wagon rack.

Building the hay loads was hard work and made my legs ache, but when the rack was finally full I enjoyed the long ride to the barn, the load jouncing and swaying over the rutted, limestone-boned trail.

Most of the rancher-farmers around Kilmore, Foxford, and Clifden used a rig called a "hay fork" for unloading hay from the wagon rack and putting it up into the mows inside the barn. It was just a pair of huge iron pincers looking like gigantic ice-tongs. The tongs were shoved deep into the hay on the wagon, then the horses hauled the great fork of hay up and into the barn through the top of the gable end where it ran along a track resembling, a bit, a railroad track. A trip rope leading to the fork allowed the operator to dump the load any place in the great barn mows. We had "hay slings": contrivances of wooden bars and ropes which were spread out on the wagon rack in the field and the cocked hay forked and built on each set of "slings" of which there were three. When the rack was loaded we drove the hay wagon right through the high, domed doors leading to the threshing floor. Up on the heavy elm-planked threshing floor, the horses' hooves thudded dully on the planking; the wagon wheels rumbling. The sling ropes would be fastened together at the top with a ring device, then the hay-car (an iron contrivance with wheels, a chain hook and a device for releasing the slings from the car) was hooked to the slings. Doherty hitched old Jupiter to the haul rope and the sling of hay would rise to the very peak of the barn, startling the staring pigeons so that they crowded out the gable air vents and went flapping in the bright sun around the eaves of the barn. When the car, loaded with a slingful of hay, reached the track fastened to run along right under the rafter peaks, the car wheels ran along the track and, like the commoner hay fork, a trip rope released the hook catch at the car from the sling and the load would drop into the mow while the

81

car, the empty rope and wood sling dangling, would be brought back to the centre of the threshing floor over the wagon and the same process would be done all over again.

Yet, although the slings saved a lot of labour, the dropped hay had to be forked about the mow and tramped down fairly solidly to utilize as much space as possible. This was always my job, for adults have a conception that boys' legs were made for dull, routine work of the fetch-carry-and-hump variety. While I was tramping wearily in the sodden-hot mow, the hay dust crawling up my nose, settling in the back of my parched throat and helping the shoulder braces of my denim overalls rub raw the still-unpadded skin which barely covered my shoulder bones, father and Doherty would ride on the wagon rack leisurely out to the hay meadow where, after I had worn my legs to stumps in the mow, I was expected to race out in time to lay out and help build the load on the No. 2 sling.

I think now I needn't have complained. Aunt Kate drove Bride as if she were a brawny maid-of-all-work fresh from the bogs of Mayo instead of being a rather slight child of nine. Bride had to carry water for the house from the Sally Brook, churn butter in the old orchard and, if there was a brief respite, Bride was forced to listen while the old woman ranted about "how hard she worked in her youth"; "what a tremendous benefit she was to her mother," and how she was dropped straight from heaven to grace the bed and board of the Fallons of Ireland.

Not that Bride didn't rebel: one afternoon she came flying out to the meadow, her brown bare feet picking their skilful way around the thistles, her frock aflounce around her skinny legs.

"Daddy!" she squared her arms akimbo. "I'm not going to do another thing for that old Aunt Kate. She's a . . . she's a bugger of a bitch!"

Father had been in a black mood since the first tumble-up song of the orchard oriole.

"You'll go back and do as you're told! And you'll be civil to your aunt or I'll hide you 'til you can't sit for a week."

I felt my face hotting up with angry blood. Bride crooked her arm over her face, turned, and walked unsteadily away toward the house. Bill Doherty rolled a cigarette and caught father in that wall-eyed stare so disconcerting because it advertised neither anger nor indifference.

That evening for supper we had stew and dumplings: chunks of gravy-brown beef, carrots, onions, and pieces of potato boiled tender and the whole seasoned to perfection.

Father, Doherty, and I sat around the old deal table and ate while Bride and Aunt Kate served us and stood by ready to leap forth with a catsup bottle, a pat of butter, or a refill of the teacups. It was an old custom and at one time it may have made sense, although what kind of sense I don't know, for the men to eat while the women stood around like coolies waiting for a word from the lords and masters.

Father ate and talked about the hay crop as though ten hours out in it wasn't enough. Doherty said little or nothing. His tremendous hands employed a knife and fork with an odd delicacy.

"Bridie!" Doherty's hard baritone cut through father's haying speech. "I'll bet you made this stew, didn't you?"

My sister's face flushed; she looked down at her toes.

"Hmmmmph! I guess if you can call being told what to do at every hand's turn is cooking you can say she made it," Aunt Kate split a glare between Bride and Doherty.

"Oh? Does Bridie have to tell you how to cook, Miz Carrigrew? I'd of thought a woman your age would have picked up a little along the line someplace."

"I'm not saying I'm the world's best—" began Aunt Kate.

"True," said Doherty, "you're not."

"But there's those that wouldn't know an apple pie from a cow flap, and it's just a waste of time trying to cook for men like that."

Doherty nodded pleasantly. "You're right, there. At the church garden party Leo Murphy swore one of your apple pies was a cow-puddle. But I knew different. I can spot one of your pies a mile away and it a foggy morning."

The day we finished haying was noxiously hot. The sun rode around the sky in a circle of yellow haze; the sky was blue-hot; not the warm, friendly blue of May or September, but a molten blue like a boiled robin's egg.

The last sling-load of hay had been warped up and slammed back in the mow so close to the peak there was barely room for the slung hay to run along the track. Up beneath the stifling rafters where no breeze flitted and little air crept I forked, tiredly, the bundled hay, spreading it out evenly across the mow and up to the very door of the gable ventilator where the pigeons lit and looked their cock-eyed looks and barn sparrows gathered in a rabble.

My arms went from plain tired to lead. The heat was sulphurous. With the hay half spread I fell on my back a few feet away from the burning metal of the barn roofing. I couldn't have got to my feet if Barnum & Bailey with ten naked girls riding elephants was passing through by way of the threshing floor.

Doherty, runnels of sweat coursing down his hard, heavy face and into the matted grey-black hair of his chest, appeared over the top of the purlin beam. He threw his leg over the beam, grabbed my three-tined fork and with a few quick thrusts and passes laid the clover out as smooth and level as a skating rink. When he had finished he looked down from his great height to where I was sprawled on my back among the coarse-stemmed clover.

"You're going to be a good man one of these days, Paddy," he said. And then he was gone—back over the edge of the purlin beam, holding my fork in one hand, stepping down the mow ladder with the rungs in the grip of the other.

As far as I can put mind to, Bill Doherty was the only person who ever called me Paddy. And apart from Bride he was the sole person to guess that I was down and on my back and needed the warp of a powerful hand.

84

We, as I said, finished about mid-day. Doherty didn't even wait for dinner. Father took out his sweat-soiled old billfold and counted several stained bills into Doherty's thick, calloused hand. Doherty shoved the bills into the pocket of his faded workshirt, and buttoned it down. He gave a hitch to his trousers' belt, squinted toward the sun, pulled his slouch hat lower on his forehead and spat into the dust and thin layer of grass lying over, curled and browning.

"I'm for Foxford and McKenna's." He half-smiled, then swung toward the old quarter-line that led toward Carden and into the Township of Daley.

"Miles is taking us in after supper . . . " father called.

Doherty merely flicked a hand and strode on without turning his head.

II

Old folks, as their years and wrinkles fold them up and pucker them in nearer the yawn of the grave, complain of speeding time: "My, how the years go by lately." And, "Seems the older you get the faster the time flies." But, unless you're waiting for a special event like Christmas or a Saturday afternoon ride into Lindsay, the minutes and hours whizz past a child quicker than the shadow of a wind-driven cloud slips across a patch of fireweed.

The months rolled into a ball and formed a year and God threw the year away to make room for another, and suddenly it was 1938 and half of it gone. Although the economy of most of the world remained depressed, father made money on cattle. We still had the surly old black-angus bull with the deep red echoes of some unquenched fire caught in the centre of his brown-black eyes. Until Aunt Kate came along the bull hadn't really been named, but when she had her first look at him, pacing sullenly around the heavily railed enclosure where he was kept 'til needed, Aunt Kate cried, "There's the devil for you!"

"Which one? Heaven was full of them at one time." Father leaned against the fence, licking a cigarette paper.

"Belial! *The sons of Belial beset the house roundabout and beat at the door:* Judges! 19:22," she said triumphantly.

"Sounds more like the old man when he was trying to get into a whore-house and it closed for taking inventory. But Belial seems a good fit.

"Belial—you black bastard; that's your moniker from now on," father said and flicked a burning match at the glistening, royal-black hide of the creature. But Belial rested his great jaw on the top rail of his prison and looked away, staring at no man knew where and thinking no man knew what.

Father had mated Belial with scrub Hereford heifers, letting the calves run with their mothers until they got too big and bunty and the cows dried in late autumn. When the calves became yearlings or two-year-olds they were shipped to Toronto on the Toronto & Nipissing.

The Fallons began to prosper.

Aunt Kate was, by now, a fixture as much as the unpainted lean-to up against the back kitchen which she closely resembled: a sort of flat, colourless look. She was still as straight as a guardsman, but of late she complained of "inner" trouble and took to what she called "doctorin'." Lindsay had capable medical people as well as a hospital; even a young doctor in his first year of practice in Kilmore had a reasonable trade. But Aunt Kate had found a gem in Foxford over in Daley Township. He lived in a squat bungalow with a hip roof and a verandah on the front commencing to sag back down from whence it came. The bungalow was shingled all over and stained a dirty chocolate-brown. A wooden sign was nailed alongside the front door. It said: DR. SULEIMAN, MEDICOLOGIST. Underneath, in smaller letters, the sign read: "Expert in female complaints, soother of hot flashes, tremors, chills, and the disorders of flatulence."

Dr. Suleiman was, even in such a small centre as Foxford, an unknown quantity. His head was large—so large his scrawny neck couldn't always keep it upright so that it tended to sag forward or loll sideways like a pullet's egg balanced on a lead pencil. His skull had bare places and tufts of rusty-iron hair in others; Timothy Connolly said the doctor's head reminded him of a rooster's ass at moulting time.

While his neck was thin, Dr. Suleiman had a huge body that was sagging all over toward the floor as though the pull of gravity was too much for it. His heavy shoulders sagged forward; his pot-belly hung bulbously into the top of his trousers; his feet were long, broad, and flat; he wore a kind of carpet slipper and as his feet splayed out there was something of a penguin look to the man. His eyes were the same colour as the exterior of his house–filthy chocolate centres with brown streaks radiating out into the whites. His hands were covered with warts which he picked at with a discoloured thumbnail so that the excrescences were either bleeding dully or scabbed over with crusted blood and sienna-coloured cells.

I had accompanied Aunt Kate once to her physician. Once the rickety steps were mounted one rang a bell-button that set up a dim, sad chime somewhere in the depths. In a few moments a slow shuffling and a parting of the nut-brown drapes over the half-glassed door advised that our signal had been heard and rescue was on the way. The doctor stared milkily out through the parted curtains, smiled too broadly for the shape of face he had, and pulled in the door.

"Velcome, velcome, Meesis T'ompson. You av' come zee your good fran' doctair, again, no? Zee bowels, I theenk. A bad zing–zee lower bowel."

"Mrs. Carrigrew," corrected my aunt. "And it's not my lower bowel; remember on the last visit you said I had an inflammation of the adenoidal spleen?"

"Ah, zee h'adenoidal spleen, of course." Dr. Suleiman chafed his hands together, dislodging tiny flakes of dead skin. "I haff so many pazients, you see, I am forget."

He led Aunt Kate into the recesses while I read the only magazine in the waiting room which was printed in English.

That was: *Agnew's Analysis of Distemper in the Horse.* All the rest of the reading matter was either Turkish, Arabic, or Dravidian.

As I waited the bell sounded and Suleiman splayed his way to the door and admitted a dumpling of a woman at least a foot wider than she was tall. After telling her he would be "weeth her in zust a meenut" the doctor sloughed on back to wherever he'd left Aunt Kate while the fat woman took up a chair directly opposite to me and glared at me with the eye of a gimlet. There are those who lay claim to a canard that fat people are eternally jolly; no greater mistruth has entered the folk mythology since Joe Smith declared himself a Mormon angel. The woman looked at me as if I had crawled up through a crack in the flooring and hissed at her.

Suddenly she leaned forward, or tried to, and said sharply, "Are you a Dillon?"

I denied not only kinship but knowledge of the Dillons.

"There's something reminds me of a Dillon about you. A Dillon traded my husband a bad horse, once."

Deep in my heart I was glad I was neither a Dillon nor a horse-trader. After that the fat lady contented herself with chewing what little remained of her fingernails. When Aunt Kate emerged she was carrying a round bottle with a second-hand cork plugged into the top. She took a little sip before we left the doctor's; she took a couple of jolts on the way home in our car (with the upturn in the family fortunes father had purchased a 1934 Dodge with wire wheels). When we reached the Clifden turn, Aunt Kate was singing "The Moon Hath Raised Her Lamp On High."

"I wonder," said father, baffled, as he garaged the car, "what in the name of Jesus was in that bottle of hers!"

Except for the occasional flash of humour father continued, in spite of his making a bit of money, to grow surlier, more remote from Bride and me, and increasingly vicious with the livestock. When old Belial, after an afternoon's work, managed to grind the top rail of his prison from its shackling wires father leaped the enclosure with a choked cry of fury. He had a pick-handle in his hand with which he smashed Belial across the face until the blood coursed out of the bull's nostrils. He sent me for fencing pliers and double-gauge wire and in silence we repaired the break while Belial, head down, blood trickling from his nose, brooded his eyes on something far away, but the red in back of the black eyes glowed like burning rubies.

I stood watching, frightened and trembling. Father, in his wrath, seemed beastlier than the bull. When father strode blackly toward the barn Bride stole from the porch where she had been watching, and slipped her hand, as warm and brown as new-laid hens' eggs, in mine. We looked in sympathetic misery at Belial standing, head down, the blood going drip-drip from his nostrils.

"Now why did he go and do that?" I tried to sound all grown up and manly and outraged, but my voice, beginning to turn husky now, nourished a seed of squeaking fear within it.

Bride scratched the back of one foot with the bare toes of the other. "I wasn't to tell this, but remember when daddy took me to Lindsay to get me new clothes and things?"

I nodded.

"Well, we saw mummy and that guy she ran away with."

"Oh lord!" I breathed.

"Yes." Bride's eyes were big and round with the burden of her news. She told me she and father were about to go into Filliard's Dry Goods when they met mother and the fellow she was living with face to face right on Kent Street.

"Daddy turned me away toward the store, but mummy hurried right up and kind of kneeled on the sidewalk and put her arms around me and kissed me. I was really scared because daddy looked just the same way when he was pounding poor Belial. Mummy said how much she missed us and stuff like that. Daddy looked right through her and he said, 'If you've finished your act, Iris, we'll be getting on.' "

"I guess that's why he larupped Belial so hard: he still has a mad on." I was disappointed he hadn't rounded on the man from the Pacific Tea Company.

Bride nodded solemnly.

We stood there for a long time, Bride's hand in mine, looking at the broken bull, each of us thinking of other broken things–toys and promises and lives. Things like that.

12

About a mile and a half west of the village of Kilmore there was a stone-crushing works that was a huge complex of quarries, steam shovels, crushers and grinders. The Toronto & Nipissing which ran through Kilmore built a branch line into "The Crusher," as it was locally known.

In those years crushed limestone was used in several employments: many county and township roads, as yet unable to afford concrete or macadam, were surfaced with crushed stone. After the passage of much traffic the stone kneaded down to a hard, durable surface especially in the wheel tracks. Powdered lime was shipped to cement plants. Limestone, crushed to small dimensions, was added to cement and water for making concrete foundations, bridges, footings, walls, and individual concrete blocks.

The owner of The Crusher was an outlander, a man of Italian extraction, from Toronto. His name was Tony Verazzi. Verazzi purchased, from the amazed but grateful owner, a tract of 200 acres composed of a sheet of limestone and shale thinly covered with an inch or two of scrambly soil on which a few sumac bushes, cinquefoil, and poison ivy fought one another for bitter survival. The main crusher was housed in a great lumpish building and was powered by electricity piped in by a direct line from a hydro plant on a river some distance to the north. A deep, massive quarry was carved and blasted out of the rock. A miniature railroad with diminutive locomotives and gondola cars freighted the raw chunks of stone, after they had been dynamited and pried loose, to the crusher. All day the monstrous jaws of the crusher ground relentlessly, weeping out the fragmented stone into railroad cars or dump trucks. The air about the plant was thick with dust; inside, where men manhandled the quarried chunks into the grinder, a pall of powder, flour-thick, crept into the mouths and nostrils of the workers and was inhaled into the lungs. Many a good man lay his length in the Kilmore graveyard after submitting to the "coughing disease."

The Crusher did not always work a full year round: the Great Depression hung over the Dominion as the grey smut hung over the plant. There was little new construction to require concrete. Only the maintenance of the roads, backed by provincial and federal funds, demanded quantities of crushed stone. Verazzi erected a number of cheap frame houses and rented them to his steady workers for a nominal amount. The wages, depending on the job and the skills that went with it, averaged about fifty cents an hour, but men, in those slack times, were happy to draw any sort of wage. Even Uncle Miles worked a few months of every year at The Crusher, operating a great, creaking, gasping, smoke-belching steam shovel, one of those colourful jobs a small boy longs for, pining to get into the thick of the smoke and heat and grease and haul on levers while wearing a striped, peaked engineer's cap and heavy yellow gauntlets.

Early in that year of 1938 Verazzi had fetched in from Toronto a nephew, Angelo Cardino, a son of Verazzi's sister. The owner appointed his nephew foreman of the works with authority second only to himself.

The Carden Irish didn't like Angelo Cardino. He was a city

93

man for one thing, an outlander for another. Also he was one tough piece of man. Angelo had had several professional fights in the boxing ring; his strong, brown hands hooked to the ends of arms where the veins and muscles jumped every time he moved them were as fast as the strike of a rattlesnake. Tom Degnan, who had worked for Verazzi longer than anyone around Carden, was sore-tailed when the owner brought in the twenty-five-year-old Angelo and set him over the crew. Degnan figured the overseeing job should have been his and he wasn't long in telling Cardino what he thought of kids coming from Toronto, still with soap behind their ears and their mother's milk in their bellies.

Degnan was reckoned to be just about the strongest man around the stone works. Even Bill Doherty, who had worked a time or two at The Crusher, couldn't lift a chunk of limerock as big as one heaved up and thrown in the maw of the crusher by Tom Degnan. Of course, Degnan never declared himself a fighting man, but his strength was so enormous none of the young fellows who liked to spar and wrestle at the noon break bothered to challenge old Tom.

As soon as Degnan told Cardino what he thought of him the young Italian told Degnan he was fired. "Get your lunch pail, if you have one, and get your ass out of here and down the road."

Degnan's was one of those thick skulls ideas find it difficult to penetrate and once in they have just as hard a time getting out. Old Tom stood like an axed steer for several seconds; then he roared and reached out his hams of hands to gather in Angelo and break him into fragments. Cardino quickly stepped aside, drove his left fist into Degnan's nose, breaking it and sending blood jets down the front of Degnan's shirt. Degnan opened his mouth to bellow, and Cardino quickly closed it with a quick punch—and another. Then, stepping back, the boxer sank one fist into Degnan's massive gut, and struck him up and under the jaw with the other. Degnan collapsed the way an old square-timbered barn collapses when the foundations have rotted and the giant hand of the wind catches it and it comes all a-tumble to the earth in a nest of tangled beams, rotting sheathing, and clots of buckled wood shingles.

Owney McCrone and Dick Rodden witnessed the fight from the loading dock. Angelo gestured them over.

"Any of you own a car?"

While Owney stared at the felled, bleeding hulk of Degnan, Rodden said he had a car.

"Do you know where this ape lives?"

Rodden nodded.

"Then load him up and take him home. I don't want to see his pig's head around here again. If he comes to, you can tell him that."

Relationships among the Irish are strong. The Degnans, through marriage, were related to the Farrells. Babe Farrell, a young fellow who worked mostly at logging for the Diamond Lumber Company, was considered a hard rock all through the county, and he'd licked three or four pretty good men, setting up a hard name for himself.

At a dance held in the school at Kilmore both Angelo and Babe were there; the natural collision happened. Angelo had a little more trouble with Babe than he had with Tom Degnan, but in the end Babe was face down on the grass in the school-yard, crying with pain and the bitter salt taste of defeat more acrid than the taste of his own blood filtering through cut lips and sharded teeth.

The Italian wasn't a fool. Sooner or later, he knew, he'd be mobbed or even shot. He took over an empty storage room behind the powerhouse at the rock works and put up a couple of punching bags and began to invite young fellows over on Saturday nights and Sunday afternoons to punch the bags, skip rope, and get a few lessons in boxing from Angelo. He was careful, however, not to allow any of the young men to learn enough to endanger his own status. In a few months Cardino was the focal point for a crowd of youths considering themselves a real rough element. They made the rounds of barn and school dances, hustling other males off the floor, grabbing girls and, once, invading Lindsay where they routed a couple of policemen. Even Babe Farrell was won over when Angelo met him on the street at Kilmore, shook his hand, and told him he was as tough a fighter as he ever faced.

Out of shyness and certain dislike for strangers I kept away from the miniature gym Cardino had set up to ingratiate himself with the local youths. But all of my peers from Kilmore commenced going, in the evenings, to The Crusher to do push-ups and spar with each other under the superior and patronizing eye of Angelo. Ed Kennedy and Niall Sweeney went; then Thad Whalen and Piper Mulvihille. John McKelvey came, and rock-hard Frank Teague of the rough, scrappy Teagues.

Frank Teague and Niall Sweeney drove into our yard in Frank's battered old "490" Chev' coupé he shared with his older brother, Jim. Frank was two or three years older than I; he had a hard, tough face set off by cold, frosty eyes the brows of which showed tracks of scar tissue.

I was bouncing a rubber ball off the brick of the house when the car came. Frank rolled to a stop.

"C'mere, Fallon!"

I tossed the ball aside, a little ashamed I'd been caught at a kid's game. I was a bit frightened: Frank was a hard fighter and his peremptory summons could have signified trouble.

"Get in and quit fuckin' around with that toy ball. We're goin' to The Crusher and spar around."

"Aw," I jabbed at the ground with the toe of my running shoe. "I don't know anything about boxing."

"And you never will if you glue your arse here all the time." Frank looked me over tersely. "Get in; you kin take a round or two outa the big wop for a starter."

I walked around the steaming radiator and got in the seat beside Niall. Aunt Kate was at the door of the back porch, wiping her hands on a dish towel and peering suspiciously at the car. I yelled at her I was going and would be back later. Her strident complaints were lost in the roar of the exhaust as

Frank wheeled smartly around and spurted down the driveway.

A few lads and the older Jim Teague were in the gym watching Angelo expertly punish the training bag, hitting it so deftly the roll of his fists merged precisely with the fluttering of the bag. The muscles along his back, arms and shoulders writhed and leaped. He looked like pictures of old Roman gladiators I'd seen in history books.

Frank gave me a shove forward.

"Here's one of them fightin' Fallons fer you." His smile was full of gaps.

Cardino came forward as lithely as a leopard, his brown thick hand extended.

"Glad to meet you, Fallon," he said.

I was about to shake the extended hand when Cardino's other palm exploded across my ear. My head rang; I staggered back a few paces, stumbled over a training mat, and sat down heavily.

While I stared up at the boxer in confusion, a ring of laughter circled among the watchers. Cardino grinned down at me, showing strong white teeth.

"First lesson: never shake hands or trust anybody you don't know."

I got to my feet, feeling foolish. My attempts to join in the laughter did not get beyond a wry grimace. Angelo tossed me a pair of boxing gloves.

"Put these on and go a few rounds with Mulvihille, there."

I gingerly stuck my hands in the padded mitts. Jim Teague, an older, even sterner, edition of his brother, laced up the wrists expertly and shoved me toward an enclosure closed off with a single rope serving as a ring.

"Go get him, tiger," he laughed.

Piper Mulvihille, a fun-loving boy a year or two older than I, ludicrous in a pair of his father's shorts, farm boots and woollen socks, was already in the ring, prancing and shadowboxing furiously. I crawled under the rope.

"Who's there?" asked Mulvihille. "I smell fresh meat. I, Lionel Strongfort Mulvihille, am about to demolish a mere Fallon. Look on me works, ye mighty Joe Louis, and despair!"

Mulvihille darted at me, flailing and punching. Startled, I backed into the rope and fell over it and out of the ring.

"You seen that, did you?" Mulvihille boasted amid the laughter. "With the mighty wind accompanying one of me mortal blows I wafted the Fallon clean free of the building."

Angry now, I ducked under the ropes and with more strength and fury than grace I waded into my opponent and sent him to the floor reeling, his nostrils seeping blood.

Mulvihille gazed up at me, stunned.

"Jeez, Patch, you didn't need to go gettin' serious."

He got to his feet and left the ring, the laughter gone. He scrubbed the back of his glove across his nose, looking at the bright blood curiously.

"Not bad," Cardino said, his teeth gleaming. "Not bad at all. You got the pizz-azz, kid; now all you need is a little finesse."

He looked around the group. "Anybody want to take big-foot, here, on?"

The youths shuffled; they looked around at each other to see if a volunteer was forthcoming. Frank Teague grabbed Mulvihille by the shoulder.

"I'll take him on. Gimme them goddamn gloves, Mulvihille."

"Aw, you're way older'n him, Frank," his brother protested.

"Yeah? Well, look at the fuckin' size of him." Frank had peeled off his shirt and was being laced into the gloves by Niall Sweeney.

We met in the centre of the ring, Frank moving in swiftly in a low crouch, his left fist waving in front of his face, his right coiled like an adder. I swung heavily, missed widely, and was immediately battered back to the rope by a flurry of hooks and straight punches. I had an inch in height on Frank, and some advantage in reach, but he was a hardened young fighter come of a fighting family. Someone pushed me off the rope and when Frank attacked again I circled away, eluding the danger in those flashing hands. Pressing close, Frank skidded on the concrete floor and I slammed him hard across the face tumbling him to his knees. He was up like a bob-cat, clawing and spitting in his anger. He battered at my face and when I held up my arms to protect my face he thudded hard blows into my belly. Again I lashed a long, looping right arm and again Frank sprawled on the concrete, a peculiar look on his face.

"You bastard!"

Frank stiffened me with a left to the abdomen, then struck up and under my jaw. The lights careened, flickered, and when they brightened again I was sitting flat on the floor of the ring, tasting the blood-salt from a gashed tongue. Frank stood over me, coldly, his gloves poised.

"Leave him be, Frank," Jim Teague spoke sharply.

"He thinks he's smart, the son of a bitch." Frank's face was red and raw where my two blows had landed.

"You ain't big enough to call a Fallon a son of a bitch, yet," his brother warned. "You went and brought him here, didn't you? You want to call somebody names go and call old Ward names; or Miles Fallon, either."

"Those two the 'Fighting Fallons' I've been hearing about?" Cardino asked casually.

Jim Teague nodded. He began unlacing my gloves. "They don't come much rougher, savin' maybe big Bill Doherty."

"Who's this Doherty?" Angelo's voice quickened so as to leave the question hanging dangerously in the air.

"The best fighter you'll ever see," I boasted. My voice was thick from the cut on my tongue. I was still angry with my clumsiness and Frank Teague's roughness which I calculated to be unnecessary.

The Italian threw back his head and let his laugh bounce off the ceiling. "Your Doherty," he pronounced it Dor'at'ee instead of the way it should have been pronounced – Do-hart-ee,

99

"will have to go some. I'm from old T.O., kid, where they make short work of the hay-shakers."

"Patch ain't bull-shittin'," Jim Teague said seriously. "You ever seen Doherty go?"

"I never saw him–period," Cardino was scornful.

"He licked Babe Farrell and Mick Rourke, both together, out behind the Benson House Hotel down in Lindsay." Frank, half-sorry he'd lost his temper, sided with his brother.

The Crusher foreman scratched his bicep thoughtfully, then flexed his arm to make the bicep jump up like a baseball underneath the hickory-coloured skin. He walked away, his laughter floating back.

The Kilmore boys forsook Angelo's gym, one by one. Most were farmers' sons or village lads working in summer for district ranchers and farmers. After heaving hay or stooking grain for twelve hours there was little energy or disposition to knock one another about under the critical, and perhaps jealous, eye of The Crusher boss. The brand of finality was marked the time Jim Teague took exception when Angelo battered the game but out-classed Frank into unconsciousness. The Teague brothers were set to double up on Cardino; a last-minute careless apology from the foreman prevented an all-out riot. Angelo took up with an older, rougher gang from west of Foxford. Only Babe Farrell sycophantically trailed after Cardino. Angelo and his bunch terrorized dance halls and took over beverage rooms. A great deal of muttering went the rounds of Carden and Kilmore to the effect that the "big wop" and his gang should be run out of the district, or the police could be brought in. No man was particularly quick to try the first proposition; the second was mere talk: an Irish community walked wide circles around the law.

13

The summer of 1938 was hot and droughty. By mid-August we hadn't known a drop of rain since June. The pastures lay scorched and sulking under the fiery sun, the grass all browned and crisped with nothing showing save the hairy stinging stalks of viper's-bugloss and the inedible moth mullein that Aunt Kate called Aaron's rod sticking up like yellow candles on the skin of the earth. All day long the cattle stayed deep in the swale-swamps where they could snatch mouthfuls of sharp swamp-grass and rub their fly-tortured bodies against the red osier and balsam fir. The rains had kept off for so long father worried we'd be obliged to start feeding the hay, stored snug in the great mows for winter, to the beeves. Even the swale, which normally carried in its bosom a shallow pond green with algæ, duckweed and bullrushes and which was fed by the Sally and lesser sources of brook water dry by summer, gave over to the searing weather and became an expanse of mud pock-marked from the hooves of the cattle.

Aunt Kate, who had no blood, gloried around in a woollen cardigan over her shapeless frock that banged relentlessly against the twisted black stockings hiding her calves and ankles from the gaze of lechers. A kind of garden, probably not cultivated since Grandmother Hannah's death, the old furrows of which, weeded over with burdock, pig-weed and curled dock, were yet visible, lay on the east side of the orchard where Belial was now quartered. Father may have regretted the terrible beating, for one day without a word he snapped a rope shank into the brass ring piercing the bull's nose, and led him into the orchard enclosure.

"I don't see why you had to put that brute in the orchard," Aunt Kate complained. "I'm thinking this while I'd be gettin' some seeds and garden. 'Twould keep these childern, here, occupied, too, and them with nothin' on their hands to do all summer."

Robbed of the orchard, Aunt Kate surveyed out a plot of gravel and clay where the wild mustard, chicory, burdocks and cinquefoil fought one another relentlessly. In the spring I was forced, after school and on Saturdays, to delve away at this crust with shovel and rake while Aunt Kate, protected from the sun by a magnificent straw hat the size of a bandit's sombrero, staked out rows and doled out, miserly, radish and lettuce seeds. She cut potatoes into sections, each section containing an eye and dropped these into shallow pits I grudgingly dug with a shovel.

By August a few dispirited stalks of sweet corn and potatoes survived the drought. An army of striped bugs fell on the potatoes, and before they were detected they had swathed through half the patch leaving ugly, tattered stalks devoid of leaves. Aunt Kate spotted this spoliation and ran crying back to the house, flapping her arms like an animated scarecrow.

"Get the coal-oil" (she pronounced it 'kile-ile'), she shrieked. "They're at me taties, the dastards. Oh, they'll burn in hell this day."

Bride and I were forced to fill cans with kerosene and then go up and down the potato rows, picking the messy little bugs from the foliage with our bare fingers and dropping them into the kerosene. As each bug was touched it emitted a loathsome stench and an acrid, orange-coloured substance. When we had deprived the potatoes of their bugs we scrubbed our hands with Kirk's Castile soap until they were red raw, but the acrid smell of the insects remained with us for days.

On a particularly sweltering morning Aunt Kate ordered Bride and me out to hoe-chop the weeds between the stalks of sweet-corn.

"It's too hot, auntie," Bride wailed.

The old woman gaped, then dug her hands into her hips. "Too hot, is it? A lot you know about heat. You'll be out and have them rows weeded or I'll make somethin' hot you don't want to be." She raised the broom in her hand and shook it threateningly.

"You touch her with that broom and I'll bust it over your old ass!"

Aunt Kate whirled and stared at me, her mouth working like that of a gaffed trout.

"C'mon, Bride," I said.

We walked out through the back porch and toward the south pastures, Aunt Kate's imprecations whizzing after us like deer flies.

"Yez wait! Just yez wait! Ye snipes! Wait'll your father hears o' this!"

"Where'll we go?" Bride shook her long hair as if to free it from Aunt Kate's barbs.

"Out to the windmill. We can always get a cold drink there and dip in the trough, too."

We walked toward the south pastures, past the barn and the flutter of pigeon wings, the toasted grass crisp as shredded-wheat crumpling under our bare feet. The soil, in places, was so thin that we walked upon the bare bones of the earth itself— grey limerock, burning to the touch, and marked with pet-rified configurations resembling long worms, fern leaves, and strange, bug-looking skeletons gone to fossil.

"What are those things, Patch?" Bride prodded one centi-pede-like form caught fast in the limestone and about six inches long.

I hadn't the ghost of an idea so I fell back upon religion.

"That's one of the old devils God chased out of heaven along with Lucifer and buggers like that. God lit a fire and

103

boiled the earth until the rocks melted, then He kicked them little shoneen devils to hell and gone all across the world, and when the fire went out they were caught fast in the rocks."

Bride shivered. "I'm glad they are stuck and can't get out."

Brave with Aunt Kate's theology I warned, "But pretty soon God's going to let the old devil loose for a thousand years and like He told old Noah, 'No more water; you're going to get fire next time.' Then there'll be a mighty old fire so hot the rocks will melt and out will pop all the devils great and small, and unless you've said your rosary every night and confessed all your sins to the priest them devils'll be getting their claws and teeth into you and pulling you down into the melted rocks. Then you'll be in the soup!"

"Jeepers!" Bride covered her mouth with her hand, her eyes widening. "I forgot to tell all my sins to Father Blaney last time I went."

"You've had it," I said, with the smug air of one who has been saved and knows it. "What didn't you tell Father Blaney?"

"I didn't mention what I said to Lydia Davis; I told her she had a face like a cow's twat."

"And so she has," I said judiciously. "It's never a sin to tell the truth."

We scrambled through the ironwood poles of the gate separating the barn compound and the south pastures. We passed a small field of ten acres or so in which, that spring, father had seeded oats. The crop was so poor the grain hadn't been worth running the reaper through it; father mowed the wreck of the oats in July and added it to the hay.

There were choke-cherries all along the fenced grainfield; the berries weighed down the branches. We stripped handfuls of the fruit; it was nearly all stone-seed, the flesh acid and puckering our mouths.

"I'm thirsty-dry," Bride complained. "I'll be glad to get to the windmill."

At the very tether end of our land—at the line fence separating our south pasture from Ed Cronin's wheat field–grandfather Fallon had, long years before, erected a windmill of metal legs and cross-braces with a huge set of circular galvanized vanes that whirled in the wind and set the suction rod of the pump to clanking and drawing up and flickering out a stream of rusty-coloured water tasting like sulphur. The water came out of an iron spout and splashed into a concrete tank brown with age and beginning to crack through its reinforcing rods on the outside. Within the tank a lazy green scum of water sporting here and there the discontented head of a small frog offered little attraction for the thirstiest of three-year-old steers. While the Sally supplied plenty of water the year round grandfather had erected the windmill to provide water for the south pasture which, at that time, was shut off, and separated young beeves from milk-cows.

There was a none-too-solid metal ladder, merely rungs, leading up to the platform where the windmill head and vanes were situated. Bride and I loved to climb the ladder and stand up on the platform and look all over the countryside. We could, on clear days, see the red-tailed hawks circling and circling the green-wooded Killylick Mountain; we could see the Talbert River flashing in the sun where it cut Cronin's farm in half. We could see our own great barn with the red paint of its sides and ends peeling and scruffing, and the twisted wire cable of the lightning rods topped by porcelain balls and a spear of iron so that lightning would take a whack at something high and handy like those rods and then follow a conductor wire into the ground where it had no show. It was a fine theory and for many years farmers fell for it; you can still see the occasional old country home or barn with the balls and spear points. The trouble was that lightning, a child of nature and therefore perverse, often took a notion to by-pass those enticing rods and zipped in through an open vent setting fodder on fire, or else it blasted a hole straight through a shingled, or even a metalled, roof sending the whole business up to glory with fire and flame.

105

South and across the Talbert just inside the Carden line was an expanse of woods generally known as "The Catholic Bush." Formerly, the wood had been part of the holding of Dermot Conroy—a valiant papist—who, so it was said (mostly by Uncle Miles), had his nose up the priest's arse so far he had to breathe through his mouth which gave him the heaves and so he died. Whatever—Dermot's wife had quit living on him, leaving him with two sons and two daughters all of whom fled home and, one after another, married black Protestants. When Conroy died and was buried in state beside his wife in the Carden burying ground, the reading of his will demonstrated that he who laughs last laughs last. Conroy's laugh consisted of his excommunicating his turn-coat offspring by leaving them neither stick, stone, nor gudgeon pin. The Conroy farm, bankable securities, and the tremendous maple and beech wood were left *in toto* to the Parish of Kilmore, the priests of that parish to act as guardians and lessees and to enjoy such monetary benefits as might accrue until the horn of Gabriel blared and the heavens opened to allow Conroy, his sparrow of a wife, and one child who cashed his chips five minutes after he was baptized, access to the Gates of Peter where they'd have the pleasure of squatting at the right hand of God forever and all day Sunday.

The sole stipulation in all this was that the hardwood bush was not to be logged, cut down, or even brushed out. Old Conroy had, in his time, made maple syrup each spring in that wood. Whether he, in making his last assigns, visualized a squad of bare-footed friars hopping about in the snow, gathering sap, and boiling it down for syrup, will never now be known. The Parish of Kilmore, or rightly the Church of Our Lady of Perpetual Help, rented out the tillable fields and the grazeable pastures. The wood they left strictly alone, and for all I know it may stand yet and will continue to do so until the last dog's hanged.

Conroy's family fought to break the will; I think they took it all the way to the Supreme Court of Ontario. They lost every suit and retired with their heretical spouses in a black rage. It was rumoured that Gid, the eldest son, got drunk one night and drove to the cemetery for the sole purpose of pissing on his father's grave. But the night was dark and Gid was drunk, so he mistakenly leaked all over poor Maude Hannegan's resting place. Maude was a poor spinster who died in her forty-third year of loneliness. Perhaps she was glad of even that little attention.

The thing that made the Catholic Bush interesting to Bride and me was the eagles' eyrie hung up in a crotch of a tremendous maple. The eagles had nested in the Catholic Bush for years, although many farmers swore the birds killed their lambs, attacked their turkeys, and slaughtered anything that was alive and belonged to a farmer. There was rumbling about "shooting the buggers" or organizing a raiding party to go over and set fire to the nest which was as big as a haystack. However, the parish priest came to the defence; the eagles, he said–and straight out from the pulpit–had been sent by Michael the Archangel to defend and keep watch over parish property. The man made it plain that the predatory birds belonged strictly to God and not to Caesar.

From the windmill platform Bride and I could watch the great creatures as they stood look-out from some handy dead limb, or came sailing into the bowl of the nest with an entire woodchuck in their talons. There was something majestic and regal and wild and terrible about those eagles. It would take small enough imagination to think of them as the wards of some avenging archangel come with a fiery sword and golden wings to slash the life from the enemies of heaven.

The metal ladder rungs were burning hot. We climbed to the stand where the vanes hung perfectly still under the scorch of the sun. The heat engulfed us.

"Let's go back down," I said listlessly. Bride thought she'd like to splash in the tank. We dropped back down the rungs, scaring away a sinuous garter snake that had been hunting frogs in the rank growth about the concrete water tank. Bride pulled her skinny dress over her head and slid out of her panties.

"Hey! what if somebody comes along?"

"I'll duck down in the water and pretend I'm a frog." Bride flung a leg over the side and tested the water. She let herself glide under the strings of green algæ, then broke into the air, strings of frog-green slime caught in her hair. Beneath the scum of the water her body looked different–older; there seemed to be an increasing roundness. When Bride turned over on her belly and dog-paddled, her buttocks looked round and enticing. I felt a nervous rasp in my throat.

"I got to go and have a leak," I said, turning toward a small spinney of basswood and hornbeam growing along the line fence between our land and Cronin's. When I came back Bride was squatting behind the tank.

"How come boys can do it standing up and girls can't?" Bride stood up and scratched idly at her bare belly.

I told her boys were made different than girls. Bride was curious. "How, different?"

"Just different, that's all."

Bride looked down at herself. "Show me. I want to see."

My mouth felt dry and stringy the way it did when we ate the choke-cherries. I prickled with excitement. I unbuckled my belt and opened my trousers. Bride came up and touched me.

"Hey!" she exclaimed. "It's growing! It gets bigger!"

A brassy taste was at my lips. I smelled sulphur. Quickly I turned away, fastening my trousers.

"You better get dressed or the sun'll burn you to hell and gone." I was gruff.

"Oh, all right. But, gee–you're funny!"

We walked quietly home through the sullen heat.

14

Usually our family went into Kilmore on Saturday nights to do the week's shopping and hear the week's gossip. For smaller, more immediate necessities we went to Mavely and bought butter, salt, and other such items from Abel Coventry. Abel Coventry it was who had loaned father money that first terrible winter and whatever his faults, father had a long memory for a favour. Abel was getting old; at one time he'd been a tall man. but he now had a stoop that was more like a crouch, and the mice got into his brown-sugar bin and laid turds in it. Coventry's wife had died screaming in anguish of womb cancer in the Ross Memorial Hospital in Lindsay some three years before.

Very occasionally we drove the thirty or so miles to Lindsay; father hated the county seat, and while we went to Lindsay on the Fair Day, the Fallons religiously avoided the town. Uncle Miles once said the inhabitants of Lindsay had the widest street and the narrowest minds of any town north of the Rio Grande.

If we had hardware to buy or when we were shipping cattle, we drove to Foxford. Foxford had more stores and more variety than Kilmore; also five trains a day made their chuffing way through Foxford on their way to and from Lindsay and Toronto. Kilmore could brag of only three trains a week; Timothy Connolly said if the service through Kilmore on the

Toronto & Nipissing got any worse, they'd take the locomotive off and just send up a hand-car. Oddly enough, Foxford was proudest of the train that didn't stop at their depot at all: that was the Limited Express which, the Foxford people liked to say, when you heard her whistle for the grade crossing south-east of town there was just enough time to see her red tail lights as she fled over the trestle bridge across Devlin's Creek.

Once there had been a blacksmith shop right on the bank of the Talbert River, but the blacksmithing trade died out about the same time as the smith himself. One of the Devoe brothers (the other was shot stone dead at Ypres) started up a little garage and auto-repair in the old smithy; the business had one door, one greasepit, and one gasoline pump. There was a sign painted on the gable end that said DEVOE MOTORS . . . WE FIX THE BEST. Uncle Miles said that was a lot of horseshit because the best didn't need fixing and all we had up in this neck of the county was the worst, anyway.

On one corner of the two intersecting main streets was the Fairbanks House, a hotel and beer parlour run by a little Irishman named McKenna. It was called the Fairbanks House because years ago when all was dry and prohibition in the saddle, old J.I. Fairbanks was chairman of the anti-saloon league and chief financial backer of the Women's Christian Temperance Union. When the Liberal government under Hepburn beat out the old Henry regime, prohibition ended; beer and liquor could be bought by the case and bottled or draught beer could be sold on licenced premises. Barney McKenna, when he bought the hotel, decided to honour old Fairbanks in the best way he knew how. The Fairbanks House was known for two things: inside all was peaceful and content-ment reigned because McKenna was quick to break up fights with a bung-starter. The other was the number and ferocity of the fist fights that took place out behind where the toilets were or out on the street where all could enjoy the spectacle.

One evening, a Saturday, when the parch of August appeared to have reached a climax, father, Aunt Kate, Bride,

110

and I went to Foxford. All four of us went for different reasons: Aunt Kate had run low on medicine that was curing her adenoidal spleen; Bride was going to buy a new frock for Etta Marie Sutter's birthday party; although I now had a gleaming blue bicycle with twin cross bars and a Sturmey-Archer brake, Foxford was fourteen miles distant and a storm was brewing up to the southwest where the Trent Canal sliced through a chunk of stump-strewn water known as the Drowned Lands. That was one reason. The other concerned pretty little Laurel Dansinger who sometimes helped tend her father's hardware store on Saturday nights. The Dansingers were German. The storekeeper had spent nearly three years on the Western Front and had a puckered hole through the muscle of his left arm to show for it where a Lee-Enfield bullet came in one side and out the other. Dansinger was in a tough spot: the Irish had no use for him because he had set up as the village atheist. "You Christians chust a boonch o' dommed fools. Vere vos your Gott when ve made manoor out each udder in der big var? I chust ask you dat, hay?" The Protestants, particularly those who had served in the Big War and belonged to the Legion and carried flowers to a little cenotaph once a year in November, figured a German was a German and still an enemy to be shot at, blown apart with a grenade, or gut-stuck with a saw-toothed bayonet.

Yet what kept the man in business was he knew his hardware; he knew it right down to the three-quarter-inch finishing nail or a monkey-wrench with knurled jaws and a wooden handle costing ten bucks. There was nothing mechanical he couldn't fix except motor cars, which he hated–the first and last automobile Dansinger owned backed itself over his foot and Dansinger never forgave it or any other motorized conveyance.

Dansinger had a wife, although she kept pretty much to herself upstairs where the living accommodations were. I think I saw her a time or two but I'll be damned now if I can recall what she looked like.

I'll never forget what Laurel looked like, although it's been many a long year since I've seen her and I've no way of knowing whether she is above ground or below. She was pretty, was Laurel, in that pink-cheeked, corn-flower blue-eyed fashion of many Germans. Her hair was the colour of corn silk—and of the same texture. Laurel wore it in two braids twisted over her head, and although she was at least a year younger than my fifteen years her little apple breasts swelled out the fabric of her dress. I was sweet on Laurel Dansinger from the first time I saw her.

My father had his own reason for going into Foxford that night, although at the time I didn't know what that reason was, nor did father volunteer about it. He drove and I sat up front in the two-door Dodge with him; Bride and Aunt Kate sat in the back, the latter dividing her acid comments on the shortness of Bride's skirt to the great blessing God was surely about to bestow upon us in the nature of the thunder storm that was lining up over the Drowned Lands. Why God had been so stingy with his rain until everything green turned brown and died Aunt Kate didn't mention.

Through the open windows the drum roll of distant thunder could be heard and, as the sun dropped behind the anvil-headed storm clouds, the wink of glare lightning was seen making an outline of the Greenbrier hills that ranged along a mile beyond Foxford.

Foxford was busy: farmers came in old cars, new cars, closed cars, and open cars. They came, a few, in horses and buggies. Women wandered the concrete walks, clutching their purses tightly lest the bit of egg and butter money inside take wing and fly away into the teeth of the storm. At their skirts and heels dogged their children: "Maw! . . . Maw, gimme five cents fer an ice-cream, maw. Hey, mummy, didja see that toy racin' car in Dansinger's windah? Didja, mummy? Mother, don't forget you promised to get me shoes with real high heels, tonight."

The menfolk stood or sat around the fronts of stores or

perched up on the counter of Foxford's second garage, in the front where they kept the tires and parts for display and sale. A lot of the farmers wore bibbed overalls, straw hats and rough ankle boots. The cattlemen mostly wore brown pants rolled up over high-topped leather boots that laced to the knees; that and cotton shirts and slouched felt hats. An occasional farmer, under the thumb of his wife, came in his "in-between" trousers which were a little too dirty for church and yet good enough so that a man hated to wear them out in the barn shovelling manure.

A group of younger men satelliting around a dark-looking fellow of twenty-five or thereabout crowded out of Skinner's pool room and headed noisily in the direction of the Fairbanks House, nudging people aside and laughing at the typically inane jests that young men in groups find infinitely humorous.

When the noisy group had passed, one of the farmers sitting on a bench in front of Dansinger's nodded in the direction the young men had taken. "That young Angelo's comin' right along. I heard he knocked out a fella from Buffalo at Maple Leaf Gardens the other night. The other lad was third in line for the belt, too."

The one beside him, a greyish-faced man with a long upper lip, spat between his feet. "Them Eye-talians ain't got the moxie when she comes right down to her. You wait— Cardino'll run into somethin' too big fer him to handle, yet."

A third man laughed. "You always said the niggers couldn't fight, either—and look at Joe Louis."

The greyish man grunted. "Twon't be long before some white man'll come along and take his number, too."

Aunt Kate had stepped along to Dr. Suleiman's; Bride, having cajoled a whole ten dollars from father, disappeared into Selkirk's Dry Goods & Notions; father, after getting a small package of cigars which he rarely smoked, went into the Men Only side of the Fairbanks House beer parlour.

I went into Dansinger's and pretended I was interested in a glass case of XL and Green River knives all costing several times as much money as I possessed. Laurel was behind the counter explaining to a farmer that, while she would ask her father to make sure, she didn't think they had a foot-valve for a deep-water well in stock.

I worked my way around the case of jack-knives and saw Laurel looking past the overalled bulk of the farmer at me, although whether it was a look smacking of interest or finding out if I was intending to swipe a jack-knife I couldn't tell. I had seen Laurel about three times and spoken to her once: father had sent me to the hardware store when he, I, and Aunt Kate had motored to Foxford for one of the old woman's "doctorin'" sprees, to buy ten pounds of three-inch common nails. While I fished in my tattered old wallet for the bill father had given me, Laurel, one white-fingered hand resting lightly on the paper sack of nails, looked me over carefully— her corn-flower blue eyes almost expressionless. I couldn't really tell from that look what the girl was thinking: did she think, "There's a fine-looking strap of a boy." Or, "Ye gods! another back-country bum."

"May I help you?" her voice had nice round syllables with the merest trace of a German accent. The farmer had departed the store grumbling about the state of the country when you couldn't buy a foot-valve closer than Toronto.

"I—no, I guess not. I was looking over those knives there. Got to get me one, sometime."

"They're of very good quality." Her mouth was generously wide and I could have sworn there was a trace of lipstick.

"Yeah. Well, got to get goin'; see you sometime again." I left with the full realization mine wasn't the most romantic parting speech yet delivered.

I stepped out into the street to hear the electric storm grumbling still in the Greenbriers as if the aspen-covered hills had caught it and were holding onto the storm so's to extract as much of the rain as the thirsty land could drink. The lightning was closer now; a flash of light brighter than the electric bulbs stuck up on the poles under tin canopies would wash the street with a flare, then whisk away with the thunder chasing after it and ripping a line of sound down the darkening clouds.

The men were still sitting or standing around; the tidier chewers walked over to the curb and spat a molasses-coloured spit into the gravelled street; others, less fastidious, plurped a mouthful of brown cud at their feet or in the middle of the sidewalk.

Down street, in the direction of the Talbert bridge, I saw Bill Doherty coming straight up the middle of the concrete sidewalk. There was just the whisper of a sway–the suggestion of a stagger–that let you know the man had a full load aboard.

"Jesus, here comes Doherty: polluted to the eyeballs again."

"How do you know?" asked the grey-faced man, testily. "You nor nobody else ever saw him down on his back."

"If he and young Cardino locked horns you'd see Doherty on his back quick enough."

The greyish man turned suddenly on the speaker. "I got fifty bucks right here in my pocket says yer a goddamn liar. That black scorpion of an Eye-talian would last about as long as you with Doherty, you stupid asshole."

As Doherty approached, the loungers greeted him casually; "G'nite, Bill." "How're yuh t'day, Bill?" "How's the ole world treatin' you, Bill?"

Doherty looked neither right nor left, ambling in that curious way straight through the knot of sitters and standers, acknowledging their greetings with a flick of one tremendous hand.

As Doherty made his unhurried and almost-even progress up the centre of the walk, Angelo Cardino and his cohorts streamed out of the hotel and headed downstreet in the direction of Skinner's pool hall. Doherty walked straight on, all but Cardino making way to let him by. Deliberately, Cardino slammed his shoulder into that of Doherty. It was as though a heavy cruiser had rammed a battleship.

"What's the matter, bo? The sidewalk not big enough for

you to walk on?" Angelo's arrogant voice rang down through the street over the muttering thunder and the sound of auto engines being warmed before the trip back to the farm or ranch.

Doherty's voice was mild. "It's big enough." His eyes focused blankly on Cardino.

"Maybe you better get out and walk on the street with the rest of the horses."

"Uh-huh." The older man rubbed his jaw thoughtfully. "I see. I guess maybe both of us'll take us a walk out on the street, kiddie."

"Any time you like," the boxer said scornfully.

At once the street loungers began to intervene; they pulled and grabbed Cardino and Doherty; they got in between and tugged and hassled, and shopkeepers came to the doors of their stores to see what was going on. Women screamed and kids ran and yelled, while all the time the storm lumbered in closer; the lightning flashes grew more vivid; the thunder ripped apart the gathering clouds.

Finally, Doherty stretched out both arms and men fell away from him as he parted them quicker than Moses separated the Red Sea. He picked his way with short, regular steps until he stood squarely in the middle of Broad Street.

"All right, kiddie," he said. "Now's your time."

The young Italian angrily shook off the half-restraining hands of his friends; he walked quickly into the middle of the street and faced Doherty. Cardino went into a tigerish crouch, weaving, dancing around the older man.

Cardino was nearly as tall as Doherty, although perhaps twenty pounds lighter which still made him a hefty man to deal with–Doherty was reputed to weigh 240 pounds. The boxer was wide through the shoulders; wide-shouldered and narrow in the waist. He wore a gym singlet that revealed brown arms with muscles almost as large as his opponent's.

For a minute or two the pair circled in the dust of Broad Street. Then the boxer leaped and struck, dodging quickly back to a crouch, easily avoiding the clubbed hand flung at him by Doherty. The sound of Cardino's fist on the flesh of Doherty's face was audible above the storm. A blue bruise beginning to well blood appeared on Doherty's cheek bone.

Twice, three times, Cardino leaped in, struck, then resumed his circling crouch; each time he left a bloody and purple mark on the Irishman's thick face. The boxer darted in once more but a blinding flash of lightning dazzled the entire street. No one, as they claimed afterward, saw Doherty strike down his adversary, yet there Cardino lay in the street, his lower jaw at a funny, loose angle, blood trickling from his open mouth. Cardino turned over, got to his hands and knees and slowly stood up. He charged in again, but it was the rush of a dying elk. Doherty's left hand caught him in a vise, the right smashed into Cardino's already-broken jaw.

A terrible "Aaaaaaagh!" went up from the crowd–a moan of something akin to sympathy and something related to horror. The cry drowned Cardino's scream just before he was struck full force by the flat of Doherty's left hand. The boxer fell forward in the street, his feet twitching.

A knot of Angelo's friends headed by Babe Farrell made a rush toward Doherty who was standing, staring down at the beaten fighter, blood dripping from his own wounds into the gravel.

Suddenly, my father was there and, to my surprise, the man with the greying face.

"Don't try it, Babe," father warned. "This fight's over."

One of Angelo's crowd cried Cardino had to be taken to a doctor. "Take him," said the grey man. He and father led Doherty away and up the street. The little hotelkeeper hurried down to meet them.

"Bring him inside; I've got some first-aid stuff."

Father said he didn't think Doherty was badly hurt. "He's more cut up than anything else."

"That Eye-talian's a mess," the grey man chuckled. "He'll be sippin' clear soup through a straw until Christmas."

15

When school opened in September after the summer holiday I fought against going back. I was fifteen, had passed the entrance exams in June, and I was tired of schools, especially the one-horse country schools like Clifden. I was no happier at the prospect of boarding some place in Lindsay while I attended the high school there; there was no secondary school closer than Lindsay. Aunt Kate lectured me on the mighty intellects of past and dead Fallons; father didn't seem concerned one way or another. It was Bride who decided me.

"Gee whiz, Patch," she argued. "I'll be all alone—the only Catholic. And that dirty Mickey Malloy—he's always after the girls."

And so I went back to school. Miss Guildforth had married during the summer break and was lost to Clifden forever. Her place was taken by a male teacher, a smallish, slim fellow with a Clark Gable moustache, spaniel-brown eyes, and a deep bass voice that made, so they said, the girls' spinal nerves flutter. I was then in the Tenth Grade, but the new teacher, Duane Sterling (Mister Sterling to the students), possessed a certificate allowing him to teach grades from One through Ten.

I neither liked nor disliked Mr. Sterling. He had a grand

voice (and knew it) for reading poetry aloud. Book in hand, the look of a concerned undertaker on his face, the teacher would stand by his desk before the pupils and in beer barrel tones he'd roll out: "*The splendour falls on castle walls . . .*"

But I couldn't listen to whatever fell on castle walls when outside the fox grapes were twining with virginia creeper around black haw trees, and crabapples were ripening in what was left of Shaughnessy's orchard. I looked out of the window of the schoolhouse and saw Mel Handford at the fall plough-ing, using a walking plough and cutting a rich, brown furrow as straight as a surveyor's string. The crows followed the plough at a discreet distance, the crows and some gulls that'd flown up from the lake to have a meal of cut-worms and other grubs uncommon around places gulls frequented.

One afternoon I was staring out the window instead of ap-plying myself to a problem in algebra when I was conscious of Mr. Sterling standing beside my desk gnawing the end of a ruler.

"Padraic," he said, more mournfully than in anger, "why don't you pack up all of your things from your desk–and there seems to be little enough–and go home and become a railroad engineer or a hockey player or a master plumber. You are not now, and never will be, a devotee of the intellect."

I got to my feet, facing the teacher; I was, even then, four or five inches taller than he. "You're right, Sterling," I said, de-liberately omitting the "Mr.," "I have a feeling if I stay in this place I'll never be anything–the same as you."

The teacher bowed, acknowledging the insult. "Very well, but we need not part enemies."

He stuck out his hand and we shook.

As I cleared out my desk, Bride gathered her own belong-ings. After that she went to the Separate School at Kilmore. Father bought her a bicycle; in bad weather he drove her to school in the car.

"Thank the heavenly angels for mercies shown," was Aunt Kate's reaction. "Now that Bride is among her own she will hear the Virgin knocking and she'll take the veils."

As September began to slip toward October and the red maples caught fire around the edges, father and I drove to Lindsay to a stock sale where he intended to buy yearlings. As we drove by the high school I saw Laurel Dansinger in a white skirt and sweater going down the walk with a good-looking boy in ice-cream pants and a school blazer. Both carried tennis racquets. They were absorbed in conversation; Laurel didn't look up as we passed.

"That looked like Joachim Dansinger's little girl," father remarked.

"I don't know. I didn't take any notice."

Father looked sideways at me, but said nothing. A grey surf of cloud spread over the sky and the rain began falling.

Father, like the frozen cascara leaves, had turned in on himself. He drank rarely, but he seemed obsessed with making money. I do now believe, after all these years, that father loved and missed my mother more than he let on, and his preoccupation with accumulating cash was his way of proving himself the victor. Once in a while some tidings from one source or another would reach us about mother and the man she was living with. It seems he lost a lot of jobs through drink or just plain damned inefficiency: at any rate the last word we had, and that came from Timothy Connolly, mother and her common-law husband were on the dole in Toronto.

We were sitting in the kitchen one evening, Bride at the table near the lamp cussing out decimals under her breath; Aunt Kate was darning a hole in the heel of one of her black stockings, father was in his easy chair over by the radio with his feet up on the book stand. I was sitting by the kitchen range listening to the rain slashing at the window panes and rattling the old shutters which had never been used and were no good for anything if you did want to use them.

"D'you remember if Tim said where she was living?" Father leaned forward and tapped into a saucer the dottle he had scraped from the bowl of his pipe with his stock knife. I noticed the grey streaks were spangling more and more through father's hair, and that there were little tremors in the hands that had once been as steady as mountains.

Bride and I shared a quick look, then went back pretending we'd not heard. We could have relied on Aunt Kate:

"Eh?" she squinted like a mole overtop her silver-rimmed spectacles that gave her a look remindful of a withered Benjamin Franklin. "Where does who live? Tim Connolly? Why he lives. . . ."

"No! where did Connolly say Iris was living?" Father was half-angry at enquiring and half-angry because he had to roar the question into Aunt Kate's deaf ear that changed sides whenever the owner thought it necessary.

Aunt Kate dropped her eyes slyly to the worn-thin stocking she was labouring to repair. "I did hear Tim say something about it, but I forget now. The way my hearing's been going lately. I think it was Vancouver–or Halifax."

Father grunted and picked up a copy of *The Farmers' Advocate*. "She'll not be enjoying the things she'd have here."

Materially, father had prospered. He had a native shrewdness about beef cattle: when to buy and when to sell. Uncle Miles had the same canniness; when he returned from the war in Europe the Soldiers' Settlement Board set him up with 200 acres in Clifden Township. But drink and the memory of some woman long married to someone else scratched and dug at Uncle Miles' innards so that he did little more than hang on and make his mortgage payments to the Soldiers' Settlement Board.

When the Ontario Hydro Electric strung poles and ran a line on the Mavely Road past our house, father got an electrician up from Lindsay and had the house and barn wired. An electric ice-box did away with keeping butter and milk in a crock sunk in a pool near where the Sally Brook sprang. We had a reasonably new automobile, and a big console Stewart-Warner radio with an outside aerial reaching, on poles, halfway to the barn.

121

Father, still holding the farmers' magazine, leaned back and put his hands behind his head.

"She won't have the luxury wherever she is she'd have here." There was no gloating in his voice; just a kind of sadness.

While October was still glowing through its own haze, father sent me on some errand or other over to Foxford. Over the years I've forgotten, but I know I was to get something at Dansinger's; probably drill bits.

It was one of those mornings when you feel the warmth will never leave and the cold never come. I once heard Uncle Miles say, bitterly, that October weather is like a woman's love: just when it's at its best and warmest is the time to expect the blizzard to come following. Before I was of an age to know better I asked Uncle Miles what had happened between his old love and himself. A quick flash of blue anger lit up his eyes, then went out. He laughed.

"The wind switched to the north," he said, and changed the subject.

I rode my bicycle to Foxford, although in those days we never called them bicycles; it was "wheels." The hills were afire with reds and yellows and oranges; even the great oaks standing lonely in some pasture showed dark red through the green. Only the hickories grumpily turned their foliage into rashes of brown spots and let the leaves fall untidily wherever the winds wished. Along the creeks the sedges and bur-reeds spiked up in chrome-yellow and burnt sienna. Mallards flew up from the marshes—whole families of six or eight. As I wheeled past the Catholic Bush a soaring shadow passed over me and the road and sailed swiftly ahead of me. I stopped and looked up, thinking to see a turkey vulture, but it was one of the great bald eagles, likely the female, because her giant wings scornfully carried her over and ahead of me as though she were the goddess Hera and I was merely a poor earthling who had never felt the lifting warmth of a thermal current, or had viewed the world from a limb one hundred and twenty feet from the ground.

I crossed the first Devlin's Creek bridge at the purlieus of Foxford. The creek (everybody said "crik") liked the town so well it hooked itself and ox-bowed back and forth until it crossed Broad Street three times under a concrete bridge and two wooden ones. The Talbert, joined by the creek a mile or so away, avoided Foxford by a quarter-mile and came no closer than where the Toronto & Nipissing crossed the river on a trestle.

The story of Foxford's three bridges is interesting and needs telling: When "Bones" Gridley ran for Member of the Legislative Assembly down at Queen's Park in Toronto, he ran on the Conservative ticket headed by a fellow named Henry–that is his last name was Henry. What his first name was I've forgotten and it's not important to the story, any more than Henry was important to the province generally and politics particularly. One of Gridley's platform planks was "three new concrete bridges over Devlin's Creek and safety for our elderly and children." I suppose Gridley figured the middle-aged, if they popped through the rotting planks, could take care of themselves.

Gridley got himself elected and his word was as good as that of any politician. Before he was elected to Queen's Park Foxford had three wooden bridges in various stages of falling down. A month after the election out came one of the wooden bridges and forms were made and concrete poured for a modern and up-to-date structure. Every carpenter and shovel-pup between Foxford and Mavely suddenly took on the glow of toryism; apparently all had voted the straight Conservative ticket that had swept "Bones" Gridley into office with a plurality of five votes.

The new bridge was a fine sight and people came all the way from Lindsay and Cannington just to look at it and compare it with similar edifices across the Firth of Tay and the Missouri River. The bridge had a beautifully arched pair of

123

concrete sides with diagrammatic edges done in the same material. The Ontario coat-of-arms was pressed into one end while the cement was still wet and pulled out a hair too soon so that a stranger wasn't sure if the bridge belonged to the Province of Ontario or the Free Masons. The thing was, as "Bones" said in his riband-cutting speech, "She's there for life, boys, you can't beat concrete." Which was true. A few weeks later a pair of tourists, a man and his wife from Toronto, splashed their brand-new Ford into one end of the Conservative bridge and had to be scraped off with hand-shovels. There was a bit of dark rumbling to the effect the Toronto pair wouldn't have lost their lives had the bridge been constructed of yielding wood. "Bones" had an answer for that, too, it came out in the *Watchman Warder*—a Tory newspaper every Conservative subscribed to but never read. Had a wooden bridge been built, declared "Bones," the unfortunate motorists would have plunged into the deeps below and drowned a terrible, gasping, choking death—not nearly as clean and quick as diving head-first into a cement obstacle at 85 miles an hour. But, as Uncle Miles pointed out, at the time of the accident Devlin's Creek was running full steam and must have been at least eight inches deep. "It is," said Uncle Miles, "an awful death drowning in eight inches of water, never mind the one knot per hour current."

But the Henry government and "Bones" Gridley with it did not remain in the exalted seat of power long enough for "Bones" to attack the remaining two wooden bridges and thus help slay more tourists. Mitchell Hepburn, the Liberals, and booze in hotels and government stores swept away the Women's Christian Temperance Union and their bottles of Lydia E. Pinkham's Compound, old Premier Henry, "Bones" Gridley, and the lot. Gridley went out of politics and into the water-witching business, stalking around mysteriously with a bit of a willow gad shaped like a catapult that "Bones" held at arms' length and made faces at until it twitched or quivered. Successful or not, I do not know; Uncle Miles said Gridley couldn't have located water if he walked across Lake Ontario carrying a whole willow tree on his shoulder.

Since leaving school I hadn't, because there was little reason to do so, kept track of days such as Saturdays and Sundays. As I put the kick-stand of the bicycle down on the sidewalk in front of Dansinger's window which was featuring axes, Swede saws, splitting wedges, and logging chains, I recollected this was Saturday and Laurel might be home or, better yet, in the store. During the school week she boarded in Lindsay. My luck was running straight down the rapids; Laurel was alone behind the counter, staring dreamily at the far wall on which, in picturesque display, were washboards, galvanized tubs, copper boilers, corn-brooms, and everything else you'd need to keep house.

She looked up and away from whatever she'd been dreaming of. "Hello," she said.

"Howdy, Miss Dansinger," I felt the title was too long but I didn't know how to shorten it without sounding familiar. The girl solved it for me.

"You can call me Laurel." When she smiled her teeth were pearly and even.

"And you," I began, "can call me—"

"Patch." She smiled. "Do you know Mr. Doherty? The great big man? When I asked he told me your name. And do you know something else?"

I shook my head.

"He said you were 'the best damned kid with a hay-fork' he ever saw."

My face was glowing like a Quebec heater. Laurel's sky-blue eyes rested as lightly as a dove's feather on my face. Somehow or other I managed to carry on a conversation, although, to father's disgust, I bought drill bits for use on wood instead of steel. I thought sure I'd get a boot in the tail when he found the mistake, but when he asked me how come I did such an ass-backward thing and I told him I got carried away talking to Laurel he looked at me strangely; his bitter mouth

125

beneath his drooping moustache worked almost as if he was going to cry. Father turned away with the package of bits and headed for the workshop.

"That's all right, Patch," he said without looking back. "I needed this kind, anyway."

Later, while I was milking the one cow we kept for that purpose, I bragged and barged to Bride who was perched on the top rail of the milking pen, her bare brown legs, already filling out trim and pert, stretching away out from her too-short skirt. Bride didn't say anything–not a syllable. This wasn't her usual way; normally, she'd have teased and tossed and stuck verbal pins in me to let the wind escape. I looked up from the milk pail I was holding between my knees. The sun was dying for the day and a cold sliver of a moon was sailing high over the Balsam Swamp. Bride was staring at the moon while great, round tears washed gently down her cheeks.

"Oh Patch! Don't get hurt. I'll hurt, but don't you get hurt, Patch–please!" And she was down from her perch and dashing toward the house until the shadows swallowed the last flash of her brown legs.

16

The parish school in Kilmore was located next to the priest's house which stood between the school and the church of Our Lady of Perpetual Help. Like most residences of parish priests of the day the house was a mighty fortress of brick, standing four-square against sin, relieved only by an open verandah on the street side, over which grew a dejected spine of rambler roses planted there by some housekeeper, long dust, with some yearning for beauty not to be found indoors where all was varnished wood and linoleum so slippery from wax and shine that old Tim Follihan, the sexton, grave-digger, and collector of contributions at mass, on a voyage to see the priest about some errand or other, went for a long slide and skate in the hall that took him clear into the kitchen where he broke his left leg against that of the stove—it being the harder of the two.

Presiding over the parish—called by Uncle Miles "Our Lady of Perpetual Penury," it seemingly forever in debt or in need of a new roof—was a great, balding, lunge of a man with a stoop to his shoulders that had his long, black-broadclothed arms hanging forward almost to his knees. Nearing his seventies and with but a monk's fringe of silvery hair rimming his skull, Father Blaney, a native of Wexford in Ireland, believed he'd been sent to Kilmore by the Archbishop of the Diocese at Peterborough out of pure spite. Forty or more years before, when Father Peter Blaney was a young man with his ordination fresh upon him, he'd been sent to assist or act as secretary and general gopher for Archbishop O'Regan then presiding. Now the Wexford and Wicklow people have a great deal of the Anglo-Saxon and Dane in their blood and, for some unknown reason, people from that region are called "yellow-bellies." The Archbishop was from Kerry, and a great quarrel arose between His Excellency and Father Blaney. It had something to do with Kerry standing still during '98 while the "boys" of Wexford smote the redcoats hip and thigh. Anyway, the hierarchy of the Church was at peace with Britain and British rule, having been bought off with the founding of the college at Maynooth and Catholic Emancipation in 1829. If Father Blaney got the best of the argument he also got Kilmore and there he stuck as fast as ever a burdock clung to a horse's tail.

The parochial school was a recent institution, being built of good red kiln brick before the crash of '29. The two teaching nuns, currently Sister Ambrose and Sister Hypatia, had a tiny den at the back where they slept, prayed, and cooked their miniature meals. The nuns had about thirty or forty Catholic children of elementary-school standing to teach, drive, and larrup. Most were Irish and ranged from the outright heathen Ryans to the purer-than-driven-snow Lynch children whose father was Lynch & Co. (Lumber At Prices You Can Afford). Lynch did his greatest trade with other Irish Catholics and his pew was right up front and on the right side. He put a five-dollar bill on the plate every mass and didn't even look round to see who was watching, and if it so happened he skinned an uneducated rock-runner like Ed Ryan the following Monday Lynch put it all down to casting five bucks, worth of bread on the waters and having it tossed back at him ten-fold, although Lynch would settle for double.

There were some Polish children, all from a single family

living back on the huckleberry rocks, going to school along with the Irish. No one knew exactly how many Gnowskis there were; some put it at fifteen not counting the old folks. There was also a very old man, probably the grandfather, with a very long beard. He had made but a single public appearance: he had got drunk at Cy Brady's, the bootlegger, and somehow got the end of his beard caught in the fly of his pants and had to walk the ten miles home to the Longford Rocks all humped over, as Uncle Miles said, like a dog shitting thumb-tacks. The old fellow was never seen abroad again; some said he died and because there was no dirt deep enough to dig a grave in all of Longford his family put him up on poles the way the plains Indians used to do, and the crows ate him.

Bride was no happier at the Separate School than she had been at Clifden. Sister Hypatia, who taught English, grammar, composition, and spelling, was a mild, decent bit of a thing and was generally well liked. Sister Ambrose had a set of whiskers to rival those of General Burnside, and a bulk to match. She delved and dug in arithmetic, history, and the Greater Catechism with the Imprimature of the Cardinal Fillion himself. It was Sister Ambrose who caught the eighteen-year-old Billy Ryan by the neck and threw him through a near window that, fortunately, had the sash up and thus saved young Ryan from decapitation.

Most of Bride's discomfiture with the Kilmore school was due to her being, already, the finest looking girl in the classrooms. This did not cause her to be the most popular pupil among the other girls; it did mean she had to swing a powerful right hand slap at leering-mouthed boys the like of Billy Ryan. That was part of the torment: Bride was assailed time and again by the sisters to take her novitiate after graduation and, in their words, "become a bride of Christ and live forever more in heavenly bliss, wrapped blissfully in His loving arms."

"I'd as soon be wrapped in 'Stinky' Ryan's arms," Bride declared. "Stinky" was two years the junior of his brother Billy, but their aim and outlook matched perfectly.

These were troubled days for Bride, and I was puzzled. She'd be as friendly as of old some days; some days she was as bitchy as a yearling colt. One evening after she cycled home from school Bride and father were talking out in the old orchard behind the house where the rain was falling on damp, fallen leaves, and there was a cidery smell of ripe apples and rain-wet hawthorn leaves.

Bride was arguing earnestly while father looked uncomfortable and kept scratching kitchen matches on the seat of his pants to keep his pipe lit. Finally, Bride turned on her heel and marched angrily into the house.

Bride wasn't at the table for supper that night. "Shall I call Bride?" I directed the question at father.

He shook his head.

"Just let her be," he said mildly. Aunt Kate looked up from her soup, her spectacles glinting.

"I don't like this hydro-electric thing," she complained. "That light," nodding her head to the fixture placed squarely in the centre of the kitchen ceiling, "is way too bright and hard on the eyes. Land's sake! Nobody needs that much light, not even the angels themselves.

"The good old kerosene lamps was good enough in my day," she continued smugly.

Father grunted. "Yes, the old coal-oil lights were just dandy. I suppose it was using them that made you unable to see past the ends of your toenails without your glasses.

"Auntie—I think you should have a talk with Bride. It's time," father looked significantly at Aunt Kate.

The old woman swivelled her eyes up in their sockets as far as they would go. "Mother Cabrini intercede for us!" she cried. "As if there wasn't toil and trouble enough for us." She looked sharply at father. "We'll have to watch her like a hawk: they get feeling their oats at this time and first thing you know she'll be into the bushes with the first young devil that takes her fancy."

"Bullshit!"

130

"Don't forget that girl is her mother's daughter," Aunt Kate's reptilian little eyes crawled with pleasure.

"Why, you goddamned old fool," father roared. "I shouldn't have said a word about it to you. You just leave the girl alone and I'll have somebody with a lick of sense tell her the facts of life. You wouldn't know a fact if you had one jammed up your arse."

There was a young, divorced woman who had a summer cottage at Raven Lake in which she lived from thaw to frost. Except for her name, which was Nancy Murtaugh, no one seemed to know much about her. She kept to herself, driving out in a new Buick to Kilmore or Foxford whenever she needed supplies. She always paid cash, and while she was friendly she had a line drawn over which no one stepped. Owney McCrone discovered this quickly when the Murtaugh woman hired him to repair her bit of a boat dock. She invited him in the cottage for a cocktail at the end of the day, the weather being hot and all. Owney read all the wrong things into what was intended as a civil gesture. What Owney could read without help from the dictionary was the bore of a .22 pistol pointed with never a quiver straight at his belly-button. Mrs. Murtaugh hired someone else to finish the work on the dock.

Father performed a small service for Mrs. Murtaugh when she had a flat tire on the Buick on the Kilmore road near the entrance to her cottage.

October's reds and yellows had turned to the hard brown of November. I was splitting hardwood and piling it in the woodshed against the winter. Father stopped on his way from the barn.

"Do you know where the Murtaugh cottage is on Raven Lake?"

I said I did.

Father reached into the pocket of his leather half-coat. "I have a note here I want you to take to Mrs. Murtaugh.

131

There'll likely be an answer; if so, wait for it and bring it back."

He turned and strode on into the house.

The road, it was more of a lane, leading into the cottage wound among beech, maple, and pine trees. The branches met at the top so, that in summer, it was like going into a covered alley. Now all the trees, save the pines, were bare of foliage except for the waxy-brown leaves on some of the beeches, rattling in the whip of the November wind.

Through the bare trunks I could see the cold glitter of Raven Lake and the dark green-stained boarding of the cottage. The eaves were wide and low all around and ended in posts making a verandah-like effect on all four sides. A huge fieldstone chimney, with a curl of smoke trifling against the sky, occupied all but a few inches of one end of the building.

There had been rain the night before and my bicycle tires made hardly a whisper on the wet leaves. The owner, her back to me, was standing before an easel set up on the dock where it held to the shore. She was painting with swift, strong strokes.

I stopped and stepped off the wheel, rattling a mud-guard with my heel. The woman turned quickly, almost savagely. She had long, black hair with a thread of grey hanging down well over the front of her shoulders and secured on either side with ribands. Her eyes were cat-green and angry-looking.

"Who are you? What are you doing here?"

I told her who I was.

"My father asked me to bring you this note." I held it out to her. "He said if there was an answer I should wait for it."

She took the envelope, slit it expertly with a lacquered thumbnail and read the contents quickly.

"Of course," she said, and her voice was all at once gentle. "Do come in while I write a note to your father. I'm sorry, but you came so silently you startled me."

I allowed as how that was a pretty dumb thing to do. She looked at me with frank curiosity.

"You resemble your father." She cleaned her brushes and led the way up the stone steps to the cottage.

A fire was burning–an old butt of a beech knot–with a bluish flame tipped with yellow. Mrs. Murtaugh sat down at a small secretary and began writing on a sheet of paper with the same bold, swift strokes she had used while painting. As she wrote I looked around the inside of the cottage. It was all one big room, a wide bed with a scarlet coverlet in one corner; a tiny set of kitchen cabinets over a metal sink; an easy chair designed for sprawling at one corner of the fireplace, and a three-quarter divan facing the glowing fire. A bit of a table with winter-berries glowing in a vase set in the middle, and a carpet stretching from wall to wall with a thick, deep pile, made up the furnishings.

She finished her letter, stuck it in an envelope and ran a sharp, red tongue across the seal.

"Do you have time to have tea with me?"

I felt awkward and gawkish.

"Well–yuh. Okay–sure!"

"Fine. It's a nice day to have company and I needed an excuse to stop painting."

She filled a copper kettle from the sink tap, put it on a swinging pot hook until it was fairly over the flames.

"I could use that little hotplate," she explained, "but boiling a kettle over a fire seems more romantic. Don't you think November's a romantic month, or are you one of those June-spoon-tune people?"

I scratched my neck, wondering if I was being made fun of.

"I kind of like October. And May. May's a nice month."

"Of course they are. It saddens me to have to leave here next week. I'd stay all winter except I can't keep the road open."

"Where do you stay in the winter?"

"Toronto." She made a face.

While she made the tea I studied her covertly; she was wearing men's denim jeans cut off around the bottoms like loggers' pants. She had big, rounded calves and her bare feet were stuck into a discoloured pair of canvas shoes. Before making the tea she had removed a grey sweater; underneath she wore a maroon piece of cloth that looked like a sash tied around her so as to barely cover her breasts and not much more. I wondered how old she was and came to the conclusion, for no good reason, that she was thirty-five.

We sat at the table and had our tea with baker's muffins, butter and huckleberry jam.

"I buy quarts of this from the Ryans," Mrs. Murtaugh said. "I suppose you know them."

"Yeah, I know them."

"Poor woman, I think it's the only hard money the poor creature sees all year."

I could have said that Mrs. Ryan didn't get to see that, either; old Ed would snap it out of her hand before it turned cool and be off to get a gallon of bingo before they closed for the day.

"You may call me Nancy," she said suddenly. "Your father calls me a very formal 'Mrs. Murtaugh.' I use that name for business purposes; it's my husband's name—my ex-husband, that is.

"You see," she went on, "I paint. Professionally. Sometimes I get fabulous sums for my views of Raven Lake. As much as fifty dollars! I've painted Raven Lake at dawn, noon, dusk, and at midnight. But I never tire of it. The lake is like a person; like me: it has moods and passions and desires. Sometimes the water is calm and even; then it grows wild and leaps up at the cottage and tries to drown me in my canoe."

I scraped my chair back from the table, wiping my lips with my handkerchief before remembering I'd cleaned some excess grease from the bicycle chain with it an hour earlier.

She held out her hand and her grip was warm and firm. "Goodbye, Patch," Nancy said. "I'm glad to have met you. You Fallons are interesting men."

I mumbled something, stuck her letter in the pocket of my

denim jumper and went out and got on my bicycle. She stood in the door, her hand against the post, and watched me out of sight.

Although it was some little time before I managed to figure everything out—the letter-writing and what-all—Nancy Murtaugh drove over to our place the following Saturday and, after reducing Aunt Kate to a small pile of surly mumbles, drove away with Bride to Lindsay.

A couple of weeks later, and after Nancy had returned to Toronto, I sat on Bride's bed as she carefully combed her long dark hair before the mirror of the old dresser that had the varnish coming off it like dandruff from "Stinky" Ryan's head.

It was the first good chance to talk with Bride I'd had since she and Nancy went to Lindsay together, and I was burning with curiosity.

"What'd the two of you do in Lindsay, anyhow? Did you go to a movin' picture or somethin'?"

Bride half-twisted her torso to catch herself in the mirror at another angle. "Just woman stuff," she said airily. "You wouldn't be interested. Do you think my hair looks better in braids or combed out loose?"

I went back to my own room and played a doleful strain on my mouth-organ, thinking about Laurel Dansinger and Nancy Murtaugh and my growing sister—Bride.

Outside a wild wind walked across the roof with prowling fingers and hurled dead branches of trees against the shutters.

17

After a night of dark, drumming rain the wind ran around to the north and the first, lazy flakes of snow tumbled along, dying as they reached the soaked, brown earth. Then the snow whirled faster, steadier, heavier. It began to cling to tops of fence rails and bare elm branches and among the stands of hickories where the blue-jays screeched. A pair of crows, black and silent in an elm top, ruffed up their neck feathers. One cawed; then both flew off toward the south. The winter, as Timothy Connolly said, "was amongst us."

I think it must have snowed for a week. Every morning came up like the one before, with the wind snarling around the clothes-line wire and the wooden trumpery hanging from the house gables, the scrolled work that carpenters call "ginger-bread." The snowflakes, big and round as half-dollars, followed in the breath of the wind until all you could see were white humps where the fences used to be, and a round, mushroom-shaped thing that was the stump of an old elm Grandfather Matt had cut down in the year of his death because he got it into his head the tree was laying for him, waiting to drop a five-hundred-pound limb on his head or some such thing. There were no sunsets: the grey cast of the sky simply got darker until the driving snow was blotted out and the line of firs hiding the house from the road pulled in closer around the roof and chimney while the wind hummed wilder and faster, singing a murder song as the cold of it and depth of it and the ice of it caught little birds and bits of other living things and killed them where they flew or stood.

We were wintering over forty head of cattle, five horses, and a pen of half-grown hogs who smelled of sour milk and curdled grain. I've never had any use for a pig. Before the winter settled in, on a day when father had gone to Lindsay, Bride had been playing around the barn with her very best doll hanging from the crook of her arm. Bride was months past her thirteenth birthday, but she'd hung onto this particular doll as long as she or I could remember, and if she had a reason she never told me and I can't, now, remember if I ever asked.

Bride had no more love for a hog than did I, so as she was passing the pen she stood up on one of the plank railings and stuck her tongue out at the occupants who looked back with little devils' eyes turned up in their heads. Bride's foot slipped from the plank and catching herself her doll dropped and fell into the mire of the hog pen. The lead pig immediately made a rush and chewed on that doll as if it was the choicest cob of Iowa corn ever to come his way. I was lying on the flat of my back on the main beam of the mow, reading one of granddad's books, when I heard Bride scream. It was sixteen feet to the threshing floor and I wouldn't take a thousand dollars and jump that far today, but I was onto the floor and down the hay chute and over to that corner where the pigs were penned before the echo of Bride's shriek quit wandering around the purlins.

Bride had one hand over her mouth and with the other arm she pointed at the pig that was wolfing down the remnants of her doll. Only a few strands of hair, like corn-silk, stuck out on either side of the hog's chompers. I gave Bride a shove toward the house and I marched into the little building that was a tack-room and tool shed and took father's .44-40 down from the two spikes that held it up on the wall. There was a half a box of greasy cartridges up on the plate beneath the rafters. I grabbed up two or three and headed back for the barn, loading the grim old shooting iron as I went. The pig, thinking I had come with another doll, snuffled and rolled a dirty eye— an eye that disappeared in a gout of blood even as the kick from the long-barrelled rifle knocked me on my butt six feet away.

I got up and looked at the pig which was so dead not a leg was kicking when Bill Doherty walked into the stable.

"Now, what in hell did you do that for?" he said, looking at the dead lump of pork and his companions huddled into a corner from the blast of the shot.

I was feeling pugnacious, not only from being mad at the pig but also because the rifle had blown me flat on my ass and I sat there in a doodle of horse manure looking foolish.

"It chomped up my sister's doll."

Doherty nodded with perfect understanding as if pigs went charging around devouring little girls' dolls and got themselves blown to hell and gone with a bald-headed slug from a .44-40 rifle and it was all in a day's work, whatever.

"Yeah," the big man said, looking at the wire-thin strands of doll hair dangling from the dead, leering jaws of the pig— jaws where a trickle of blood the colour of beet sap was dribbling.

He shoved back his old, sweat-stained slouch of a hat and ran his fingers through his mat of grey-black hair. "What we got here is a justified killin', and no jury between here and Fenelon Falls'd convict you of more'n bad temper. The thing is, it's no jury you got to convince—it's your daddy and that's another horse entirely."

"I ain't scared," I said, with more bravado than good sense. "I'm getting too old for my old man to lick."

"Come the day you get too old for Ward Fallon to lick it'll be because he's taking pity on your grey hairs." Doherty snapped ped his hat back down across his eyes. "What we'll do is—I come in Barret's old pick-up with an idea to borrow some hand tools to fix up the old Dalton shack I'm going to winter in. I'll drive up and we'll slide that cannibal there onto the back of the truck and you can tell Ward I bought my winter's meat off him for twenty dollars."

Doherty allowed himself a tight smile at the relief sticking out on my face. He vaulted over the pen planks and sliced a gash in the pig's throat to let any spare blood out. We had the pig loaded and away in less than twenty minutes.

As the truck got lost on the road where it crooked around the bare balm-of-gileads near Dorgan's Hill, Aunt Kate came out, arms akimbo, eyes narrowed, where Bride and I were silently watching Doherty drive away.

"What's he doin' with one of our pigs? And what was that shot I heard? Like to fright me out of the few pitiful years I got left."

"Father sold Mr. Doherty a pig," I lied. "We shot it first; he didn't want to take it alive."

The old woman searched me with her icy bits of eyes, then turned and hobbled back into the house. I noticed a hole in the back of one of her black cotton stockings.

18

Christmas came and went and the New Year followed after. I was looking forward to my birthday which came early in February. Bride, who puddled in such things, told me I was an Aquarian and that I was interested in legs—female legs. I gave a great scoff, but just the same I felt there might be a trickle of truth in this astrology business; certainly I warmly admired the trim legs of Laurel Dansinger, and the shapely calves of Lila Kennedy who already wore silk stockings and liked to pause on the village sidewalk and adjust a garter. In fact, legs and girls and girls and legs and bosoms and thighs were, of late, haunting my nights, bringing dreams of a strangely exciting, yet wistful fantasy time, and I would waken in the middle of the night with my pecker erect and reaching for some mysterious region just out of range. I found myself exquisitely sensitive to the touch of my own hand; one night I chafed at my penis until it gushed and I threw myself back against the brass bed-head, gritting my teeth in a spasm of emotion that was bitterly delightful.

It was wrong. Father Blaney had asked all adolescent boys to remain after mass the preceding summer. He herded us into the vestry and in his Wexford dialect—which was, surprisingly, much like English, only softer—told us about this thing called carnality. The terrible sin, he said, was the one which drove Adam and Eve from paradise, and that was the sin of lust. Not lust for money or land or a new Ford coupé the mate of Jerry Lynch's; it was lusting after the bodies of women and young girls.

"Why—our first parents walked about stark naked and didn't even realize it, they were that pure and innocent," the priest rumbled.

"Not even when they stepped on a bull-thistle?" enquired Thad Whalen.

Father Blaney said there were no thistles in the Garden of Eden.

Father Blaney paced up and down the length of the vestry; he threw his arms wide. "They'd everything right there at their beck and call. The sun shone day and night and beautiful birds sang and the finest fruits you might wish for were there for the taking. Then," the priest's voice dropped, "came the Evil One in the shape of a serpent, winding himself round and round against the only tree in the entire Garden the fruit of which had, by God, been forbidden Adam and Eve."

"If," asked young Whalen, "Eden was such a perfect place, how did a snake crawl into it in the first place?"

Father Blaney speared him with a hard eye. "There's a young heretic for you. Oh, Martin Luther and John Knox would've been proud of you. Don't you know the Tempter is listening in right now and he's getting out his notebook and he's jotting down the name of Thaddeus Emmett Whalen, and he's saying to himself, 'There's a coming devil to be made use of in the years ahead.'

"Now who did the Adversary choose to tempt, in whose ear did he coo and whisper about the joys of biting into the Forbidden Fruit? It was the weaker of the two sexes—the woman, Eve. Always remember that, my lads, women are the weaker sex. They must be protected, of course, as we protect our mothers and sisters. They, the women, must also be protected from themselves, for the Devil does be getting into them so that they do be using paints and dyes and other devices of Satan so they can be entrancing poor, foolish men into rolling with them in their beds of lust."

We gaped and shuffled our feet, looking uncertainly at one another.

He continued. "Satan knows when young men and boys are most vulnerable to the damnable sins of lust and impurity. Sometimes when you are alone he will slip filthy ideas into your head and you will play with your private parts until you do exactly what the Adversary wants you to do. Oh boys! you must be strong and resist all temptation; you must save your innocence for the holy marriage bed for the Sacrament of marriage is most beloved by our Blessed Saviour and His holy Mother Mary."

We stumbled out into the bright glitter of the summer's sun. I felt clammy, as if I'd touched a finger to a slug.

Ed Kennedy, who was Lila's brother, hummed a dirty bit of a song:

"Did'ja ever get your finger
Where you couldn't get your hand. . . .?"

"Jesus! it's all a cod," laughed Thad Whalen. He turned down the corner of his lips and gibed, "Save it for your holy old marriage bed! Asshole! I'm savin' mine for Delia Leger–in bed or out of it or up against a snake rail fence."

"Yeah? 'N have old Antoine take an axe t'you," warned Piper Mulvihille. "Keep away from that French Settlement stuff."

The French Settlement lay in Grandmaison Township directly east of Clifden. It had been settled largely by French loggers brought in by the timber companies because of their skill with axe and crosscut saw. Also the French Canadians tended to be more reliable, less apt to go off on a drunk or get in a barroom fight than the Scots and Irish of Daley and Fraser Townships. Their descendants went to mass at Our Lady of Perpetual Help, but they had a parochial school of their own and mainly kept to themselves, neither being accepted by nor mingling with the Irish Catholics. The girls and younger women were dark-haired, fair-skinned, and subtly graceful.

"Fartin' Jenny's more in your line, Thad." Niall Sweeney lit a tailor-made cigarette.

Riding my bicycle on the way home I tried to reason marriage, women, sin, and rubbing peckers. I couldn't make sense of it, somehow; I still haven't, although, to be sure, I no longer think of such things as frequently as I did then.

It seemed to me that I was either an awful fool or awful slow, or maybe both, to know as little about sex and the way of boys with girls and vice-versa as some of the other fellows my own age or even younger I met in Kilmore or Foxford on Saturday nights. I wished I was as smart as Thad Whalen: Thad talked with great expertise about Sheiks and Ramses which I learned were "rubbers" or "french-safes" that men were supposed to wear when they screwed women so the women wouldn't get knocked up or the men get some kind of a disease a lot of women were supposed to have. Thad said there was a lot of the "black syph" going around; the "black" kind was worse than the regular because it made your penis rot off in less than three weeks. The "black syph" was mostly got from nigger women or squaws, but sometimes a white woman would have it—especially those that travelled around with the striptease acts that came to Lindsay Fair.

I couldn't find out about this excruciatingly interesting thing called sex unless Uncle Miles volunteered some cryptic, half-jeering information; or when the town boys, gathered together beneath a street lamp around which the miller moths flew in summer madness, hands in their pockets, rocking on their heels, and corner-eyeing any female that passed, added luridly to my small store of knowledge. At home there was a weighty volume called *Dr. Pierce's Golden Medical Book* in which were line drawings of the male and female bodies from the waist down. Every farm boy knows what a cow looks like; a cow or a mare. And he also knows how farm animals breed. It's the human women and girls that remained forever mysterious: did the men mount them from behind while the females were down on their hands and knees like cattle, or what?

In the medical book there was a passage on something peculiar to boys and young men called "the terrible habit." The "terrible habit" weakened and dissipated youth and strength; it caused foaming at the mouth, madness, and bad breath. The best cure, said the book, was *Dr. Pierce's Golden Medical Prescription*, which claimed to drive impure thoughts of lust and the desire for "secret practices" completely out of the heads of those afflicted.

Unfortunately for my peace of mind, I hadn't read about secret practices and terrible habits until I became a victim. I fought mightily against the tendrils of desire worming into my brain, but in the end I nearly always lost and the imp bestrode me while I sweated, conjuring images of Lila Kennedy, Laurel Dansinger, and a pretty, young married woman, Edith Browne. I even imagined Bride co-operating with me: Bride with her ripe little breasts thrusting at the front of her dress; Bride flouncing up or down stairs in her pants and bra, her bottom wiggling in unconscious seduction. I knew then I was lost; that I could never be a manly man or the youth who would bring the admiration of the world down on his high school as he scored the winning goal or kicked the football for a 150-yard field goal. I looked at myself in the mirror and saw with horror I was an old, bent, weak boy breaking out in "hickies" (cured only by Fleischman's Yeast) and ruptures of the skin to which all victims of the secret practice fell prey. I had dandruff; all the ads said a boy with dandruff could never get *the* girl: *the* girl was only attracted to men with smooth, marbled hair glistening with good health and Vaseline Hair Tonic; hair that was without a stray lock or a flick of dandruff.

One day Ed Kennedy threw me a half-dozen "comic" booklets. These were little, brown-covered books with pornographic reproductions of standard comic characters: Blondie & Dagwood, Tillie The Toiler, Maggie & Jiggs, Boots & Her Buddies, things like that. One booklet showed Dagwood making one of his end runs to catch the bus to work; when he was gone Blondie opened the back door and let the milkman in, after which he shoved an impossibly long penis in between Blondie's legs as she lay, smiling happily, on the sofa. After reading those comic books I no longer believed that men and women mated the way farm animals did. But the worms of desire ate at me worse than ever. They hadn't seemed to have bothered Ed Kennedy. At least he didn't let on if they did. He just handed me the books and said, "Want to take a look at these? Don't go home and chase your old Aunt Kate around the barn, now."

I looked at the books and let the terrible habit wash over me. Afterward, I sprawled tired and dispirited across the patchwork quilt of my bed. I knew I was licked; I could never grow up and be a man. I was too full of vice and impure thoughts. The Devil was waiting with a grin.

Thirty-five years is a long time in the lives of men. Thirty-five years are half the three score and ten mentioned in Christian Bibles.

In this, the fiftieth year of my life, I stare back through the funnel of time, gnawing the ends of my grizzled moustache—the kind of moustache my father and Uncle Miles wore so long ago—and count the years and those events that filled them; I count the graves and think of those that filled them.

The seasons change and Time spins relentlessly on. In winter the snow heaps about the marble and stone markers; by spring the grass, greening now and dotted with dandelions, blushes in the sun where lately lay the snow. Sandburg said it well: I am the grass; let me work. Summer brings *a handful of visitors from Toronto and Calgary and Detroit. They walk slowly among the tombstones, bending over to peer at the weathered inscriptions carved in granite so long ago. Some are elderly, leaning on canes or stronger arms; some are middle-aged, rosy with fat and good living; some are young and heedless of all that and those lying so close below. The young scamper over the mounds and play tag among the markers, stopping to exclaim over red roses set in blocks of clear plastic—caught like ants in amber—like souls in Purgatory.*

And less and less frequently, when no one is about, a tall man with a grim face above a grizzled moustache wanders silently over in the shadows of young pines growing above a rusting iron fence. He reads again the legends on the stones he has read so often. He looks out at the country road; when there are no automobiles in sight he takes a pint flask of whiskey from his pocket and drinks wordlessly and without pleasure.

19

On the 5th day of February in that year of 1939 I became sixteen. Aunt Kate had gone out of her way to bake a cake, grumbling because there were no candles to be bought nearer than Lindsay. Undaunted, the old woman set a single votive candle in the centre of the cake where there was a great sag caused, Aunt Kate said, by the heavy boots of Bill Doherty who had dropped in from his winter-bound shack over against the Talbert River where he was cutting cordwood. Bride gave me a huge book, *The Birds of America*; it had black and white photos as well as paintings. She must have saved her allowance money for months. Father gave me a rifle: a little carbine saddle gun of .22 calibre that held seventeen rounds of long-rifle ammunition.

"I don't want you putting holes in any more pigs," father said with a slight, crooked smile as he handed the gleaming weapon to me.

Aunt Kate squinted frostily as I exclaimed over the rifle, sighting it out of the window at the clothes-line pole. "A shooting gun, now, is it?" she complained. "Ain't he kind of young for them things? There's enough shooting and stuff going on these days without him adding to it."

Later, when we were alone, I told Bride, "I sure admire the

149

rifle, but I guess I like the book you gave me best."

"You do? Oh Patch, you're sweet," and she threw her arms around me and gave me a hard kiss full on the lips—a kiss fresh with spearmint-flavoured toothpaste.

For a moment I tingled to the touch of her strong young arms about my neck, to the swelling of her breasts against the front of my shirt; then I backed away, gently loosing her arms. I felt the words of Father Blaney, "unclean lust," burning in my head. My face was hot, my tongue gritty.

"You got perfume on," I sniffed. "It stinks."

"It does not! Did you know daddy is sweet on Nancy Murtaugh?"

"Sure." I didn't, but I wasn't about to play dumb. "Where'd you get that smelly perfume?"

"A very good friend of mine at school. A nice boy, too."

"Huh. Stinky Ryan?"

Bride wrinkled her face. "Jerry Lynch, that's who. So there."

"Not that lumber dealer's kid—the one that wears knee pants and plasters his hair down with brilliantine?"

"He cleans his finger-nails, too, and that's more than you do, mister smarty."

I felt the rats' teeth of jealousy for no good reason. Jerry Lynch was a pomaded pin-head who wafted deftly around the priest at mass in his role of altar boy. Jerry had his own Ford coupé, too, because he was seventeen and old enough to drive, but not even his old man's money could buy him out of public school where his slow-witted brain imprisoned him. Four years older than Bride they were in the same grade—VIII as the Separate Schools called it instead of Senior IV the way they did in the public system.

"I could lick him the best day he ever saw."

"Oh my! Another big, bad Fallon. Big in the head, too."

I sulked under Bride's taunts. I made a fist and studied the already-big knuckles standing out. A Fallon's fist, I thought proudly; and a wrist thick as a rope already—like a fighting

Fallon's. Only the arm lacked the bulge of biceps and the heavy, corded forearm muscles. There was a white scar trailing across my knuckles. I was proud of that scar and liked to think I'd marked it on somebody's teeth. The only thing was I'd scratched it on a rusty nail sticking out of the toolshed door. The thing had festered for a week before the scab went away and left the scar. It's been nearly forty years and I've the scar still. I lost the pride in it long ago.

We were in Bride's room, on the south side with a gable window looking out over the old orchard and a second window staring off across the white, snow-drifted pastures. My sister's room was always a cheerful mess. I examined the clutter on her bureau, and picked up an unfamiliar looking box.

"Hey! What's this? K-o-t-e-x. . . ."

Bride grabbed the box out of my hand and shoved it into a bureau drawer. "Don't be a nosey-parker. Gee, you're dumb, sometimes. It means I'm a woman now, not a kid anymore."

I remembered then. Something Thad Whalen called "having the rags on." I wasn't too sure what he meant and I was too afraid of being laughed at to ask. I left Bride's room and went to get down *Dr. Pierce's Golden Medical Book;* it was all there for the reading.

The winter dragged on toward March. Father came downstairs one morning in a new black suit with a thin white stripe he'd had tailored for him in Lindsay in the fall preceding. His great-coat of blue cheviot was over one arm and he carried a travelling bag.

"Going to Toronto on business," he said curtly, answering Aunt Kate's and my unspoken questions; father rarely travelled except when buying cattle. To go to Toronto was, for him, akin to catching a boat for Tokyo.

Bride was spending a week with the Lenehans who lived in Kilmore; Bill Lenehan was a foreman of the track gang on the Toronto & Nipissing, and the Lenehans had two girls of about Bride's own age. The prospect of being winter-bound in a

151

great ramble of a house with none except Aunt Kate for company, not to mention the extra work of feeding stock, cleaning the barn, and all of the chores that went with running a cattle ranch, did not enchant me.

"How long will you be away?" I poured coffee out of the blue granite pot into a thick, white mug.

"About a week. Save me some of that coffee."

Aunt Kate and I watched the Dodge disappear up the road between the heaps of ploughed snow on either side. "Ward's got the woman-itch. I can tell it just by the way he's been actin' of late." Aunt Kate wrinkled her face in an evil grin.

"An' I know who 'tis," she went on. "That woman that does be havin' a cottage on Raven Lake; the one all the men is after. I know her kind."

I buckled on my sheepskin and escaped to the barn. While I was working hay onto the threshing floor from the mow two pigeons on an end beam caressed each other with their bills; they made a soft, cooing sound; soft and ventriloquial. The female fluttered to the air vent, looked out, then winged away. The male followed. Listlessly, I climbed down the mow ladder; clouds drew together across the sun and began to drop huge flakes of snow.

On the third night of father's absence I had turned in early, reading myself to sleep and making my eyes sore from the too-fine print of Hugo's *Les Misérables*. I was awakened by a faint wash of light in the room; my eyes were heavy with sleep. Numbly, I sought the alarm clock on a chair near the bed; the hands said two o'clock. The faint whisper of footsteps made me look up to the source of the light: it was a candle held by Aunt Kate.

For a moment I was terrified: she wore an old-fashioned nightdress that swept the floor; her white hair was unbound and hung in front of her bony shoulders on either side her neck. Her eyes were wide and seemed, in the faint glow of the candle, unfocused. I opened my mouth to speak, but Aunt Kate laid a finger to her lips and hissed me into silence.

"I don't want *them* to hear," she whispered conspiratorially. She looked slyly back in the direction she had come. "They *can* hear, you know, them wans . . . "

"What ones? What are you talking about, aunty? Look, it's only two o'clock. Why don't you go back to bed?"

She looked at me, an odd smile wrinkling her face, as if I were a toddler without understanding or knowledge.

"Her that was Hannah Dorgan and the three daughters that was hers. Them and Matt—that was brother to me. They hated me whilst they was alive and they hate me whilst they're dead. All but Hannah, Matt's wife, that is. She felt sorry for me. Sure, and I'd rather she hated me along with the rest. I wanted none of their pity.

"Did you know they made Rodney stop writin' me?" Aunt Kate moved closer, lifting the candle so she could look into my face. I recalled I had never seen the woman without her spectacles before. Without them her eyes were huge and round and grey-green, but as blank as new note-paper.

Still holding the candle in its brass holder Aunt Kate sat on the edge of the bed and transfixed me with her grey stare.

"Matt sent my fare to me in the ould country. He sent me my fare and a great glowin' letter tellin' me of the fortunes to be made here and the fine young men of family 'n fortune I'd meet 'n marry." She flung back her head and I could see the chuckles bubbling up her throat.

"Sold! Bought and sold like a sheep at a fair! And to that dirty-handed old Con Carrigrew . . . Him wid his dirty hands and his spits of tobacco and the mouth of him and the breath of him like a manure pile. Sold by my own brother Matt so he'd have the walkin' boss's job for the Carrigrew Lumber Company. The pimp! Worse than a pimp! A man who'd sell his own sister to a pig that walked like a man and grunted like a hog!" Her voice raised to a shriek and the candle jiggled dangerously in her hand.

"Aunt Kate, go on back to bed. You're dreaming or something."

She paid no attention.

"Oh I played me part. I played the dutiful wife, and I cleaned up Carrigrew's vomits when he was drunk and sick. And I lay in his arms when he wanted my body and him grunting a pig's grunt and his breath that would curdle milk so that I'd turn the head of me away and shut me eyes and pray–pray for his death. His or my own.

"And when he died of the cancer that started as a scratch in his throat and then grew and grew 'til it strangled him, I went down on my knees and thanked the blessed saints that live in heaven, even did I be left a widow woman with next to nothin' what with the company bein' near bankrupt 'n all. I got on me knees and thanked the angels and I thanked the saints when they all died–Hannah an' the three girls after–an' then Matt. Oh, I prayed a long prayer of thankfulness when Matt died. Died alone like a dog writin' to some whore or other, they said."

The old woman rocked back and forth, the candle swaying and throwing weird, mutilated shadows.

"It's the Crowley blood. Not from my mother; not from the mother to me and Matt and the rest of them what's dead and gone. She was old Dan Crowley's daughter, and her mother before her was Katie O'Dowd–a saint on earth as was my mother after her. But the taint of blood came through to Matt; the taint of the Crowleys–of that old whoremaster, Dan! Ha, young Miles had it and Emmeline Foxe turned him down because of it. And your father married a slut of hell if there ever was one, and him now chasin' the bitch of Raven Lake. Even you," and her eyes ceased to stare and narrowed evilly. "You and the spots on the sheets. I know. And there's your sister buyin' underwear like them whores do be buyin'; oh, I know the taint. Yez all got it." Her voice rose to a cackle.

I made as if to get out of bed; I was angry. I hadn't thought about the "secret practice" spotting the sheets, and the knowledge of Aunt Kate's awareness infuriated and shamed me. But it was in her lashing of Bride made me savage.

"Go back to bed," I ordered, my voice as curt and whipping as my father's when he was spurred by temper. "Go back to your room and stay there or I'll tie you down and send for you to be taken to Whitby." The small town of Whitby on Lake Ontario was the site of the nearest asylum for the insane.

Aunt Kate rose and stood looking down at me, the candlestick held high over her head. She looked like one of the Three Fates, but which one I couldn't tell. She turned and faded from the room and down the hall, a pallor of light following the footsteps that were so light they could not be heard. I heard the snick of her door, and the light was gone. I lay on my back staring at the dark ceiling until I fancied I saw patterns and whorls and the unsmiling faces of my grandmother and aunts.

For a long time I looked and my thoughts were not those a boy of sixteen should have. I went to sleep at last, to be awakened by the clear burring of the alarm clock. The eastern sky showed a widening crack of light between it and the earth. I rose and slipped into my clothing.

20

On a night in early March a great storm went raging through the firs and elm trees set about the house, harassing the lichened old apple trees and tearing with wrenching gusts at every eave and gable. The wind smashed rain by the pailful at the many-mullioned windows; and the decrepit shutters, long unused and rusting to death on their hinge plates, rattled and shuddered like a skeleton in a tin coffin.

Aunt Kate, who had been mumbling by the kitchen range, had moped upstairs to her bed; Bride was in her room cussing furiously at the inventor of the decimal system. Father sat in his captain's chair, reading *The Winnipeg Free Press & Prairie Farmer*, a rural weekly the subscription to which he brought from Saskatchewan with him. "Do you know," I once heard father say, "I never knew of a single case where the *Free Press* cut a poor farmer off because he hadn't been able to keep up his subscription."

I sat at the other end of the oil-clothed table polishing my carbine, pushing an oil-soaked rag again and again down the barrel, then, squinting through it at the light where it gleamed, silver-blue–alluring–polished death.

Father laid aside his paper and filled his pipe with Canada Straight. "I wouldn't get too fond of that goddamn thing." He eyed me over his match flame.

"Heck, it was your birthday present."

"Yeah. And I'm wondering if I was wise."

"I got a rabbit with it the other day and come spring I'll get at the woodchucks. You said woodchucks make holes where the stock can put their feet and bust their legs."

"I know what I said." Father puffed irritably. "I heard my old man say the same thing, but I never knew of any farm beast broke a leg that way, come to think of it."

He was fixing to proceed when a pair of dim head lamps of an automobile turned in the driveway, poked hesitantly among the firs, then jerked on up the short lane.

"Now who in hell would that be coming at this hour of the night?" As father spoke the elderly wooden clock on the mantel above the calendar advertising Dr. Bell's Veterinary Drops gurgled and commenced tiredly counting out the hours which were ten.

I looked out the south window where a ruby tail-light showed through the last of the rain; the head lamps feebly washed the orchard in yellow light. "It looks like Danno Moran's car."

"Danno Moran?" Father stalked over to the window and glared out. Danno was the most successful of Daley Township's bootlegging industry. "Put the back porch light on . . . Danno Moran, for the love of Jesus!"

With the winking of the porch light, the car lights went out and three rain-driven figures staggered onto the porch and hammered at the back door. Bill Doherty, Luke's-John Coffey and Danno Moran–all in various stages of intoxication–came roistering in, stamping their wet boots and throwing rivulets of water from their hats.

"Ward, ye shoneen bashtard!" Doherty seized the rungs of a chair in a hairy ham of a hand, twirled it around before the stove and sat facing father, his huge arms resting on the back of the chair. "Give the man a drink, Danno."

Danno had the long, sad face of a used-up horse or an undertaker. He reached into the damp recesses of his shapeless suit and brought out a flat flask of rye whiskey. Doherty opened his mouth to shout, but Danno raised an admonishing hand.

"There's more in the buggy," he said, setting the pint on the table in front of father.

"We been on a jag for a week," said Doherty jovially. "Miles was with us for a couple of days."

Father took two or three swallows from the flask, gasped and wiped the back of his hand across his lips.

"That's not vendors' stuff—it's homebrew!"

Luke's-John, an amiable bachelor of forty who had spent a lifetime of sitting in the chimney corners and drinking the liquor of others, beamed at the room with his drink-reddened face.

"Danno made a great run last week." He showed brown teeth in a grin. "Ten gallons, eh Danno?" Luke's-John was so called because of three Coffey brothers of old who had married and had boy-children each of whom was named John. Mark's-John was out in Regina; Tim's-John had been run over by a disc-harrow after which the pieces had been gathered reverently together and buried in a packing case. Luke's-John remained in the district, doing odds of jobs for a place at the table, a bed in the barn, and enough drink to ease the pain of failure.

The first flask was followed by a second and a third. All save Doherty were getting drunk. Irishmen, being congenial, prefer to drink in small squads made up of males only. An Irishman detests drinking with a woman about, for most of them long ago were firmly wedded to reincarnations of their mothers or drink—or both. With the former there was no getting along;

Luke's-John was tearfully recalling his father, a parent who had passed along twenty-five years before and had been, mercifully, spared the sight of his first-born toddling down the road that's walked by fools. "Yez'll all mind my poor father," mourned the dutiful son. "Had I listened when I was at his knee I'd o' bin a better man this day."

Danno nodded lugubriously.

"I doubt it," remarked Doherty brutally.

"Oh it's a turrible thing to be deprived of a father and me nought but a boy," Luke's-John wept. Danno handed the orphan the bottle from which he drank, tears and slobber from his nose and mouth adulterating the whiskey. Doherty grinned and tolled out a bit of a song:

"I'm as free a little bird as I can be,
I'm as free a little bird as I can be,
But I'm sitting by the roadside and mourning all my days
'Cause there's no one in this world cares for me."

with the latter there was no doing without.

He had a strange, enchanting voice when he sang–not at all the vast rumble of his everyday speech.

Danno Moran nodded solemnly, while father, the strong booze taking hold, did a little shuffle and step as he headed out the back door for a leak. When he returned he cajoled Danno into singing.

"Yeah, c'mon Danno," Doherty said, "I haven't heard you sing since your mother's wake."

Danno temporized. He'd no voice he said; no voice at all. He had once–maybe twenty years ago Danno Moran had a voice, but the years, you know; the years take their toll. We're all aging fast, said Danno morosely.

"I've aged five years just listenin' to you now. Come on, Danno, give us one of your cheerful numbers." Doherty's hand closed around the bottle.

"Danno has the voice of an angel," mourned Luke's-John.

Encouraged, Danno hemmed a couple of haws, tried out a

few notes, and after a false start or two enlivened the raging night with "The Baggage Coach Ahead," a long, tortuous account of a man journeying aboard a train with the body of his wife. Every verse ended with: "Her body now lies sleeping in the baggage coach ahead." There must have been seventeen verses, and all the while the wind raved and tore at the shutters. Whenever I went outside to go to the toilet I could see the sparks from the towering kitchen chimney caught and carried away on the backs of the wild, black horses galloping unseen along the roof-tops and through the swaying branches of the tossing trees.

When Danno concluded his dirge, Doherty, who was enjoying himself immensely, clapped his great palms together loud enough to jar the clock on its shelf. "'Atta boy, Danno! It takes the Morans to liven up an evening. You ought to sing that in church, Danno, you'd bring the steeple down."

Luke's-John was sobbing glutinously. "That's how they took me poor father to his last resting place—in a baggage-coach; but I do forget which one—was it the one ahead or the one behind?"

"It was neither," said Doherty cheerfully. "Old Luke went to the cemetery in the back of Joe-Bob McNulty's wagon. I remember it well because I drove the team. Christ, it was an awful day: something like this. The wind was blowing so hard the two Duggan brothers had to sit on the rough-box so's old Luke wouldn't have been blown clear over to the Methodist graveyard. It was raining hammer handles, too; there must of been a foot of water in the grave. Luke went in with a splash—the only splash he ever made in his life and he had to wait 'til he was dead to do it."

That touched off another howl from Coffey and some sombre reminiscences from Danno about funerals great and small he'd attended and where he'd been entertained. "Long Mike Heffernan's widow was the worst I ever seen," he said gloomily. "The undertaker laid her in the back of the hearse on the way home from the funeral."

Doherty chuckled. "She did well to wait; she might have screwed him on the way over. Anyway, I never saw the woman that was worth a good goddamn, widowed, wed, or waiting."

Father, who'd been drinking steadily and saying little, twisted his lips in his bitter little grin. Holding the bottle in front of him and beating time with his finger against his knee, he sang:

"On a bright and sunny day
When a young wife went away
From the husband who had filled her heart with pain . . . "

The other three men were silent. The song of the storm filled the house. Father eyed the contents of the pint flask he held, then put it to his lips and swallowed the remainder.

"Go and fetch us another jar, Danno," Doherty said.

"That was it. There's more at home."

"Then by all means let us go." Father was on his feet and fumbling in the closet for his hat and slicker.

"We'll go to Orillia," said Doherty authoritatively. "I'm tired of swamp-juice. There's a bootlegger in Orillia who'll have the real m'coy."

"Orillia it is, by Jesus!" Father turned to me, his eyes fighting the fog of liquor he'd drunk. He swayed, his tall frame reeling like a limb in a gale. "Patcheen," he put out a hand and roughed my hair. "Patcheen, look after things. I don't know when I'll be back."

He paused at the door and looked at me. "I don't know when I'll be back," he repeated, and he was gone.

I heard the roar of the car's engine being raced. The auto jerked down the driveway, turned west on the road and disappeared into the storm, the sound of the motor hanging like a wisp for a few moments.

"Daddy went too, did he?" Bride had come up behind me as I stood at the window. She wore a long, flannel nightie with ribands laced across her bosom. Her hand slid into mine and she stood closely by me. I felt her trembling.

161

"It's all right, Bride," I said, trying to be reassuring. "He'll be back soon."

She didn't answer, but when she turned her face up to mine her eyes were pools of tears.

For a long time we stood together at the window, looking out into the night and the storm; and what I saw I didn't like, and what Bride saw I'll never know but she shivered with every blast of the gale.

21

It was Uncle Miles who broke it to us. He came a few minutes
before the hour of noon. His face was as grey as the ends of his
moustache. Sometime in the night, the storm had blustered itself out and went chasing its tail across the maple ridges far to
the south. The rain had blasted the remnants of snow that
clung to the bottom of ravines or in the deep woods, and the
world about us was raw with mud and littered with boughs
and branches ripped from their mother trees.

It was a Saturday and Bride, having no school, was hanging
out a few bright bits of things upon the clothesline in a March
sun suddenly gone friendly. A tender, uncertain haze of green
showed through the mud. When Uncle Miles drove into the
yard and stopped the car he beckoned his head at Bride and
she ran lightly down the steps of the clothesline platform and
followed him into the house. Our uncle opened his mouth but
no words came. He ducked his head grimly, then he said what
he had come to say:

There had been an accident; a car accident on the highway

to Orillia. Father was dead; father and Luke's-John Coffey. Danno Moran might never walk again. Only Bill Doherty was unhurt. The auto had been stopped on the highway to allow Doherty to get out to leak in the ditch; Danno, who was driving, shut off the lights and a second car hurtling through the storm-wracked night struck Danno's automobile from behind. Luke's-John, who had been in the back seat with father, was killed outright; father died in the rain a few minutes later with Bill Doherty holding him in his arms and crying like a baby. Father had spoken, or tried to speak because the life's blood of him kept welling up in his throat from where his lungs and chest had been mashed. "Tell Patch . . . Bride . . . " And the rest was all a gurgling groan and the drum of his dying heels on the wet pavement.

The occupants of the second car were shaken up, but not badly hurt. They were all young, in the late teens, coming from a dance. The four young people stood around, wet to the skin, and shuddering from the cold and death and bright blood washing down the concrete of the highway. The police came, eventually; the police and an ambulance. Doherty had walked off down the road into the night, carrying our father's body in his arms as easily as Bride carried her doll. When the police and the ambulance men caught up to him Doherty was looking straight ahead, muttering over and over, "It was all my fault–it was all my fault."

When she first heard father was dead Bride screamed–once. Then she sank into a chair with her hand over her mouth staring at Uncle Miles with horror. I seemed frozen except for my hands which kept fumbling at the seams of my farm jeans. We all turned at the sound of Aunt Kate's voice from the stairs. She had come silently halfway down and leaned over the banister.

"I knew it. I knew it all along. And that Doherty man is to blame. He's the one. There was none of 'em any good, 'ceptin' Ward and he had too much of his father in him–same as you, Miles."

"You go back upstairs or I'll kill you." Uncle Miles' tone was deadly mild. "And pack your belongings. Soon as the funeral's over you're leaving this house for good."

The old woman turned and went back upstairs without a word.

"Now there's lots to be done and we've got to hold up until what needs doin' is finished. Your dad 'n Luke's-John are at the undertaker's at Woodville, but we're going to wake them here. Both of them, and I'll tell you why: Luke's-John hasn't chick nor child to mourn his comin' or goin'; he was lonely all his life and he shouldn't be alone at his wake. We'll want to get the parlour redd up and some saw-trestles made for the coffins. The bodies'll be comin' here this afternoon sometime. Bride—you're the woman around this place now; what you got to do is set by the coffins and meet them as comes in. Have you got a black dress you can put on? If not I'll run in to town and get somethin'."

"I can't! I can't! Daddy! Daddy!" Bride broke down completely. I went over and held her shoulders.

"Can't you let her be? Get somebody else to look after the wake," I said fiercely.

Uncle Miles put on a dogged look. "It's best this way, Patch. Father Blaney'll be along and I asked some other women to step over and do some bakin' and help out. I've got to go clear to Lindsay yet 'n buy whiskey and candles 'n one thing 'n another."

"Our dad's dead, goddamn you!" I could no longer hold back the tears. "And you're going to have a party."

"This here, Patch, is a wake. It's the custom among our people and Ward wouldn't want it no other way. Now I've got to get goin'; I should be back against dark time."

The neighbours, friends, and acquaintances began trickling in about seven o'clock that evening. I met them at the door and ushered them to the parlour where the dead men lay, each in his simple black coffin, with all of the ravages of their death healed by the cosmetic arts of the undertaker. Bride sat at the head of father's casket where two tall tapers flickered sending tiny, scuttling, mouse-like shadows across his face so white and quiet; only his red-grey moustache above the lips now free of all bitterness offered a spot of colour. Bride's face was as white as chalk behind her black veil that hung, shroud-like, about her shoulders and over her simple black frock loaned her by Lila Kennedy who had it bought when her grandmother died the year past. The Irish and the Clifden Anglo-Saxons came in in knots of twos and threes; the Catholics genuflected, some awkwardly because of aging limbs, and crossed their breasts. The Protestants went by the casket with hands folded in front, heads bent; sometimes lips moved in silent prayer.

I suppose we all, by times, feel that when our own hour has struck the world and its work stops with the last tick of our hearts. Father lay in the parlour in his last sleep, his big hands clasped over his chest, a rosary of black beads wound through his fingers. Luke's-John Coffey, despite his years of dissolution appeared almost cherubic. No one sat at the head of his coffin; the two death candles twinkled and sent spirals of waxy smoke toward the ceiling. Luke's-John's only known relative was a sister in Detroit. She had been notified and was expected on the morrow.

Meanwhile, the earth–pulsating with life–spins on as heedless of the death of men as if they were dried oak leaves sinking silently through the clear air of autumn, coming to rest among the squirrel-hulled acorns on the ground. The hungry cattle lowed plaintively; the horses stamped in their stalls. On the second day neighbours came–Mick Clancy and his three grown sons, Art Dawes from south Clifden, and others. They cleaned the stables, watered and fed the stock. Their women-folk came, too; work-thin women who had too many children, too much bone-cracking toil, and not enough of life's ameni-ties. They scrubbed the floors, brought hundreds of sandwiches and dozens of pies that loaded the kitchen table. Uncle Miles had bought bottles of dark amber Irish whiskey, a keg of draught beer, and sherry for the women.

For two days and nights the wake went on. Bill Doherty didn't show up until the last night. He was a terrible sight: unshaven, his clothing unchanged and still showing traces of father's blood. He reeked of home-brew. Yet, withall, he came into the house with a grave dignity, shaking hands solemnly with me. Only when he went into the parlour did his emotion give way; he sank his great grizzled head on Bride's shoulder for a moment, then straightened and looked into father's casket. Doherty placed a huge hand, trembling now, on the still hands of my father–hands that were nearly as massive as Doherty's. After walking around Luke's-John's coffin Doherty came into the kitchen and poured a glassful of raw whiskey which he drained at a gulp.

He poured a second tumblerful, raised it level with his mouth and looked about the room almost truculently. "To the Fallon," he rasped.

"To the Fallon," the murmur ran round the room.

"To the Coffey."

"To the Coffey," echoed the room.

Mary Lenehan came into the kitchen. "I think they're going to say the Rosary now," she whispered. All save Doherty and I went into the parlour. The big man looked at me quizzically, but said nothing. He walked to a window and looked out.

"It's raining again," he spoke without turning.

From the parlour we heard the drone of the Our Fathers and the Hail Marys.

"Shouldn't you be in with the rest of them?"

"I don't believe in God or God's mother or his old Aunt Sadie," I answered bitterly.

"Neither do I. But speaking of aunts, where have you stuffed old Kate Carrigrew?"

I shrugged. "Uncle Miles chased her upstairs the day after the accident and no one's seen her since."

"Car coming." Doherty squinted through the rain-streaked

window. "Looks like a Buick—nearly new at that. Who to hell around here owns a new Buick?"

"A Buick?" I moved to the window. "That's—that's Nancy Murtaugh—the woman who has the cottage on Raven Lake. I think father liked her."

"Did you or little Brigid tell her about your father?"

I said we hadn't.

"Then it must have been Miles. He's got more sense than I gave him credit for. That woman, if she was Ward's friend, deserves to be here."

I stepped out on the back porch and waited until the Murtaugh woman came from the wet and the dark and entered the circle of light from the porch lamp. She was wearing a dark red leather coat, unbelted and unbuttoned as if she'd thrown it on her in a careless rush. Her grey-streaked jet hair tumbled almost to her bosom; there was a wild look upon her like a doe-deer bursting from a thicket and her with the hunters' hounds savaging on her trail.

She came up the steps with a little run and flung an embrace tightly about me; I realized I had gained inches through the winter: I could look down on the dark cloud of her hair misty with the March rain. Through the open door of the kitchen I saw that several people were gathered around the table loaded with booze and eatables. I motioned to Owney McCrone.

"Would you ask Bride to step out a minute?"

Bride, all black dress and veil, came from the parlour; she looked twice her fourteen years. She held out her hands to the older woman and raised to kiss her cheek.

"Do come in," Bride said softly. "We've been waiting." My sister led the way into the parlour and Nancy Murtaugh, head bent as though against the drive of a gale, followed after.

It was the custom of the times for two persons, usually a man and woman, to sit up through the night beside the dead in a "death-watch"; like many another of the old ways I suppose it's given over to funeral homes, "reposing & slumber" rooms and canned music piped through some hidden hole in the ceiling. On this, the last wake night before the burial, the deathwatch was taken over by the chief mourners. When the last of the wakers had filtered out, Bride, Nancy Murtaugh, Bill Doherty, Uncle Miles, and I remained.

Bride was near collapse.

"This girl has to go to bed," Nancy exclaimed.

Bride protested, but Doherty caught her up in his vast arms and started toward the stairs with her. "Which room is hers?" he asked over his shoulder. We told him. Bride's dark head fell against Doherty's arm and she was asleep before he reached the landing.

The four of us sat in the dance of candle-light, listening to the sigh of the wind in the firs that now and again fetched a sweep of rain against the heavily draped windows. The parlour clock, a dismal concoction of dark walnut and Grecian columns, chimed a silver chime three times. We swivelled our heads to look at the clock as if we expected it to say something. It was then I noticed that Nancy Murtaugh was crying and had been for some time. The tears chased down her cheeks like the rain washing down the window glass, but there were no sobs.

Uncle Miles had poured himself a whiskey. To his great credit this was, I knew, his first drink since the accident. Bill Doherty was gazing fixedly at the dead features of Luke's-John Coffey as if he was seeing something in that characterless face he'd never noticed before.

"We were lovers."

The words startled the air and hung for a moment in the vitiated atmosphere.

"Once," Nancy spoke again. "For one night when he came to Toronto. He wrote later saying he would get a divorce so we might marry. 'You need a man,' he said, 'and Bride needs a mother and I need a wife.' 'What about Patch?' I asked, and he smiled and said Patch needed to see more of the little girl whose father had a hardware store someplace."

We were silent, but the tears continued to wash down her cheeks. The dreadful clock on the mantel of the long disused fireplace ticked at the night hours while we sat, each wrapped in the cocoon of our own thoughts.

We must have been half-dozing when some subtle, indistinct sound brought us frighteningly awake. Aunt Kate–a spectre in her long, yellowing-white nightrobe entered the parlour, much as she had come into my bedroom weeks before. There could now be no doubt the old woman was completely mad: she ran her lichen-coloured eyes around the room, letting them rest on Bill Doherty for a long moment. Ignoring Luke's-John she went over to father's coffin and looked a long time at the waxen face. Then, going to the head of the casket and placing herself between the flickering tapers, she raised her folded hands to her breast and began to sing in her clear, pure soprano that pierced, eerily, the room of the dead and trans-fixed her listeners where they sat.

"There's a little rosewood casket
Sitting on a marble stand;
There's a package of love letters
Written by my true love's hand.
Go and bring them to me, sister,
And read them all tonight;
I've often tried but could not
For the tears would blind my sight . . . "

We listened in a kind of horror, but no one moved to inter-fere. Aunt Kate bent forward and looked again at father's face, then as silently as she came she glided out of the room and disappeared.

"Christ!" Uncle Miles muttered. "I suppose the old fool's been up there without a bite to eat or a sip of water since the wake started." He turned angrily, saying to no one in particu-lar, "Well, goddamit I can't look after everything!"

"I heard my mother sing that song forty years ago," re-

170

marked Doherty. "Haven't heard it since. Funny thing to sing at a wake," he mused.

"Can't you see she's battier than a pig in the buckwheat?" Uncle Miles said irritably. "She'll have to be put away–quick."

"After everything's over," Doherty replied. "After everything's over."

The wind grew stronger and the dark spruces flailed their arms against the house.

The morning broke grey and drizzly and the windshield wipers of the automobiles bearing those coming to the funeral slish-slashed across the streaming glass. The house quickly filled with ranchers, farmers, shopkeepers, and a few professional men from Lindsay who had known my father. The parlour door was shut and Bill Doherty, much too large for the suit loaned him by Uncle Miles, stood guard to let no one in. Uncle Miles was conferring with the undertaker in one corner of the kitchen.

"When do I screw down the lids?" the man asked.

"Right after the chief mourners have gone in and looked for the last time. No one else is to go in, y'hear? Now the mourners'll be me and Patch, here; young Bridie; that woman from Toronto; and Luke's-John's sister." Uncle Miles gazed pensively around the room bursting with people. "Yeah–and Bill Doherty, there. He's a pallbearer, too. After the mourners come out the piper will go in–and the two fiddlers; then the pallbearers."

"Who's piping?" asked the undertaker with professional interest.

"I got Long Donald Cameron from the Scotch Line, and the fiddle-players are 'Leghorn' Mullaney and Joe Kealey. Where is Long Donald? Is he not here, yet?" Uncle Miles shouldered his way through the crowd to the back door.

I followed my uncle outdoors where a tall, bone of a man wearing the full highland regalia of the Clan Cameron was standing on the back porch wiping beads of rain from his pipes. Long Donald stood six feet six inches and the hair on his head and the backs of his hands was the colour of new-threshed straw.

Uncle Miles told me to go back inside and get a bottle of whiskey for the piper. "Hae ye ony scotch?" Long Donald asked. "I hae nae use fer yure Irish distillations. I micht as well aye pipe wi' lemonade."

I went in and came back with a partial bottle of White Horse scotch. Cameron tilted the bottle, his Adam's apple bobbing up and down like a shuttle on a weaver's loom. We went back inside where Uncle Miles pulled the two fiddlers away from the drink-loaded table. Then he, Bride, Nancy Murtaugh, Mrs. Byrnes (the sister to Luke's-John), Bill Doherty, and myself passed into the parlour and the door closed behind us leaving us for the last time with our dead.

Bride gave way utterly, then. She flung herself across father's coffin and I do not want to hear such grief again. Doherty, after a time, led her gently away, talking softly to the weeping girl. Nancy Murtaugh, too, cried as she kissed the forehead of the man she loved. Uncle Miles said nothing, but his lips under his moustache were set and strained. Doherty again placed a hand on father's clasped fingers, and two great tears started from the fathomless blue of his eyes.

We left, then, the undertaker slipping by us into the parlour, Bride being all but carried by Bill Doherty, her sobs tearing at her small, black-draped figure. The three musicians, the six coffin-bearers lined up at the parlour door and when it was thrown open by the undertaker Long Donald Cameron struck up the high, keening dirge of "Sarsfield's Lament" and marched into the room and round and round again about the coffins, the fiddlers' violins moaning in unison with the wild piping. Father's pallbearers and those of Luke's-John took up their positions by each casket, now with the lids tightly closed and screwed down. The tall Scot changed key and broke into "The O'Driscoll's Farewell" and marched out of the room, into the kitchen and out of the house to where the hearse, rear doors opened wide, stood waiting. There, flanked by the fiddlers, the piper sounded the ancient Gaelic wail as the coffin-bearers shouldering their burdens came out bringing the mortal remains of my father who was leaving for the last time the house he was born in.

After the Requiem High Mass at Our Lady of Perpetual Help and the brief, graveside ceremony, I rode home with Uncle Miles while Bride came in Nancy Murtaugh's car along with Bill Doherty who had hardly left Bride's side all day. As we wheeled out of the cemetery I turned and looked back at the raw, sand-red mound that marked father's final resting place in the Fallon plot where slept his parents and three sisters.

"You'd better start looking ahead and leave the dead behind you," said my uncle tightly. "We're going to have our hands full, you know."

"What do you mean?"

"I mean Ward left a sound enough will leaving everything to you and Bridie, but neither of you is of age and that means the fucking Official Guardian of the province will be around horning in, and they're apt to put the whole shebang in escrow until you're both twenty-one. And you know goddamn well you can't let a cattle business sit on its arse and rust for eight or ten years. I ain't got no time to look after it; besides, it wouldn't look right; it'd look as if I was tryin' to screw you out of what's yours."

I said I didn't think anyone would say that.

"What? These sons o'whores in this county? Like fuckin' hell, they wouldn't!"and he went into an obscene tirade that was more to relieve his feelings than to bad-mouth the people of the district. "Ward has a little money in the bank; not much, but there's a little: enough to make a couple of mortgage payments and take care of the funeral expenses. The thing is, kid, there's a lot of work to be done around the ranch in the meantime and it's too much for you to handle alone. We'll get Bill Doherty to stay on for the summer, at least, until we can get you and Bride a lawyer to try and keep everything from going over to the Official Guardian or some other government son of a bitch. Those cocksuckers'd rob a widow of her gold teeth or an orphan of an all-day sucker."

The auto splashed on through pools of muddy water. The still-leafless branches of the roadside elms dripped moisture wearily onto the soaked earth. Along the horizon a grey scud of clouds tumbled along ahead of the rolling wind.

22

The unreality of death must forever give way to the realities of living. After the funeral the neighbours who had performed the farm chores returned to their own affairs. Bill Doherty and I took over feeding the stock, cleaning the stables, and doing ninety out of the hundred things a day any general farm requires to keep it rolling. Uncle Miles had his own place to look after, although he'd hired a lad to tend the farm for the week of the wakes.

Aunt Kate remained in her room throughout except for that one eerie night visit to the parlour. Bride had taken her soup which the old lady grabbed, peering suspiciously around the door partially opened to Bride's insistent knock. After the funeral Bride reported that Aunt Kate's room smelled terribly; rather than come down to use the outside toilet the old woman had filled a vast china chamber-pot until it bulged, then commenced on an old-fashioned hand basin and water ewer.

"Well, she's got to go. The old folks' home won't take her, I doubt; she's clean gone is what she is. I'll get a doctor out to look at her." Uncle Miles scratched his head.

Dr. Maclean of Foxford was a greyish man of greying years. Whatever skills he possessed he picked up on the Western Front during the war. He entered the house gravely, his secretive-looking bag carried in one mouse-coloured hand. Bride led him upstairs.

"You may leave," the doctor told her firmly. "I wish to be alone with the patient."

Bride returned to the kitchen where Doherty and I were finishing dinner. We heard the sudden rise of disturbed voices of which Aunt Kate's was the loudest and most profane. There was a crash, a high-pitched squeal of triumph from Aunt Kate; then silence.

"She's killed him," Doherty said comfortably, pouring himself a cup of tea.

Dr. Maclean descended the stairs and stalked to the door with as much dignity as possible for a man who has just had a brimming chamber-pot emptied over his head. We gaped at him.

"This," he said, mopping at his face with a handkerchief, "is a matter for the police."

As the doctor left we noticed a large piece of excrement clinging to the shoulder of his grey suit, like an epaulette.

The provincial police and two medical men in an ambulance came, but Aunt Kate had barricaded her door until it was proof from frontal assault. It was Bill Doherty who finally coaxed her out and into the ambulance by declaring his love for her and offering marriage.

"Why do yez want to be marryin' me?" Aunt Kate asked, not unreasonably, from behind her fortifications.

"Because you're the first person I know who ever threw a pailful of shit over old Maclean's head," Doherty answered. "He looked good in it. It matched the tie he was wearin'."

We all waited for an hour while Aunt Kate dressed for the "wedding." She emerged from her fortress wearing a suit of full-length underwear, a pullover wool sweater, rubber galoshes and a bath-towel worn like a tarboosh on her unkempt head.

"You're beautiful," said Doherty, taking her arm. "Off to the bridal altar; the coach is at the door."

Aunt Kate happily climbed into the rear of the ambulance

and out of our lives. She was to live until 1941, an inmate of the Whitby Asylum until her death.

Doherty had disappeared on one of his periodic "jags," and Bride had not recovered sufficiently from father's death to return to school. At Uncle Miles' advice we sold all of the farm stock excepting Jupiter whom nobody wanted and none of us wished to shoot. Along with the stock we had disposed of most of the machinery so that the money made from these sales plus the yearly rental of the pasture land to the Clancys provided Bride and me with enough to live on. After some hesitation we sold the automobile as well.

Late in April a man and a woman, both of middle years, arrived in a car as I was replacing wooden shingles blown from the back porch on that night of storm and death the month before. Bride was cleaning the outside of the windows with Bon-Ami and a pail of warm water.

The man was a short, potty, jenny-ass of a man with thin-rimmed spectacles and a high, balding brow that is often mistaken for a sign of cleverness. He wore a slightly rumpled suit and a drab tie that did not quite fit the collar of his shirt. His hat brim was turned up all round like a cheap homburg. His companion was a spider-legged, gaunt creature, dressed in a style some three or four years out of date. A hat weighted down with a dyed turkey feather cleaved to a head badly sprung on a neck not calculated to stand the strain. Her calf-length tweed skirt of narrow cut gave her a canter like a hobbled goat. The pair had official Victoria County written all over them.

"I think we got trouble," I said to Bride. Together we watched silently as the pair approached.

The man spoke first, holding the lapels of his coat in hands. "Would this be the Fallon place–estate of the late Ward Fallon?"

I nodded. My throat felt sticky-tight. I made no move to get down from the short ladder I was using to fix the shingles.

The little man looked around almost jauntily. "And would I be correct in assuming that you are Patrick and Bridget Fallon, children of the deceased?"

"You would," Bride spoke up. "Only our names are pronounced and spelled P-a-d-r-a-i-c and B-r-i-g-i-d." Bride carefully spelled out our names.

The female of the pair cracked her face in something like a smile so that the wire of her dentures showed. "Well, these Irish names can be terribly curious, can't they?"

Bride stared at her, coldly. "Only if you're English and don't know any better."

"We represent the Children's Aid Society for Victoria County," said the little man, puffing into the breach, "and it's our information that both of you are under the legal age ... "

"And that you haven't been attending school recently," said the woman triumphantly.

I replied that I didn't have to go to school and that Bride was going back to classes in the Kilmore Separate School within a week.

"But you must have adult guidance and supervision," the woman cried, stretching her neck as though about to crow.

I said we had Uncle Miles living less than a mile away as the pigeon flies.

They told us we didn't understand–that we would have to go to some kind of home or "shelter" until accommodation could be found for us with some family or other.

"I don't suppose you've heard from your mother since ... since your father died?" The woman looked sourly at me.

I shook my head.

The man scraped his hands together, looking around. "Well, then, suppose you get your things and come along with us. We'll keep you over in Lindsay until arrangements can be made to find a nice family to take you in; maybe both in the same place."

"We're staying here."

The man, he called himself Mr. Anderson, looked up sharply. "I'm afraid you don't understand. You have no choice; the law is very clear on the matter, very clear. Isn't it, Miss Pennyfield?"

"I guess you didn't hear me right: I said we're staying right here."

"In that case," the Pennyfield woman started forward, "we'll simply have to force you."

I stepped down from the ladder, reached inside the door of the porch and caught up my little saddle rifle leaning just inside the edge of the jamb. I levered a cartridge into the chamber.

"You're standing right where I'm figuring on shooting." I met them stare for stare. The Pennyfield woman gasped and put a hand to her throat; she began stepping backward toward the auto, but Anderson tried to smile his way out of a dangerous situation.

"Oh come now, come now. You're making things worse for yourself." His smile trailed off. "Give me that gun this minute. This minute, do you hear?"

The high-powered little carbine took a spiteful chunk of dirt two inches in front of Anderson's polished toe-caps. He leaped backward and fled into his car. As he started the motor he rolled his window down as though to say something. I jacked a fresh cartridge into the breech and raised the muzzle. The car dug its wheels in reverse and shot violently back until it reached the road where it roared out of sight.

"You should of killed the dinky little bastard." Bride's face was set and white.

"I can't do nothing for you now," Uncle Miles threw his hands up when Bride and I confronted him with the situation at his little farm shack. "What a dumb stunt to pull! Christ, you might as well have shot the Grand Master of the Orange Lodge. You know what this county's like."

"Well, we're going to no Children's Aid home or whatever," I said angrily. "We'll brush out back on the huckleberry rocks for the summer and they'll never find us."

Uncle Miles told us to do whatever in hell we liked and slammed out of the shack.

"I'm going to phone Nancy Murtaugh," I told Bride as we walked home.

We sat with Nancy Murtaugh in the lawyer's office in Lindsay and told our story while the attorney pulled his ear lobes, the end of his nose, and his bottom lip. When we were finished he got up in his salt-and-pepper suit and stared out of his office window overlooking the dirty grey of the Scugog River.

"Jesus!" he said. "Jesus!"

He turned suddenly and aimed a cigar-browned finger straight at me. "Did it ever occur to you that Manfred Anderson's wife and the wife of Judge McCabe are sisters?"

"Who's Judge McCabe?" I asked sullenly.

"Who's Judge McCabe?" the lawyer mimicked, then roared. "I'll tell you who Judge McCabe is! He's the man behind the bench who is going to send you to gaol for seventy-five years: that's who Judge McCabe is."

He shook his head at Nancy. "You see what we're up against. They're all like that in the north end of the county. Savages! Drink and fight and shoot: that's all they know. All they want to know. All they live for."

He sat wearily down behind his desk and studied his hands. "I knew old Matt Fallon before I went into law. They'd have had a manslaughter charge against him if they could have found the body. Ten'll get you one if a man was to go over that Fallon lay-out with a pick and shovel you'd turn up something besides nigger-head rocks. And the father of these . . . "–he spread his hands–"beat a man half to death in a lumber camp and lit out for the Saskatchewan prairie."

"This is all very interesting, Mr. Slattery. But our concern at the moment is for the living Fallons. Specifically, what do you propose?"

The lawyer looked at her shrewdly. "You intending to take

custody and responsibility for the youngsters?"

"I am."

"And you haven't heard from their mother nor do you know where she can be contacted?"

Nancy shook her head.

"What's your marital status?" Slattery shot at her.

"Single. I . . . I was married. I'm divorced."

"For what reason? Adultery, I suppose?"

She nodded.

"And the offending party?"

"I was."

The lawyer bounded from behind his desk. "Oh this is wonderful," he shouted. "A young Dillinger headed for the gallows tries to blow the foot off a county official who is prominent in the Free Masons . . . Free and Accepted Masons, not to mention the Scottish Rite and the Orange Lodge and the Scarlet Lodge and the Black Lodge, and for all I know maybe a Shriner and a Bashi-Bazook and a Klan Kleagle. Then for a guardian our Jesse James selects a woman who has been divorced for adultery." He paused and looked furiously at a photograph of a solemn King Edward VII on one colourless wall. "Do you know what the greatest sin in the town of Lindsay is? I'll tell you: it's getting caught. Adultery's next greatest."

"Perhaps we need another solicitor," Nancy said stiffly.

"What you need is a Judge McCabe for a brother-in-law. Now don't *you* start acting the damn fool. We need you, adultery or not.

"We'll move to be heard in chambers; that way no snoopy reporters and tittering tillies. I'll talk to the Crown and see if he'll keep his nose out of it. He isn't a bad fellow, the Crown: crazy–crazier 'n a bear and its arse on fire–but I'll have a go at him.

"We'll likely get a hearing tomorrow. Make these kids younger looking than they are: put Wyatt Earp, here, in knee pants and stick an all-day sucker in his mouth. Tie a bandage around the girl's chest–she's got bigger boobs than Mae West.

And have her carrying a doll, or a teddy-bear, or both. Now as for you," Slattery eyed Nancy not altogether without appreciation, "try to look something like Judge McCabe's wife: sort of thin and brown and dried up–like a penitent monk. It'll be hard, but try."

Judge McCabe was a tiny, doll of a man whose miniature body was topped by a large, round, florid head totally devoid of hair. He wore gold-rimmed pince-nez; he had the look about him of a very angry tomato. His wee hands, pink nails carefully groomed, sprouted from the sleeves of his judicial robes and tapped irritably with a gold pen. Mr. Anderson and Miss Pennyfield stood together, grave and drawn. The Crown attorney lolled in a chair, picking his nose and examining the findings with minute care before stowing them away reverently in a pocket handkerchief.

The judge's chambers was a dark, walnut-coloured cave, ranged round with shelves of mouldering tomes containing every statute, decision, declaration, and legislation handed down since Moses was an altar-boy. A manure-coloured rug joined the four walls. The judge lolled in a huge, leather chair the hue of a deceased elephant, and which utterly dwarfed the occupant. Bride and I stood self-consciously and not a little frightened in front of the judge; Nancy stood behind us, her hands warm on our shoulders. Slattery, hands jammed in his side pockets, listened without apparent interest as the Children's Aid pair intoned their tale of horror. As they spoke the judge darted fiery little eyes at us from time to time. When the two had completed their testimony and answered a few questions put to them by the judge they stepped back and stood in an attitude of respectful adoration.

In a voice as musical as a small stonecrusher Judge McCabe said it was perfectly clear that a hand–a strong, guiding, firm and chastising hand–was needed here; the only thing to be settled was the choice of institution. "Even you, Mr. Slattery," the judge grated, "will admit some action is necessitated."

Slattery took his hands out of his pockets and clasped them behind his back. "Indeed, m'lord." County judges required no more than a "your honour" but Slattery knew his jurists.

"I do have," he continued apologetically, "a minor question or two to put to our faithful servants of the county: a mere clearing up of one or two points I didn't quite grasp during the presentation of their evidence."

"Get on with it then," the judge said irritably.

Slattery, hands still behind his back, walked in small circles on the rug. "Now, I gather when you went to the Fallon *estate*" –he chose the word carefully–"you found the two children outside, did you not?"

Anderson and Miss Pennyfield chorused that such was the case.

"And," pursued Slattery, "what were they doing? Playing tag? Causing a disturbance? Stoning passing automobiles?"

It was admitted such was not the case. "Many years ago," the old lawyer mused, "when I was a lad in Ireland, we played a bit of a game we called 'Aunty High Over The Barley Mow'; we tossed a ball back and forth over a stack of barley. That was in County Tyrone, in the *north* of Ireland. You may have heard of the game from your parents, m'lord; I believe they came from County Tyrone, did they not?"

"No–County Antrim."

"Ah, yes. County Antrim: the *loyal* county, as her late Majesty, Victoria, was wont to say to her beloved Albert.

"But what I wanted to ask," turning back to the representatives of child law and order, "was–the two youngsters were not playing Aunty High Over The Barley Mow, by any manner or chance?"

When he received the reply to the negative Slattery rubbed his fingers over his long jaw. "Hmmmm. Tell us, then. What were they doing?"

Miss Pennyfield spoke up. "He," indicating me, "was repairing the porch roof and the girl was washing windows."

"I see: repairing the roof and washing windows. Two lone

183

bits of orphans, their mother fled, their father dead, struggling to maintain a decent front: doing the necessary chores about their pitiful home. Maturity," turning to the judge, "such as this is seldom seen in the young today. It's obvious they were brought up to respect property and the home."

Anderson smelled a trap and rushed to close the water-tight bulkheads. "But—he shot!" he stuttered shrilly. "He grabbed a rifle and aimed it square at me, he. . . ."

Slattery held up a restraining hand. "Now, Mr. Anderson, we've already heard your little tale. I might remind you this is Judge McCabe's chambers we're in; his lordship'll tell you when you may or may not speak up. I advise you not to take liberties in *these* chambers." The attorney looked around the room aggrievedly.

"Yes, Anderson," said the judge sharply. "*I* will decide who shall give evidence and when."

Slattery bowed appreciatively to the judge, then button-holed Anderson with a hard stare. "Did you or did you not have your proper identification and credentials on your person when you invaded the Fallon property setting forth unequivocally that you were a proper person authorized by the Children's Aid Society of this county empowered under such Acts and Patents as to legally proceed to secure the persons of the Fallon children and carry them off, willy-nilly, to a public shelter?"

Anderson smiled disdainfully. "Of course. I have been with the society a number of years. I think I know enough by now to always have on my person all proper identification."

"To be sure. And did you know enough to present such identification to the Fallon children in order to assure them that you were, indeed, what you professed to be—the manager of the Children's Aid Society for and in the county of Victoria?"

Anderson leaped back but not in time; the jaws closed gently about his neck. He looked angrily at Miss Pennyfield who gave him glare for glare.

"N-nno, but I thought–"

Slattery pounced. "I don't know what you thought, but I'd like to tell m'lord what this brave boy, here, thought: he thought he was protecting his little sister from a child-molester."

"Oh, come now, Mr. Slattery." The judge came to his brother-in-law's rescue. "A child molester would hardly take a woman with him on a criminal errand."

"But a white-slaver would," hissed Slattery. "We read about it in the papers every day. The Mafia, m'lord. They travel about in the guise of respectable citizens, sometimes with false papers: very clever, these wops–sorry, m'lord–I mean Italians. There was a case in Chicago, just a few weeks ago. Your lordship may have heard about it: a pair of white-slavers–a male and female–their pictures were in the *Toronto Telegram*. In fact the man looked somewhat like Anderson, here. Caught red-handed, so's to speak." Slattery studied the floor mournfully. "It turned out the man was an ex-priest."

Anderson opened his mouth like a gaffed trout, but Slattery cut him off. "So Paddington here, named, by the way, after William Paddington–one of the heroes who defended the walls of Derry against James II, who had been reading of the Chicago case in the *Telegram*–his father always subscribed to the *Telegram* and the *Watchman-Warder*; the late Mr. Fallon was an ardent Conservative; not politically active, but staunch– immediately suspected the Mafia ring was about to strike again. Here were two total strangers, faces set and grim, advancing in a threatening manner on this plucky boy and his helpless sister. Even then, having so strong a respect for law and order, the boy fired but a warning shot. Had he intended to kill," glancing significantly at Anderson's paunch, "he could hardly have missed such a target at that range."

Slattery did another turn about the rug while the Crown attorney still sprawled in his chair, silently applauding with professional appraisal the old lawyer's performance.

"So, friendless and alone, who did they turn to–and it was

only natural—but the lady, the very dear and concerned lady before us now, with whom their late father intended to marry once divorced from his wife—a woman who deserted her family for a scoundrel and who has not been heard from since."

"True," replied Slattery sorrowfully. "The Roman Church is dictatorial and high-handed in such matters. Shortly before his untimely demise it is my understanding that Mr. Fallon had sought spiritual advice and counsel from Mr. Calvin Ussher, pastor of St. Andrew's Presbyterian church at Mavely. Had he lived and remarried Mr. Fallon and his intended would, in all likelihood, have become part of the Reverend Ussher's little flock."

It took five minutes for Judge McCabe to write out an order assigning Bride and me to the care of Nancy Murtaugh.

Afterward we had dinner with Mr. Slattery in the Benson House Hotel's dining room.

"I never heard so many damn lies in all my life," I declared, digging into my apple pie.

"You've never been in court before, either," replied Slattery. "Bring me another mug of coffee, will you, Gertie? And trickle a little something into it, eh? About so much." He held up four fingers.

Nancy wanted to know about the fee.

"A hundred dollars. Ahhh, this is more like it." He sipped his fresh cup of coffee. "These kids are worth it. I checked on the estate. They've got bags in the Foxford bank; they owe on a mortgage, but there's enough coming in from rentals and interest to meet the payments and taxes as well as to keep them in shoe leather. I'd say they were sitting pretty."

Nancy counted out ten ten-dollar bills. "It was worth it to watch you perform."

The lawyer chuckled and carefully stowed the money away in a huge, brown billfold. "I never asked what you did for a living."

"I paint," Nancy replied.

"Barns or portraits?"

"Neither. I'm an Impressionist."

Slattery winced. "Lucky I didn't ask you in chambers. McCabe would have thought you were a Communist.

"Say," he mused. "Did you ever play Aunty High Over the Barley Mow? No? Boys o boys, those were the days of real sport. The boys were on one side of the stack, the girls on the other. If you caught the ball you ran around the stack and kissed the first girl you came to. I remember young Maurya Mulligan . . . "

We got up and left the old man alone with his dreaming.

23

Nancy Murtaugh let her cottage on Raven Lake stand empty while she moved into the big farm house with Bride and me; this was part of the agreement made with Judge McCabe. Nancy considered renting the cottage – it had a first-rate location and any number of well-to-do city people would have paid good hard money to rent the little one-room cottage from spring through autumn – but in the end she decided against it. "I can't let perfect strangers trample in and out of my little place," she wailed. "It would be like shooting poor old Jupiter."

Jupiter was the last animal left after the sale. Bride and I considered getting a dog, some sort of watch-dog that would bite everybody except us. Then one night before the fuss with the Children's Aid people old Belial came back. We got up in the morning and there he was grazing quietly around the bole of an apple tree in the orchard. A great crust of dried blood about his nostrils showed where the great, black bull had ripped the ring from his nose. I never knew a bull to pull a ring through his nose before or since–ever. We had sold Belial to the Clancys, and that same afternoon Clancy and his two sons came with chains and a whip to fetch their absconded property.

"No," I said, "I guess not. I'll give you your money and five dollars more for your trouble. We were thinking about getting us a dog; old Belial, here, will do just fine."

So we didn't pen the huge beast up again in his confining corral. We fixed the fence around the orchard and allowed Belial to crop in luxury. We even ran a lane of rails down to the Sally Brook so's the bull could waddle down and ease his thirst and rub off the pestery flies in the four-foot stands of squaw weed. Sometimes he'd come up to the fence near where Bride was hanging out clothes and stick his massive head over for Bride to scratch under his jaw and behind his ears. He was alive and with us at the time I went away to war. Sometimes when I go back near the old burned-out ruins of the house I can feel Belial's black presence and hear his low, throaty rumbling, like horizon thunder on a summer day.

Although we burned pans of sulphur and brimstone in Aunt Kate's room we never did quite get the smell out; at any rate we always imagined we could smell the results of her last tenure. It was decided then that Nancy should take over father's room. It was a nice room; the south dormer looked out over the orchard and the little swamp where ran the Sally, while the west window showed a cloud of aspen and balm-of-gilead masking the Dorgan Crossing.

Bride and I had not been in father's room since before he died and not much then. The only person who had entered that bedroom was Uncle Miles when he went to get father's new suit–the one he was laid out in. We opened the door and it was like opening a grave. Spiders had run webs in corners and closets; the bedding was rank and mouldy with damp; the air was still and dead. A rough briar pipe lay in an ashtray partly filled with dottle on the bureau. Beside it was a photograph of Nancy taken at her lake cottage; she was standing, short skirted with one hand braced against the door jamb, smiling. Nancy caught her breath and went quickly over to the south window. "Is—is any clothing of your mother's left in here?" Her voice was catchy, and she looked at the fast run of the Sally without turning her head.

Bride said mother had taken most of her personal things with her and those she left behind father had burned.

"Well, then," Nancy said brightly, turning around, although her voice still quavered, "we'd better get to work. If you can open these windows, Patch, this room could use some air."

Bride went back to school. She had a new bicycle and the four mile run into the Kilmore Separate School was nothing but a bit of exercise for her. I was left alone with Nancy.

Like many with artistic, creative temperaments Nancy's long suit wasn't model housekeeping, cooking, or domestic drudgery. One could not visualize her in bare feet and a poke bonnet following after a team of oxen. Despite her fondness for the country and her lake cottage Nancy was a creature of the city and the amenities of the city. Lugging water from the Sally Brook two pails at a time did not, for Nancy, represent the good life where one turned a tap and out came enough to boil tea or have a shower bath. She painted a good deal, often several hours a day, and sometimes she loaded up her Buick with paintings and took them into Toronto where, she said, she had a showing. Once she spent most of a week with her easel and frame set up outside painting a view of the orchard and Belial snuffling contentedly through his nose which was still sore from his escape. When Nancy finished she dried her hands on her blue painting smock and asked me what I thought of her picture. I studied it for awhile and I wasn't sure whether she was funning me or not. Finally I told her it looked like she'd spilt a mess of paint on the canvas and the cat had sat in it. I caught the full gust of her anger and it was ugly enough.

"Clod!" she spat. "That lawyer was right: Irish red necks given to drinking and fighting. You couldn't even spell culture!"

"No, maybe not," I admitted. "But if that's culture I can get along fine without it."

"*That* and others like them pay for a lot of things around here."

My head went up quickly. "We've money of our own and we never asked you for a penny."

"All right, Patch; I shouldn't have said that. People just don't understand an artist's feelings."

"Do artists ever try to understand any but their own feelings?"

Nancy put her easel under her arm and went into the house without replying.

I picked up my rifle and strolled off across the pastures. The new May sun was still setting early; already it had worked around to the poplars lining the Crossing. I saw Bride cycling home from school, her blue cape floating out behind her. I whistled tonelessly between my teeth and continued walking. I passed Jupiter dozing, hip-shot, under a black oak. I wished I had a dog for a companion; a dog understands things, even the moods of people, and mine was a strange mood I was far from understanding.

Later I heard Bride calling me for supper, her voice rising high and clear over the turmoil of the brook, but I sat on the five-barred gate that opened into the maple bush so beloved by my grandmother I never knew—the bush Abel Coventry had tried to buy from father. When was that? five, six years ago? Closer to six, maybe. A rail fence enclosed the maple bush. Two great sentinel sugar maples attended the gate which was hinged with iron-roll hasps on one tree and was secured by an iron bar-latch to the other. Years ago old Matt Fallon had tapped the trees and made syrup out of the sap. A few rusty sap buckets stacked one inside the other lay sprawled about beneath the trees among the bright green of dutchman's-breeches and the speckled leaves of trout-lilies. The boiling-down place could still be seen: a great ash pole eight inches thick chained horizontally between two trees was where the big, cast-iron pot—bigger than any witch's cauldron—was hung and a fire built under it in a kiln of limerock. The kettle was filled with sap and a fire of hickory and maple built in the kiln and the sap boiled and the bubbly scum ladled off every so often and flung into the granulating snow where it cooled, and father and Uncle Miles and their three sisters grabbed it up in their mittened hands and ate it because it looked and tasted like taffy.

Somewhere deep in the black-boled depths where the blue cohosh was just unfolding its wet leaves—the way a new-born calf is wet when its straining mother drops it—a hermit thrush tried a single note, then rang out a melody, clear and lonely because it was forty years and more since children ran and laughed under those trees and chewed maple taffy, and forty times forty and times that again would go by and no children would come, and the hermit thrush fluted to the lengthening shadows and the pale green star of Venus rising just over the budding trees.

"Patch!"

I turned, startled, swinging around, my rifle coming up.

"Don't shoot, Patch; it's only I—not the Children's Aid beadles." Nancy's solid figure loomed out of the dusk. She was wearing an old cardigan sweater unbuttoned over a thin blouse, a dark skirt, and she was in her bare feet.

"You're going to catch pneumonia running around barefoot this early in the year. Christ, the snow's hardly gone!" I tried to sound grown-up and huffy like my father.

"I'm a wild thing; I'm a dryad, a wood nymph. I'm proof against such things," she said and drew closer in the gloom until I could sense the woman-warmth of her and smell the woman-fragrance. I tried to turn away but she caught my arm.

"Are you so very angry with me, Patch?"

"I'm not sore. Well, I was, maybe, but I'm not now."

"You didn't come for supper."

"Wasn't hungry."

"Was it because I'm really not a very good cook?"

"Bride and me didn't ask you to come hire on as a cook. Nor a dishwasher. Nor a maid-of-all-jobs. I—we needed you. We still need you. And maybe it's not all a one-way street. Maybe you get as much good from staying here as we do having you."

Nancy grasped my two arms. "Look at me, Patch," she said.

I looked and in the coming night the two eyes of her loomed and seemed to grow and glow as great and green as Venus now climbing steadily high over the dark flare of the Catholic Bush.

She leaned forward and pressed her mouth tightly against mine and I realized I'd never been kissed full on the lips by a woman before—or a girl. My mother used to peck my forehead and Bride planted great smacks on my cheek when she was leaving for school, smacks that left traces of lip-rouge, now. For a long moment we stood, our lips held together by some invisible force that had risen out of the night like the bog-lanterns some call "The Fair Maid of Ireland" rise and dance and lead the lost traveller into his boggy grave.

I could see and hear nothing but the drive of blood through my head until Nancy let leave of my arms and my lips and stepped back. I realized I was foolishly grasping the rifle. I leaned the weapon against the gate and turned toward the woman again but her ear had caught the notes of the thrush and she was letting her soul rock gently in the waves of it. I was about to speak but she reached up a finger and placed it against my lips. "Shssssh." Her whisper hung between us like mist. The thrush called again, re-arranging and running over his bit of a symphony, then the sound dropped and fell back into the shadows and the trunks of the great trees drew closer together in the dark.

We walked together toward the house glowing with lights

like a ship abroad by night on the ocean. Once Nancy let me put my arm about her shoulders and we walked several paces, our hips meeting and swinging together; then I let my hand drop over her shoulder and slide beneath her blouse to the nestle of her breast—round and firm and warm. She removed my hand gently with both of hers, then she fled ahead of me toward the house—toward the lights—and my heart sank because I thought she had done something cruel and unnecessary in a world where already so much useless cruelty flourished as thick as ever the bitter weeds growing rank in the flower beds of my long-dead grandmother.

Bride was at the kitchen table, hunched over her school work, when I came in. Of Nancy there was no sign. Bride threw me a quick, searching look, then bent again over her books. A flush spread rapidly up her face.

I hung the saddle-gun on the pegs high on the wall and went and stood by the stove. I removed one of the lids and stared at the little pine fire that had been kindled to chase the night's chill.

"Somebody was asking about you today, Patch." Bride's voice sounded scratchy and too unconcerned.

"Yeah? Who?" I replaced the stove lid.

"Somebody real pretty. Somebody like Lila Kennedy."

"What was she asking about me for?" I was determined to be dense.

"Oh, why does any girl ask about a boy? Because she's interested in you, that's why."

"I thought she was going with Niall Sweeney."

Bride made a face. "I bet if you asked her to go to the Swiss Bell Ringers show next week she'd be happy to go with you."

The Swiss Bell Ringers, as they billed themselves, were a hold-over from the days of vaudeville now ousted in the cities and urban centres by the movies. A pair of aged and versatile vaudevillians gathered a troupe of entertainers, musicians, puppeteers, illusionists and cross-cut saw fiddlers and drove from town to town around the continent, playing to crowds of

194

fifty or a hundred where the tickets cost only fifty cents.

"Lila's more your age, too," Bride said maliciously.

"She's a year older'n me."

"That's better than twenty-two."

Nancy came down stairs enveloped in a bathrobe chastely covering her from neck to instep. She was carrying a huge china basin full of water which she took out and emptied in the tile gutter behind the woodshed.

"There's my bath for the week," she laughed. "How did people ever manage to get clean in those things?"

"I don't think they did," I answered. "Aunt Kate used to say that if you washed too much the water would soak into your pores and get drawn up into your brain."

Nancy told us she would be leaving early in the morning for Toronto with several paintings she intended displaying on an exhibition-sale. She said she would probably be away three or four days. In the morning when I got up from a tossing, restless sleep Nancy was gone. Bride, a notorious late riser, offered no sign of life from behind her closed bedroom door. I kicked rudely at the door and when there was no answer I pushed open the door. Bride's head was tangled in her nightie which she was struggling to remove. She stood by the bed, naked from her neck down, arms flailing at her nightie. I stared.

"Why, she's like a woman," I thought. "Like those women in the sexy comic books Ed Kennedy gave me."

Her breasts were like pear-apples, and a dark V of hair was spreading up toward her navel. Bride worked free of the nightie, her face flushed with exertion. "See everything you wanted to?" she jeered, tossing the gown to crumple in a corner while, naked as a shorn sheep, she walked over to the closet. I backed away, my face flushed and embarrassed. I was stirred more than I wanted to be. This wasn't like comic booklets or Thad Whalen's stories of Lila Kennedy, or even kissing Nancy Murtaugh by the light of a solitary planet. There was something black and twisty, yet honey-sweet: it was Father Blaney's serpent coiling in ring upon ring around the Tree and Eve, naked as my sister Bride, listening in wonder and then with desire as the flickering tongue of the snake flew like lightning and the acid-sweet words dripped upon the mind of her that listened until she walked, wide of eye, and heaving of bosom into the coils—into the darting tongue.

I fried bacon and eggs for Bride's breakfast and made sandwiches for her lunch. Left to herself she'd never be up in time to get her own breakfast or make herself lunch. But when she came downstairs in her short skirt and shoes with heels that were almost spiked, I mumbled something to her about having a good day in school and I almost ran from the house and away south through the pastures until the house was out of sight. I walked until I came to the five-barred gate where, on the night before, Nancy Murtaugh had come stealing in her bare feet to look for me and set within me a jangling, cutting feeling as though I'd swallowed a pair of Spanish spurs. The sun sent a warm glow through the maple wood, drawing the new leaves out of their buds and causing a million white trilliums to dance and shine among the black-trunked maples. Trilliums white and trilliums red as blood or a woman's painted lips, as far as the eye might roam. Spring beauties and hepatica, shy as squirrels, carpeted little vales, and the bright green of leek tops scrambled with the cohosh and trout-lilies to find the sun. I climbed over the gate and gouged out the new-sprouted leeks; they tasted hot and wild and succulent. I knew the little wild-onions would do terrible things to my breath, but I dug up several, slipping from the bulb the thin sheath protecting the white root, before biting into the rank flavour.

"Mighty good, ain't they?" I jerked around sharply. The speaker was sitting on a lightning-felled maple, looking at me with the bright eyes of a weasel although the eyes and a huge crooked nose were all that was visible of his features so hidden they were by heavy brows and a dirty grey streaked beard that surged up to his hairline and hung down to his chest. With a wretched old hat, the wide brim turned down all round, and clothes that would have disgraced a scarecrow the man looked like a troll or the terrible dwarf Alberich who had hidden the treasure of the Nibelungen. I recognized him: Old Man Kavanagh he was called; if he ever had a first name he'd either forgotten it or wouldn't give it because no one alive by that day knew him as other than Old Man Kavanagh. No more could any one remember when Kavanagh was anything but an old man: an old man who lived in a shack in a deep stand of tamarack beside the Talbert River. The shack was little better than a badger hole: a tangle of logs, mossed over, with pieces of tin tacked over some of the larger holes.

"Sure," continued the old man, "I always do be comin' here this toime o' the year to be gettin me a diggin' o' wild scallions. Them and ginger-root. Ever et ginger-root, bucko? No? See them round-like leaves there. Them over agin that butt of rocks stickin' out. Got a little red flower down near the bottom; hard to see. You get the roots. You get them roots n' eat 'em in the spring of the year and they'll make your old snapper rise up like a trout to a May-fly," and the old man went into a great cackle of laughter ending in a fit of coughing. He thumped a weathered old hickory stick on the soft ground at his feet, his eyes like broken bits of glass studying on me and looking as if their owner was possessed of some mighty joke no one else knew.

"Ward Fallon's get, ain't ye? Yez got the look. Knew him when he was a pup no older'n you. Knowed the brother, too. Miles. Knowed them three gals; all went young with the consumpt'. Too bad; fine lookin' women them Fallon girls. Come by it right: mother was a Dorgan. Prettier than a harebell in a June wind. Yep–Hanner' Dorgan. Knowed her when she was goin' to school at the old Log Corners. They was a log school n' a log church–kind of a meetin' place. Yeee-ah, knowed your gran'daddy Matt. Bad bastard that; don't keer a bust 'n the arse was he your kin or no; Matt Fallon was a bad un. His kids was all right, though. Funny how she turns out, hey?"

He filled a stump of an old pipe with a handful of tobacco

and chaff dug out of the side pocket of the wretched overcoat he was wearing; he looked like a big gnarl you sometimes see growing out of a stump or a downed tree.

"Yee-ah. Ward Fallon left a jump ahead of the constables. Got clear out west I did hear. Came back to die, didn't he. Ought better to have stayed put. Miles was sore old Matt didn't leave him but one dollar bill; figured he looked after the old daddy and should o' got the home place. Know why he didn't? No, eh? Because Miles went and fit in the big war with Germany, that's why. Matt figured no Irish should go fight fer England. Didn't speak to Miles fer two years 'n more after he come back from overseas. I was in the British army once. Long time ago. Sent me to Africer 'n fought the Zulus there. Meaner 'n cat-shit them fellers. Big black heathen bastards."

"I guess you must be pretty old."

That set Kavanagh into another fit of cackling. "Nobody know how old I am, jasus be forever thankful. Fellow runs the post office in Kilmore said the govermint'd send me a pension was I to be after tellin 'em me age. I say fuck the sons o' bitches!"

He relit his pipe and looked up at me again. "I do be seein' yez out a lot lately with that shootin'-iron o' yours. Good shot; too good. Just like Matt wuz. I see you knockin' over squirrels and woodchucks, things like that. Now, you listen to old Kavanagh: them's our own brothers 'n sisters—all things what live out in the bush and in the fields. They not be harmin' yez. You go shoot at tin cans or knotholes and lay off'n the little creatures or you'll be bad's old Matt."

Kavanagh looked around, chuckling somewhere in the depths of his evil-looking beard. "This here bush was a favoured place of yer grandmaw's. Used to come walkin' in here a lot, pickin' flowers 'n such. Was somebody else liked fer to come here, too. Come once too often and stayed. He's over in that holler yonder, eight foot down 'n rocks to hold him there. . . ."

The old man got up and hobbled away slowly through the

198

trees. Now and then I'd hear him laughing as he went. I heard him laughing after he was out of sight.

I walked toward home, passing a couple of woodchucks out for a nibble at the new clover, but I didn't raise my rifle barrel. I kept hearing the old man's words: "Eight foot down 'n rocks to hold him there."

24

In the end it was Bride made the date for me with Lila Kennedy to go to the performance of the Swiss Bell Ringers at the Orange Hall in Kilmore. I felt foolish riding into Kilmore on my bicycle to go on a date with a girl who I knew went out with young fellows who could drive, and maybe owned, automobiles. While Bride ironed furiously at my one white shirt, I strode worriedly around the kitchen, desperately examining the crease of my trousers to see if the edge pressed into them by Bride was holding. I felt one of my socks slipping down; the elasticity had all gone out of the garter: men wore garters in those days; they were of elasticized fabric that hooked around the calf of the leg and fastened to the top of the sock. "I can't go!" I roared frantically. "Me bloody garter's gone limp and I've no other. I can't appear on the street with a sock trailing down to me instep."

"Wait!" Bride fled upstairs and was back with a pair of garters clutched like vipers in her hand. "There were a pair of daddy's among his things when we cleaned out the room for Nancy."

I knocked with some timidity on the side door of the Kennedy house in Kilmore. Ed Kennedy was, by the day's standards, reasonably well-to-do: he was head foreman down at the sawmill owned by the Sigerson Brothers. The Kennedy house was an old-fashioned, yet very attractive house of gables, sun porches, bay windows, and all sorts of carved gimcrackery done up with narrow white siding. A concrete walk, barely old enough to be cracked, led from the little metal street gate to the side door.

Lila's father opened the rear door and looked at me quizzically through the screen; he was in his sock feet, carried a newspaper and his glasses were pushed up on his forehead.

"Yes," he said. "What can I do for you?"

"I was wonderin'," I said foolishly, and feeling faint, "if your daught–if Lila was home?"

He chased a fly away from the screen door with his newspaper. "She is, but she's going out tonight. Who will I say called?"

I was set to turn and flee when Mrs. Kennedy came into the kitchen and peered out past her husband. "Who is that? Is that you, Patch? Ed, this is Patch Fallon, the boy who is taking Lila to the performance tonight. Come in, Patch; Lila will be down in a jiffy. Can I offer you anything while you're waiting? I've some fresh chocolate cake."

I declined everything and perched on the corner of a chair with the pale sweat of death trickling down my scalp, the dandruff of which I'd spent the better part of an hour attacking with Vitalis and the "60-Second Work Out" as the ads advised.

And then Lila was coming down the stairs, her skirt flaring to show a delicious amount of silk-stockinged legs, and she ran over and pecked me lightly on my scalded face.

"What d'you think of all this trouble over in Europe?" Kennedy growled around the edge of his newspaper.

I said I thought it looked bad over there and might get worse unless they did something quick.

Kennedy said as far as he was concerned Neville Chamberlain didn't know if his arse-hole was punched, bored, or reamed out with a teaspoon. As my knowledge of Neville

Chamberlain had not reached the point where I could supply an answer I played dumb – an easy thing to pull off because I'd never felt dumber in my life.

Somehow Lila and I got out on the street where the perfume of lilacs and horse-chestnuts was as fragrant as the subtle scent Lila was wearing. The sun had just set, leaving a lavender blush on the western horizon through which writhed dark, roiling clouds like locomotive smoke. It was four blocks from the Kennedy house to the Orange Hall and we were obliged to run the gamut of stares from couples too old to do anything but disapprove, and youngsters hanging from tree limbs who shrieked and tittered. We had to pass old Lizzy MacCluney's cottage and were unfortunate enough to find her poking among a bed of geraniums set near a rusty ornamental fence. Lizzy wanted to know how I was doing, how my sister was doing, what that Raven Lake woman was doing, and she also enquired if we owned a bed of geraniums and Dover's wire-haired terrier came and dug and crapped in such a geranium bed, what action, short of shooting the dog and the Dovers, might we suggest.

It was fun sitting on the hard maple chairs beside Lila, watching the performers going through their acts; they rang bells, played hand saws and cross-cut saws, thumped out tunes on jugs, played melodies on crystal goblets, and pulled a lot of old vaudeville gags that were brand new around Kilmore. The touch of Lila's silken knee against mine was almost unbearable; her hand stole into mine and I felt my huge Fallon hands were so rough and calloused and coarse compared with her slender, soft, trimly manicured hands. When the company pulled off some particularly funny bit Lila leaned against me, rocking with laughter; when they sang some sad, old song like "Among The Budded Roses" Lila dabbed at her eyes with a tiny handkerchief and nestled even closer, letting her head fall back against my shoulder until I was nearly crazy with the clean, windswept fragrance of her hair.

During the intermission the lights came on and a hand

grabbed me by the shoulder. I turned and Thad Whalen was grinning at me. "Come on outside a minute, Patch, I wanna see you. Hi, Lila."

Lila excused me, and with some annoyance I followed Thad outside.

He led the way around to the rear of the hall where a dark alcove offered shelter from the street lights. "Here," Thad shoved a pint flask at me, "have a snort."

"What is it, shine?"

"Not on your mother's grave! That's the pure cat's ass— Gooderham & Worts."

I took a long swallow, pretending the fiery liquor was not suffocating me in the least. "Whee-yuuuuuu!" I came up for air and handed the bottle back to Thad, fighting the tendency of the whiskey to come back up through my nostrils.

"You're a Fallon, you old son of a bitch you, you're a Fallon," Thad exulted. He raised the jar and took a couple of swallows. "Got another in the car. But say—you got Lila, eh? I brought Rose Hanley. Tell you what. After the do we'll all go in my car for a little spin, say, back to the sand quarry?" Thad winked and shoved the bottle back at me again. I drank, but more slowly this time.

"You got any rubbers?"

I looked down at my feet and shook my head; I was about to say I was wearing oxfords, but Thad went on.

"Never mind, I got some. Here," and he handed me a little tin box. I opened it and took out one of the silkily-powdered condoms. I didn't know what to say.

"Y'know somethin'? I was out with Frank Teague a couple o' weeks ago, eh? I had Rose and Frank had one of the Bell girls. But you know how dumb Frank is! We were at the dance hall in Foxford and I gets Frank out in the can and I asks him does he have any french-safes. He said no, so I gives him a Sheik and do you know what the stupid arse-hole said? He says, 'Will I put it on now, or wait until after the dance?' " Thad staggered around, doubled up with whiskey and laugh-

203

ter. I laughed too, but mine had a hollow sound: I had been set to ask Thad that very question.

As we went back inside the hall I stealthily read the instructions on the back of the tin, although it still wasn't clear to me how one could get a roll of slippery rubber over a soft pecker or what good it was supposed to do when it finally got there.

Back inside Lila nuzzled into my arm. "You were gone a long time. I missed you."

She sniffed. "I smell liquor. Have you been drinking?"

I nodded.

"Oh, I hope you saved me some; I'm so dry!"

I blinked. I knew that Lila was seventeen, but I didn't think anyone got dry for booze that young. I said Thad had more in his car.

"Oh, that's fun. Are we going with Thad? I think he's got his father's car. The big Olds. Who's with him? Rose Hanley? She's okay. We'll go driving after, shall we Patch?" Lila dug her fingers into my biceps and rubbed her knee tightly against mine.

The remainder of the Bell Ringers' show became a hazy mist of music, the close warmth of Lila's lithe body against mine, and a great feeling of exhilaration as though God had just unlocked the world and thrown it wide open for me. I swayed slightly at the finish when the house stood for the singing of "God Save The King," but I remembered I was a Fallon—one of the drinking Fallons—so I made the best show I could manage of standing erect. Lila and I merged with the crowd outside; I looked around for Thad Whalen. A car horn sounded.

"There they are, Patch." Lila clutched my arm and we ran over and climbed into the rear seat of the Whalen Oldsmobile. Thad gunned the motor and we swooped down the street and whirled out onto the highway. Rose Hanley, a red-haired girl of sixteen, was in the front with Thad. She turned around.

"You two going steady?"

While I was trying to think of something to say, Lila answered, "If we weren't we are now. Aren't we, Patch?" She put her arm around my neck and hugged me to her.

"Thad, you got any more of that drinking liquor?" The night air rushing through the no-draught ventilators was clearing my brain-fog.

Thad chuckled and reached into the glove compartment. "Bust the seal on this, Rosie-O."

Rosie broke the seal and handed the pint bottle back to me. "Save some for old mom and daddy here."

Lila took a long sip, made a face and grimaced at the bottle; she took a longer drink, then handed the jug to me. "Where we going, Thad?" she asked. "Lindsay?"

"Lindsay!" Rose shrieked. "Who in hell wants to go to Lindsay!"

"Why, me and ol' Patch there figured you girls'd like to see the moonlight over the stone quarry." Thad up-ended the first bottle we had drunk from out behind the hall. He opened his window and slammed the empty flask against a rock.

"Rattle up the stove-pipe–
Johnny shot a bear;
Shot him in the arse-hole
And never touched a hair . . . "

"Thad, you sing magnificently," Rose crooned. "You ought to've been on stage with the bell-dinglers."

"How's your old 'bell-dinglers'?" He reached over with his free hand and flipped at Rose's breasts.

Lila swung her legs up and over my lap, tugged my face down to hers and kissed me firmly on the mouth. Her hands, her fingers were doing strange, wandering things up and down my neck, behind my ears and along the muscles of my arms. Not quite intentionally but more for the want of something to do with it I let my palm rest on Lila's stockinged leg above the knee; she moaned softly and let her legs fall open. She nibbled like a rabbit at the lobe of my ear. We didn't even realize the car had come to a stop in the stone quarry.

205

I kissed Lila repeatedly, almost savagely, while she clung to me, her lips, her hands wandering and touching and driving me through a field of fire. My hand, unskilled and unsure, roamed higher beneath her skirt, fumbling and feeling at strange and exotic things—lace and silk and soft, curling hair.

"Patch," Lila whispered urgently in my ear. "Is it your first time, Patch? Is it, Patch?"

"Yes," I gritted.

"Oh Patch!" She held my head to her bosom so that I could feel the thrust of her taut little breasts. Then she became instructive.

"Let me help . . . I'll show you. Wait, Patch, wait . . . " and she fended off my eagerness—my ineptitude.

Then we were together, close and enveloped in the warmth of her flesh, surrounded by her slim thighs, her eager little breasts bared and nipply in the half-dark. I felt like I was the High King of all the World; I felt like old Belial felt when he rested his black muzzle on the top of his railed enclosure and watched from the red corners of his eyes the heifers grazing or gambolling in the distant pastures. I learned that sex was a wild tearing at one's back with blood-red finger-nails; it was a clawing, biting, shaking, animal thing with a soft, yet firm body moving swiftly and in perfect unison with my own, until the sky tipped and one corner of Paradise showed through.

I lay on Lila's breast, exhausted; dulled with whiskey and freed suddenly of that terrible torment that racks the uninitiated. I lay quietly and she spoke softly, almost maternally, to me, running her fingers through my hair and stroking the back of my neck.

"I love you," I said.

She didn't answer, just kept on fondling my neck, now and again squeezing me with her thighs.

"I love you," I repeated.

"Not now, Patch," she said softly, "not now; not yet."

"What do you mean, 'not now—not yet'?" I demanded, half rising.

"Patch! Patch!" she cried, pulling me back down to her, smothering my protests with the carmine of her lips. "Wait . . . Wait awhile. Maybe later, later on, if you still feel this way."

Lila pushed me gently and sat up, pulling her skirt down and trying to undo the tangles of her taffy-coloured hair.

"It's always like this the first time, Patch," she explained. Then seeing the anguish in my face, she faltered. "I know what it's like, Patch; oh God, I know what it's like and I'm not that much older than you. It hurts and it hurts and you think it will never go away.

"Do you know the first time I did it? It was with a man, a mill-hand down where daddy works. Oh, he told me he loved me, too. And I believed him! I had just lost my pretty little cherry and I was so in love, too. He was married and had three kids up around Timmins. Boasted to everybody down at the mill about 'fucking' the boss's daughter. Daddy heard and fired him: chased him down the road with a cant-hook. That man was thirty-six!"

"I'm sorry, Lila," I said quietly. "But I feel something very powerful for you; if it isn't love, I don't know what it is. Maybe I just don't know."

The other couple, all unknown to us, had left the car; now they were returning, carrying a blanket and singing an off-key country ballad:

"O, she then removed her corsets
  And on the floor she laid
  And I shoved me whole eight inches
  Up Maguire's hired maid."

T*ramp, tramp, tramp, the
ghosts are marching. They tramp as only a ghost
can – slipping into the dark of my lonely bedroom
on the four winds of the world. The ghosts rise
from their graves; they leave their wards in the
asylums; they take flight from the agonizing
beds of cancer; they come from behind cold pen-
itentiary walls; from across the sea.*

*As I lie, staring into the dark, the ghosts sit si-
lently at the foot of my bed. They are silent, but
I hear them; they are invisible, but I see them;
they bring no odour, but I smell graveyard clay
and the dry-spice scent of old wreaths long browned and blown with wind and weather.*

*The ghosts allow me no rest – no sleep. I put out
a trembling hand and grope for the friendly feel
of the bottle. I drink; I gulp the fiery Irish whiskey while the sweat beads break out on my fore-*

head and the ghosts stare at me from rimless eyes and whisper to me with mouths the tongues of which rotted long ago.

O God! give me whiskey. Bring me whiskey. Hot, burning, mind-soothing whiskey. Whiskey chases away the grey, silent things hovering about my bed. I drain the last of the bottle. I want whiskey! My roars echo and rock through the silent house–I have been long alone. . . .

> *O, it's whiskey, you divil–*
> *Ye've been me downfall;*
> *Ye've kicked me, ye cuffed me*
> *But I love ye for all. . . .*

I rise and stumble about the house, fumbling in closets, peering into crannies. Were They here whilst I was out and hid my whiskey? Goddamn the sons of bitches to hide my whiskey! I reach and my hand closes around a quart bottle. I've won again!

> *Whiskey, rye whiskey,*
> *O how I love thee;*
> *Ye killed me ould father–*
> *Now damn ye, try me!*

25

A full calendar month had passed since that night when Thad
Whalen had dropped me off at the road by our yard gate, and
I had stumbled, staggered, and crawled my way in through
the back porch, scratching and plucking at the door like a mis-
erable dog scrabbling to be allowed in out of the weather. The
open door and Bride standing there in her flannel night-dress,
Nancy behind her in a terry-cloth housecoat through which
her breasts threatened to tumble out.

I got to my feet and plunged through the door, crashed into
a corner of the table and fell into my father's old captain's
chair. I hung my head down; the stink of my own vomit curdled in my nostrils. I had left my suit coat in Thad's car; my
tie was lost forever; my white shirt Bride had so tenderly
ironed was shy a few buttons and ripped at one shoulder. My
trousers were not quite buttoned and they bore deadly evidence.

"It seems our boy Patch has reached his majority." Nancy
was coolly amused, but she began to brew coffee.

Bride sat across the table from me, her face white as milk
and the wild Irish-blue eyes fringed with jet lashes were wide
and filled with something that may have been misery had I

but the wit and my senses about me to read them rightly. Her breasts, already larger than Lila Kennedy's, heaved with the depth of her breathing and the pent emotions.

"Hell, Bride," I mumbled, "I guess I went and saw the elephant." And I slid forward on my face and knew no more until the noon following.

Of all the months, save that of October, the month of June was the best Victoria County had to offer. It was then the great green pastures, alive with meadow larks and bobolinks, rolled like the waves on the sea to cool, grey dikes of stone walls or the darker grey of rail fences. There the mighty beef cattle ranged and grazed, to the depths of their knees in succulent limerock grasses shot through with clinging vetch, nodding daisies, and the cream-rich yellow of butter-and-egg plants. The three-year-old steers with sides like marble slabs flung up their heads as one approached, gazed at the intruder, then fled in mock terror, their tails over their backs and their iron hooves drumming on the sod. At the far corner of the middle pasture where the galvanized frame of the windmill stood against the sky while the vanes swung lazily and the pump rod complained rustily, a concrete watering trough, years old and gone brown and crumbly, hosted a net of green slime, and bits of frog faces peering warily from the water. Garter snakes sped lithely into the cover of sorrel and burdock flanking the trough. The surplus water flowed over one end of the trough and slid quietly away among hilly tussocks of twitch-grass and miniature stands of St. John's wort.

There must have been a million birds that summer. I remember the birds because, while I didn't know it then, it was the last summer I was to pay heed to birds. It was the last summer of joy and youth and the proud strength of the arms and tireless legs.

Nancy spent hours from dawn-up to lights-down out with her easel and her palette. I kept away from her because she didn't like to be watched or talked to while she worked. Bride was in her last month of elementary school and she was, following the summer holiday, planning to board in Lindsay and attend the collegiate there.

I had been out with Lila Kennedy but once since our first date; that was to a movie in Lindsay, Lila driving her family's car. We had parked and kissed a lot, but nothing beyond because of something called a "period" Lila was at some pains to explain about.

"Jesus, I'm one ignorant christer," I told her.

Lila laughed. I'll never forget the way she sounded when she laughed. It sounded like the silvery chiming of a very old, and very expensive, clock.

"Weren't we all," she said and played the gentle tips of her fingers over my face.

There were other changes: I seemed to have a grown a foot taller, although it was only a few inches. I was now over six feet and I had put on a lot of body weight and muscle where it counted. And I was beginning to drink. Whiskey was expensive and beer was hard to conceal from Bride and Nancy. I rode my bicycle over to Danno Moran's and bought wine from him either by the quart or the gallon jug: cheap wine that left the footprints of a giant headache on the temples when I sobered.

On a day in mid-June I cut across fields and leaped brooks the four or five miles to Danno's lay-out. Danno owned a rickety bungalow to which he had, at some time, intended to add an extra room. In fact Danno had got as far as pouring the concrete foundation and laying a few floor joists, but then the bad weather set in, according to Danno; the bad weather lasted for years, perhaps as long as twenty years. The floor joists turned grey and twisted in the sun; the concrete, never too hefty, crumbled under the drive of spring and autumn rains. And now it was too late: the accident that killed my father and Luke's-John Coffey had left poor Danno with a gimp on one side and a twist on the other. The use of his right arm was near gone; the rubber in his left leg had turned to a steel

213

rod embedded in it for life. Now when Danno walked he jerked and kicked like a three-legged donkey going to the fair.

Danno had married Sadie Murphy who may have once been comely. Now she matched the wallpaper in her parlour, wallpaper that was original and of a thick texture, a blessing for it seemed to be all that was keeping the roof from tumbling in. There had been a child who had died young of black-throat diphtheria. Danno and Sadie had never tried again. Sadie grew gaunt and the corners of her eyes turned bitter and she wore the same dress for a month at a time. Danno lurched and bucked around the house, popping corks, lifting tops of beer bottles, and setting out balls of malt in none-too-clean tumblers. He was raided ritually and without malice by the provincial police who rarely found anything beyond a glass or two of Shankers' Extract of Boggle-Root which Danno's wife took for the female miseries. Danno's cousin was the county constable and if collusion was suspected it was never proved.

Danno was in the front yard when I reached his house; he was dispiritedly kicking at a Russian thistle growing by the side of his leaning porch. It was the only Russian thistle I'd seen since I left Saskatchewan.

"Here's a turrible weed, a most ferocious plant growin' right in me front yard and threatenin' to spread and destroy the universe," Danno lamented. "And what does yer governmint be doin' about it? Nothin'. What are we paying taxes for when them as runs the show will allow poisonous things like this to take root and spread on a man's property and not lift a hoe against it?"

Danno had paid no taxes for years; the township would not seize his property because they didn't know what they would do with it, and the cost of issuing a writ and sending round a sheriff would be more than the lay-out was worth.

"Bill Doherty's inside," Danno mourned as he led the way up the jiggling steps. "He's been on a jag for a month and has the cryin' blues. I can do nothing for him. I've sung for him and everythin', but he's deep in the blues. It doesn't make for a cheerful atmosphere in the home when a man has the cryin' blues."

In the parlour the massive Doherty was sitting at a round, dining-room table, a bottle of Burke's before him and a glass. He turned slowly, his bloodshot eyes trying to concentrate on who I was.

"Patcheen, me darlin' boy!" Doherty shoved out an enormous hand the back of which was heavily veined and covered with a bristle of black hairs a few of which were turning grey.

"Bring us another tumbler, Danno, and be quick. Jesus, you ought to stick a roller-skate on that short foot of yours: you'd gallop like Finnegan's ass. Patch, you long butt of a Fallon, you; you've been avoiding me. I've not set my twinkling blue eyes on you since Christ won the sweepstakes. What has old Bill Doherty ever done to you that you'd run a mile to hide behind a tree from him?"

I pointed out that he had gone off on a bat and never returned. I might as well have saved my breath for the mighty drink of Burke's Irish Doherty slopped into my glass.

"I know," he said brokenly, covering his face with his hand. "I know why you hate to set the sight of your eyes on me: it's because I murdered your father; your father and poor Luke's-John Coffey. I murdered the two of them and ruined Danno here—he was fuck-all to begin with and now he's worse." Large tears trickled down behind Doherty's sheltering hand.

I looked helplessly at Mrs. Moran, but she was pouring herself a glass of muscatel, a wine that Doherty said would give anyone the flying shits for three months. Her face was aloof. The ways of men and drink were not unknown to her, neither were they of supreme interest. She took her glass of muscatel and flopped into a rocking chair with a five-year-old copy of *Hollywood Romances*.

"Danno," Bill commanded, "sing us a bit of a song to cheer us all up, here. Here's young Fallon come all the way to see Bill Doherty and there's no music to make him welcome. What kind of a goddamned bootlegger are you, anyway, Danno! Strike up the band and leave the parade follow."

"Me voice, Bill," objected Danno. "It hasn't been right since the accident. I—"

"Sing us a song or you'll have another accident that'll finish what the first one started."

"I'll get me melodjen; I always sing better with me melodjen." Danno scooped a tattered old melodeon off a shelf and wheezed a bar or two:

"John Brown's body
Lies a-moulderin' in the grass—
Blackbirds 'n beetles
Playin' checkers up his ass."

"Grand, Danno," said Doherty ironically, "just grand. Give us a bit of history along with our music. Was that John Brown that went to free the niggers or John Brown that used to run the livery stable over in Foxford?"

"Bill," I broke in, "I heard you sing at our house, once. Would you sing again?"

He turned his stone-blue gaze on me as if baffled by something, as though he was trying to catch a thing the sieve of his mind had allowed to slip through. Then he smiled, gestured at Danno and told him to open with "The Blue Velvet Band." Doherty's voice was almost perfectly pitched; a deep, rich baritone free of all the jerks and jumpings and theatrical side-effects tossed in by many Irish singers.

"'Twas in that city of wealth, wit and fashion—
Dear old 'Frisco where I first saw the light;
And many the grand old frolic I have had there
Is fresh within my memory tonight."

The song, to my chagrin, was interrupted by two men coming through the yard. Danno peered out at them from behind a filthy drape. Doherty stopped singing.

"Who's comin', Danno?"

"I—I think it's Babe Farrell and Gully Malloy."

216

"I've no damn use for either. Kick their asses to hell out," Doherty rumbled.

"It's business, Bill," Danno pleaded, hopping like a wounded crow to the door.

The newcomers ordered whiskey. Doherty answered their greetings curtly. They turned their attentions on me.

"Ain't you takin' a big chance lettin' little orphan boys drink here, Danno?" gibed Gully Malloy. Farrell grinned through the gaps in his teeth.

Danno raised a trembling, cautionary hand, but Doherty swung his chair around to face Malloy.

"What was that you said about orphans?"

"Wasn't talkin' to you, old man."

"Well, by the black-haired, blue-eyed Jesus I'm talking to *you!*" Doherty lunged from his chair, but tripped and went sprawling. Malloy swung a wicked, iron-shod boot at Doherty's face. The boot never connected because I struck Malloy squarely in the mouth as hard as I could swing so that blood and bits of broken teeth came away on my knuckles. Malloy was up like a bob-cat and we went fighting and swinging wildly across the room and out the front door where Malloy caught me above the eye with a hard-boned fist. I dived down the steps, stunned and half-blinded. I would have been a dead pigeon had not Malloy been distracted by the body of Babe Farrell hurtling through the front window, carrying with him the sash and part of the frame as he flew. Doherty had gained his feet and entered the war.

I was sick with pain and fright. I'd never fought a grown man, and Malloy was several years my senior and work-hardened: the Malloys, when they weren't drinking or thieving, worked at cutting logs or cordwood. All of them, including the old man, were as tough as boot leather.

I climbed to my feet, blood misting my left eye. Malloy was at me; we clinched, rolling about the yard and thoroughly flattening Danno's Russian thistle, settling his botanical problems for years to come. Malloy was getting in some pretty good

217

clouts to my head until I jammed my thumbs into his eyes; he bawled in agony. I leaped clear and to my feet and drove the heel of my boot against Malloy's ear. He slid slowly forward on his face. I aimed a second kick, but Doherty grabbed my shoulder.

"When they go face down like that they're out of the game."

Babe Farrell, more shaken than hurt, came up, picking slivers of glass out of his hide.

"What in hell you sore at me for, Bill?" Brawny as Babe was, he almost cringed before Doherty.

"You forgetting the time you sided with that wop in Foxford?" Doherty spit on the palm of one huge hand.

"I'm apologizin' right here an' now."

Doherty grunted something. Danno's wife emerged with a basin of water she laconically emptied over Gully Malloy's head. Doherty prodded him, not gently, in the ribs with his foot.

"Get up, you whore's scut. Get up and get going. The sight of you would chase a goat away from a garbage dump."

Malloy rose, slowly, balefully. His musk-rat eyes gleamed malevolently.

He dribbled a line of obscenities, raising his fist at me. Doherty roared and moved at him. Gully fled, running awkwardly toward the road. Farrell followed slowly. In a way I felt sorry for Babe Farrell. He was a good hand at the mill and was better than a fair fighter, but Angelo had whipped him in his own turf and now Bill Doherty, too contemptuous of him to hit him, had thrown Babe through a window as though he was a cloth doll. He walked away and his walk was that of a beaten man. Babe was killed in the war, I heard. Killed in the army driving up through Italy, and I guess he's buried there.

"Let's get some iodine on them cuts," Doherty advised.

"Danno!" It was a bellow. "Get out the Rawleigh salve and iodine and do us some doctoring!"

We went inside together.

26

Toward the end of June I walked to Uncle Miles' place – about a mile as a heron flies – because we had not seen or heard from him since the affair with the Children's Aid Society. He had shown little avuncular concern for either my sister or me, but he was a Fallon and kin. I went to see him in the evening as the sun was stretching the shadows of the great, vase-shaped white elms, and night-hawks were sounding "beep" high in the thin air where an early star was taking on polish. Uncle Miles was sitting on an elm block that must have been three feet in diameter, beautifully carving a single-tree of white ash with a draw-knife.

My uncle's "house" was a shack of two rooms, one of which, Uncle Miles said, was the kitchen and the other wasn't. The barn was large, well-built, and had an adjoining silo because Uncle Miles grew a considerable acreage of corn he chopped into ensilage to put extra heft on the beeves he stall-fed all winter. In addition to these out-buildings there was a garage, a workshop excellently equipped with a full range of power and hand tools arranged with neatness and precision. Other than a rickety toilet, there was a singular building known as the "battery shack." Uncle Miles was a radio buff. He owned one of the first receiving sets in the district and was continually tinkering with tubes, circular objects wound with green wire, tuners and other contrivances unidentifiable to all save a technician.

Before the arrival of rural electrification, radios were powered by batteries: usually a "wet" cell that was nothing more than a 6-volt car battery, and a pair of "dry" cells that when their energy ran down were not, like the larger car battery, rechargeable and had to be discarded. Even the car battery had to be taken to a garage once a month or more, depending on how long the set was turned on, and put on the electric charger. In the early days of radio, in the 1920's, this meant a thirty-mile drive to Lindsay as no automobile repair garages had recharging equipment nearer than the county seat. Uncle Miles had rigged up a shack with four-vaned metal sails that, theoretically, were supposed to turn round and about in times of wind. The windmill shaft was connected to an old auto generator that was in turn hooked to a wet-cell battery that took on a charge when all went well. On the day of the Big Wind of 1929 – a hurricane that cut a swath through middle Ontario like a giant bulldozer – Uncle Miles was in his shack setting the brake on the vanes to prevent the approaching storm from hurling them clean off the shaft they were attached to. Playing no favourites, the gale picked up the shack, vanes, and Uncle Miles and deposited them, somewhat ungently, in a newly ploughed field a quarter-mile to the east. The next day, unhurt but savage, Uncle Miles retrieved the shack with a logging-chain and a team of horses. Now it stood, vanes bent and draggled, a neglected ruin among the wild mint and cinquefoil a few rods from my uncle's dwelling.

"Well, what kind of trouble are you in, now?" was his greeting. I said there was no trouble I couldn't handle and if there was I wouldn't come to him to set it straight.

"Getting big in the mouth since Gully Malloy tripped and you kicked him in the face, aren't you?"

"You suddenly got to be buddies with the Malloys?"

He snorted. "I licked the old bear and his cub, Len, at the same time at a dance in the schoolhouse."

I allowed as how I'd heard that; I said it was a good chore that needed doing. Uncle Miles was mollified. The man had greyed. His moustache, thicker and heavier–beginning to look like Wyatt Earp's–was grizzled. Uncle Miles had a red-grey stubble a week old furring his face; his eyebrows, thick and the colour of his whiskers, were lowering across his bitter eyes. And I guess he had a right to be bitter. He lost his sweetheart; he lost his father's affection (for whatever that was worth) when he enlisted and went overseas in the First World War. Then he lost his sister Rosie, and I think that was the heaviest blow of all. I looked at my uncle through older eyes; not wiser, maybe, but older.

I set myself on a saw-buck and watched Uncle Miles' razor-sharp knife slice methodically through the finely grained wood.

"Going to get a tractor in the fall, now that prices are going up because of the war scare in Europe. I've got a hundred acres of oats headed out the best I've ever seen."

"You were in the big war; d'you think there's going to be another?"

Uncle Miles held out the whipple-tree at arm's length and examined it with a critical eye. "Yeah. England and France were too tough on Germany after the Armistice. Broke her back. Clemenceau and Lloyd George: meaner than catshit, both of them. The Germans went haywire and this Hitler bastard came along and the square-heads followed."

"But I bet we can lick them again."

Uncle Miles spat between his feet. "*You* can 'lick' them if you're eager. I had enough of Jerry last time."

We sat silently for a few minutes. Far down where the Sally Brook flushed out wide beneath the marsh-marigolds before it cut across the far corner of Uncle Miles' land on its way to join the Talbert, a night-heron squalled.

"I wonder why we never hear from mother. You'd think she'd come back and try to claim something?"

"Her right of dower? I wouldn't let it worry me. Ward had her sign away her rights in front of a notary public. The paper's in the bank at Woodville along with the rest of your documents and money."

"It's still funny we don't hear from her. Maybe she didn't like me much–I don't know–I thought she'd at least want to see Bride."

My uncle looked at me curiously. "She's out on the coast. Vancouver. I got a letter from her not long after the accident."

"You never told me 'n Bride anything about it."

"It wasn't addressed to you. Somehow she got word about Ward's death and she wrote asking if you and Bride were all right. I wrote back and said you were doing just fine and a lot better than if she was with you."

"What's she doing out in Vancouver?"

Uncle Miles shrugged. "I wouldn't look into it too far if I were you." He stared bleakly at the sliver of moon beginning to clear the peak of the barn.

"Another thing you ought to know: you thought I ran out on you and left you to the wolves. Well, if I'd horned in people would say I was aiming to rob you kids of the home place. I was mad at the old man when he left the whole shebang to Ward, and I let it be known around. I'm not taking a hand in anything. You're there and I'm here."

"Yeah," I said. "Yeah, I guess that's right."

Uncle Miles stubbed out his butt of a cigarette and got to his feet. "There's something I want to listen to on the radio. I'll see you again some time."

"Tell me something," I said on impulse. "Who did grand-mother Hannah used to meet back in the maple bush?"

"The father of your Aunt Rosie," and the shack door slammed behind my uncle.

When I reached home Bride and Nancy were playing a noisy game of two-handed euchre. They didn't hear me come in. I went to my bedroom and lay on the bed, staring at the darkened ceiling, for a long time.

27

July and August are two months I've always hated. For one thing I cannot abide hot, muggy weather; for another, Victoria County was, and still is, a roosting ground for tourists and cottagers. This was because, in the northerly parts of the county at least, there was nothing but scenery. The locals couldn't plough, milk, or pickle the scenery until they found out that urban-weary millionaires from Toronto and Detroit had a penchant for buying lakeside lots where, in summer, they could ooze into deck chairs, booze, fish, and peek at better-looking females than their wives through field glasses.

July and August, therefore, to me are synonymous with heat, mug, and outlanders in ferocious costumes. Thirty-five years has brought about no change in my thinking.

Looking back on it all from the vantage point of years and whatever wisdom I can lay claim to, I believe that summer of 1939 found me with not enough to do. What with the pastures rented and the stock gone and enough income for the support of Bride and myself, I had not a thing to occupy my time except in the reading of books far beyond my simple education and wits. I had grown into a slab-sided brawn of a boy who had, perhaps, picked up and kept intact some of the poorer virtues of his parents. I had periods of almighty gloom—a gift from my father; I had little skill in grappling with problems that were not purely physical in nature: this was inherited un-blemished from my mother who, as I recall, never had two consecutive thoughts about anything in life greater than which pair of shoes should be worn with what dress. I may be doing the woman an injustice because I've not laid eyes upon her from the day she walked out until this time of writing. I do not know if mother is dead or alive. Nor do I care.

Nancy Murtaugh had been given the power of attorney to handle the financial part of our affairs; and this she did with scrupulous honesty. I believe she enjoyed life at the Fallon house as much as she did her summers at her Raven Lake cot-tage. She had re-opened the cottage and often spent days there alone without coming near the Fallon place, although by no means was the woman neglectful of those things she had con-tracted with the Children's Aid Society and the County Judge to do. Bride and I were plenty big enough and old enough to take care of ourselves in most areas.

Nancy was generally friendly and aloof at the same time; she circumspectly avoided any occasion or a furtherance re-sembling that spring night at the maple bush gate. She and Bride got on well, possibly because of the gap in their ages; Nancy was thirty-eight to Bride's fourteen.

When the school in Kilmore closed for the summer vaca-tion, Bride, who had topped her class in her highschool entry examinations, was free for the summer. She had grown—changed. Traces of the girl were still there, but Bride's was the body of a woman. Her thoughts were woman-thoughts and my little kid sister was gone forever.

One afternoon I came in the house to see Bride standing in the centre of the kitchen in a new dress. Nancy kneeled beside Bride, a mouth full of pins, examining critically the cut and fit of the material. Bride twirled lightly on heels that must have been three inches high. "How do I look, Patch?" She swished her body around again. "What do you think of it?"

"Your little sister has a very heavy date, tonight," Nancy advised, narrowing her eyes at a tuck in the waist of Bride's dress.

"Yeah? Whose birthday party—Ann Lenehan's?"

Bride stuck out a pink tongue.

"No birthday parties: Bride is going all the way to Lindsay to a real, live, talking picture," Nancy said.

"To Lindsay! Who are you going with?"

"Jerry Lynch."

My face flamed. Deliberately I went over to the cupboard where father kept his whiskey; there was a third of a bottle of Seagram's rye. I took a swift belt from the bottle.

"You are going no place with Jerry Lynch," I turned, letting my back rest against the counter.

"When you are old enough to drink *and* handle whiskey, you might be old enough to advise others." Nancy coolly removed the dress she was fitting on Bride. Bride stood in her short satin slip against the ray of the sun; her legs played shadow magic beneath the slip; her breasts jutted full and fair; in the black corner of my eye I could see foppish Jerry Lynch reaching out to fondle those warm, living globes, lifting them like eggs from their nest, putting his face to them, his tongue. I could hear him yapping to the corner-boys that hung around Kinch's Novelty Shop: "Hey! You guys ain't seen nothin' yet. You wanna see the boobs on the Fallon broad!"

"I'm playing a man's game I drink a man's drink." My voice was thick with the boil of rage, but I fought to keep it steady.

"That's right. You're just playing at being a man. I think your sister has as much right to be a woman."

I took a long, heavy pull at the Seagram's. "Bride," I said, trying to keep my voice calm and reasonable, "do you really want to go to a movie in the town of Lindsay with that titty-rag of a Jerry Lynch?"

"Oh, Patch, don't be silly. Nancy's coming with us. Jerry asked me several days ago when we met him in town, and I said, 'Sure, I'll go to the moving pictures with you if Nancy goes too.' And that's all there is to it. I wish you wouldn't drink that strong old whiskey, Patch. I think it brings out something mean in you. I really do."

"And we're driving my Buick," Nancy said in mock grimness. "I don't trust Master Lynch's sporty coupé."

I wheeled into Kilmore in the evening on my bicycle, still smarting from the victory Nancy and Bride had won. I felt like a cheap braggart and would-be he-man. The whiskey had run out of me, leaving a bad taste and so little wind I was obliged to get off and push the machine up Dorgan's Hill, a rise that any other time I could have pedaled up sitting on the seat and bracing into a ten-mile wind.

Kilmore lay tired and dusty after three hot weeks without rain. The horse-chestnuts and red maples were covered with a fine grey ash that had been laid on by wind and automobile tires; there were, as yet, no paved roads leading in or out of Kilmore. The closest pavement was the Portage Road a mile south; it was called that because Champlain, when he and his Algonquin guides made a little pasear up through the district, had run a chain of lakes, but were forced to portage several miles and the road was so named after the Frenchman's old route.

I propped my machine against the front of Canfield's garage and service station and went inside to get a drink. I picked a stone bottle of ginger beer from the cooler. Sib Parker, who was a mechanic for Jack Canfield, came out of the repair part where the grease pit and ramp hoist were, wiping his hands on a tangle of dirty waste. He wore greasy coveralls and a cloth cap with the peak ripped off. The cap was lettered with an advertisement for A.C. spark-plugs.

"*Mister* Fallon," he said, with some emphasis on the "mister." He reached into the cooler and fished out a coke. "Know what this stuff does to yer innards?" he asked, holding the bottle up to the light. I shook my head.

227

"Had an old U-bolt, one time; couldn't get the nut off her. Rusted tight, eh? Stuck her in a tin can with some coke in her," he rested his vulpine eyes on me, enjoying his lecture, "an' the next mornin' bolt and all was near eat away."

Parker dug into his pocket and brought out a bottle-opener. "Only tool in the whole shop that's worth a damn or gets the most use." He showed brown stubs of teeth.

I looked around at the stacks of auto tires and boxes of tubes on grimy shelves over the counter whittled and scarred by years of loafers.

"I think I'll learn to drive and get me a car." I leafed through some tattered folders of advertisements put out by the Ford people.

"Thazzo? What'ja do with your old man's car? She was in pretty good shape, wasn't she?" Sib coughed out a lungful of blue smoke from a Sweet Caporal cigarette.

"It was sold when we held the auction. I'm thinking of buying a Plymouth coupé."

Sib mulled that over thoughtfully through his cigarette smoke. His face pursed. "Dunno. Harder'n ol' Jesus to start in the winter time; aluminum pistons, y'know. Expand with the heat and contract with the cold, that's what them kind of pistons do. You take your General Motors cars, now–Chevy and them; they got cast-iron pistons and you don't get that kind of trouble that way."

"What do you think of these Fords?" I gestured toward the folders.

"Well, we sell 'em here, but I'll tell you straight out: these here V-8 motors is bound to wear your rings out on one side. Bound to, runnin' on a slant that way. Was I you I'd get me a Chevy. Oh, say, 1932-33 coupé; somewheres in there. Nice little set of wheels for a kid your age. Easy on gas." Sib stubbed his cigarette out. "Gotta get back inside: puttin' in a new rear end for Reg Poole."

I stuck my hands in my pockets and wandered dispiritedly out onto the street. Piper Mulvihille and Johnny McKelvey were sitting propped against the window ledge of Calvert's old harness shop. Calvert was long dead and the shop closed for years, although old Mrs. Calvert still lived in a pair of bleak rooms up over the empty shop.

"How's your hammer hanging?" Piper licked the edge of a cigarette paper. I sat on the ledge where the flakes of green paint were still clinging to the grey, weathered pine.

"Christ, this place is dead! Any of you got a drink?"

Johnny lifted his head. "Haw-haw."

I raised my arm to cuff at him.

"G'wan," he said. "Just because you got the best of Gully Malloy . . . "

We sat and watched the street lights come on under their tin reflectors, and the big orange Shell sign over Canfield's gas tanks began to glow. A middle-aged farm couple ambled past, the man in braces and a dark grey work shirt around which he had knotted a brown rag of a tie in honour of his visit to the city. Although it was mid-July with the temperature crowding 80° the woman wore a heavy, black cloth coat the bottom of which reached to her stubby calves; a potty brown hat was jammed over her ears and wispy grey hair; the cuban heels of her shoes were so worn she slopped over on each side so that her walk was remindful of a sailor struggling down deck in a gale. "That's what we're all going to come to," remarked Piper, the glow of his cigarette following the backs of the farm couple. "We stay long enough around this country we're going to wind up just like that. The arse of our pants gone and an old woman that looks like Mary of the Wild Moor."

"Shit, yes. That could be my old man and woman," Johnny said thoughtfully.

"No, it couldn't," Piper said ruthlessly, "yours look worse. Patcheen the Gombeen is the only one of us with brains. Is he set up, or isn't he? He doesn't do a lick of work; he fucks the dog all day and that Murtaugh woman with the big boobs all night."

More people were drifting into town, parking their Fords

and Pontiacs self-consciously at the curb, then getting out and shaking hands heartily with neighbours they hadn't laid eyes on for nearly three days. The farm girls between the ages of twelve and sixteen, mostly too big and gumpy for the clothes their mothers made them wear, stayed close to their old ladies lest the Kilmore Mafia drag them into an alley and set fire to their virginity. The women and girls passed on into the general stores, the girls pretending to examine things they couldn't afford to buy while their mothers whined about canned tomatoes going up another three cents. The men stood in front of the pool hall or went over to Canfield's and perched up on the counter beside the new batteries and stacks of the new sealed-beam headlights.

A pair of well-dressed young fellows of about twenty, with belted-in-back suits and glued-down hair, walked briskly up the street, carrying musicians' cases. They halted under a street light, took a guitar and mandolin out of the cases, stepped to the curb and began, in pretty fair harmony, to play and sing.

"No matter where on earth I go
I see these girls in calico.
You want to go to Heaven—
You want to be free;
You want to go to Heaven—
You better do like me."

"Glory be to Jesus! What've we here?" said Mulvihille.

"Them's that Holy Roller outfit from the States. Didn't you see the signs on the hydro poles?" Johnny informed him.

After singing a few "Come-To-Jesus" songs one of the young fellows said out good and loud that they represented the Angels of Mercy Redemption Group that right now had a tent on the cow-flats back of the sawmill. And in that tent was the great and well-known Reverend Peabody Thatcher Sloane— he who had saved souls from Yellowknife to Brownsville, Texas, and across from Halifax to Walla Walla, Washington. And there was more: there was the Milner Trio, three of the prettiest sisters ever to save a hell-bound soul; there was Heavenly-Grace Eccelstone, soloist and second preacher of the Angels of Mercy. There were another half-dozen lay girls and boys, and anybody who felt that old Devil sin sitting heavy on their necks could come down, listen to the music for a mere twenty-five cents, and if they felt the words of the healing message of salvation seeping through, for another ten cents they could come forward to the Seat of Grace and be saved against the time the Lord should come to judge heaven and earth and Victoria County. Heavenly-Grace Eccelstone would also lay hands on any of the sick and ailing and bring down on them God's healing touch.

"Jesus! I got something here she could lay her hands on and heal," muttered Johnny.

"I like the sound of them 'lay gals'; they say them religious heifers are hotter than a Ross Rifle after the third shot." Piper dug around in his pockets. "Patch, you rich bastard, lend me a dime and we'll all go and get saved. Johnny and me will tend to the lay gals whilst you're looking up the Seat of Grace."

The two singers belted out another hymn and then strode briskly in the direction of the cow-flats, followed slowly, and sometimes sheepishly, by small groups of farm folk. There was a huge bell tent with tin chairs set out before a plank platform on which was a piano being tinkled by a whopping great woman with corn-yellow hair and black eye-shadow. She was dressed in a long blue gown hitched tightly across her fanny. Two girls of about eighteen and a younger one holding up a bull-fiddle, all wearing short blue frocks, appeared to be the Milner Trio. A tall man, with cavernous cheeks and a frock coat under the tails of which he kept his hands hidden, walked slowly about the stage, keeping a close look on how fast the metal chairs were filling. He looked like Abe Lincoln – a long time after Booth shot him.

The tent was slowly filling with Protestants from Clifden; a few Scots from Fraser Township, and a handful of religious

231

ends and oddities from Kilmore and Carden. Piper, Johnny, and I sat as close to the front (the better to see the girls) as we could, slumping down in our seats with our legs over the backs of the chairs of the next row ahead. Piper lit a smoke, but a thin chap, all eye-glasses and Adam's apple, crept down off the stage and croaked that God didn't allow smoking in His house. Piper said if God was that fussy why didn't He put up signs, but in the interests of peace, salvation, and a squint up the legs of the Milner sisters, Piper stubbed his cigarette out on the plastic-covered purse of a fat farm woman who had just grunted and huffed her way between the chairs, settling like a lead ostrich into the one immediately in front of Piper and ruining his view.

There was any amount of singing and praying. During one soaring harangue from the Reverend Peabody Thatcher Sloane, "Dummy" Quigley, who had a cleft palate and only part of a tongue, grew excited and capered up and down making the unusual noises only Dummy could make.

"God hears!" roared the preacher. "God hears and my good friend down there is speaking in tongues."

"Quigley hasn't any fucking tongue to speak with, you stupid ass-hole," Johnny muttered. After awhile Adam's apple went down and led Dummy up to the seat of Redemption and he was taken backstage and kicked out—saved, no doubt, but as silly as ever.

An occasional sinner started drifting up on the stage; the men were hugged by Heavenly-Grace while the women got theirs from the Reverend Sloane. Levi Barker, whose teeth were so rotten his breath could be heard, limped onstage and was saved in jig time by Grace who kept her head turned toward the back tent flap that was open and letting in the reviving airs of the cow-flats.

I thought the whole thing so much bloody tom-foolery, but Piper was out for religion. "C'mon round to the back," he said, when the show ended, "and we'll pretend we want the girls' autographs."

We trooped to the rear of the tent where a couple of hard-looking grips were already pulling tent pins and stashing away props, including a big harp done all over in gilt paint, but the strings were just parcel-cords from a Red & White store. "This here's a classy show," observed Johnny.

The grips gave us a hard look. "What d'you guys want?"

"We want to see the Milner sisters," said Piper gamely. "They promised us their autographs if we come forward for Christ."

The biggest hand, a six-foot lunk with a face badgered with small-pox scars, swung his chin over his shoulder. "There's their dressin' room. You knock before you go bargin' in, eh? Else you get knocked as you come flyin' out."

We started toward the dressing room. "I'm getting scared, Piper," I said. "I don't think that pair of buffers walk in the gentle ways of Christ."

Piper put his finger to his lips. "Hang on, Patch, we need you. If you don't want one of the girls you can stand sentry."

Piper tapped at the canvas until one of the girls stuck her head around the edge of the makeshift door. She was wearing a white slip instead of the blue dress she had worn for the show. "What do you want?"

Piper held out a chocolate bar wrapper turned outside-in. "Could we three Christian chaps have your autographs, please? We've only lately found God and The True Light. We'd be ever so grateful."

"Well . . . " She took the stub of a pencil Piper held out. She had to hold up her knee to rest the paper on while she wrote; also she had to take away the towel she was holding to her breast when she came to the door. Whether one looked up or down the scenery was far better than you generally found out on the cow-flats.

When she had scrawled her name she turned and called: "Beth! Allie! Some nice boys would like your autographs."

Beth and Allie, still in their blue frocks, came and signed the chocolate wrapper. "I'll treasure this forever," said Piper,

233

stuffing it in the pocket closest to where he kept his heart. "I don't suppose you young ladies would care to walk along the river a way? The Talbert is a most beautiful stream this time of the year; the groves on its banks are sublime; the . . . "

"Are there any trout?" the one called Allie asked. "I'd love to catch a fresh trout; this show doesn't feed its performers too well."

"Trout!" shouted Piper. "You could walk on their backs clear from here to Danno Moran's and not get your toes wet."

"Sure," Johnny added. "And last week me father spotted a swordfish. Ow!" Piper had just jammed his heel on Johnny's instep.

"Let's go, girls." Allie was excited. "Can I take my rod and reel?"

"You can bring your harpoon and a lobster-net." Piper was all agreement.

The six of us strolled along the cowpath that followed the winds and twists of the Talbert. Piper and Allie were in the lead; the oldest one—the girl who had first come to the door—Debby, walked with Johnny McKelvey. The youngest sister, Beth, a girl of about seventeen, and I brought up the rear. It was a fresh, dewy night with little gems shining on the cowflaps in the moonlight; somewhere a night-heron let loose a raucous blast; Beth shivered and held tightly to my arm.

"What was that!" she shuddered.

"Sounded like a mountain lion." I knew my fauna.

Beth said she and her sisters were three out of a family of fourteen east Kentucky kids whose father, when sober, went down in a pit and rousted coal for thirty-five cents a ton. She had a soft, gentle accent, like water music. The show paid the girls fifteen dollars a week and what passed for bed and biscuits. Ten out of the fifteen dollars went home to Kentucky. I began to feel sorry for the girls and I wished we hadn't brought them out just to job them.

We walked alongside the gentle murmur of the river, holding hands, hearing the distant tonk-tonk of some restless cowbell whose owner was up and prowling for her night feed. The face of the near-to-full moon was reflected in the water, the current wrinkling it and taking a twist at it until it was the image of an old man.

We found a white cedar leaning out over the river by a slab of limerock growing on a slant forming a natural back rest. We sat down on the turf while a whip-poor-will whooped across the river in the still deeps of a scratch of deciduous wood. Beth slipped off her shoes and waded ankle-high in the current. She came and sat beside me, her toes savouring the water.

"I surely do know that night bird," she said. "Travelling round the way we do I just miss the call of those whip-poor-wills. They're that pretty.

"When I'm all alone and still
I can hear that whip-poor-will;
And he calls all the night—
He's a lonesome whip-poor-will."

"That's a pretty song. I like it better than those Glory-be-to-Jesus things you girls sang at the tent meeting."

"Yes-ss," she answered slowly. "But it seems like people got to hold onto something. Folks down where I come from are *that* poor! You have to believe there's a better place than this cruel world; you have to think someone, like God, cares about you long's you're alive and after you're dead."

I placed my hand on the bare flesh of her leg just below the hem of her dress; she caught my hand gently but firmly with her knees, but she did turn up her face to be kissed. Her lips were as fresh as daisies.

"It's not because of religion and all that stuff, but my folks depend on what we girls send home and I wouldn't want to walk in on my mommy and daddy with another little'n to feed and tote for."

I felt shame rising red up my neck. "Heck, I didn't ask you all the way out here just to get . . . just to do *that*," I lied.

She squeezed my hand and smiled up at me, then got to her

feet. "Allie! Debby!" she called. There were a pair of indistinct answers from various points along the river.

We walked the girls to where the tent was knocked down and loaded on a truck. The troupe rode in a couple of beat-up buses. We said our goodbyes and we left.

"Now goddamn the fish-tailed luck," Piper complained. "Another five minutes and I'd had that little hill-billy spread from the Perch to the Talbert."

"Why don't you shut up, Mulvihille? Why don't you just shut up?" Johnny kicked a stone out of his path.

When I got home the house was in darkness and Nancy's Buick wasn't in the garage. I took what was left of the whiskey from the kitchen and went up to my bedroom. I drank it all before I fell asleep.

28

I do not, now, recollect how the gang of young fellows I ran around with came to be called the Kilmore Rakes, but it had a dashing sound and we put effort into trying to live up to the title. Aside from myself there was Thad Whalen, Ed Kennedy, Johnny McKelvey, Niall Sweeney, Piper Mulvihille and, occasionally, we were joined by Johnnie Joyal, a slender, good-looking boy of seventeen from the French Settlement.

We spent a lot of time holding up storefronts on a Saturday night, going to Lindsay to movies, drinking cheap wine at bootleggers, getting into fights at Saturday dances. A lot of the bloom of my victory over Gully Malloy was lost when Alec Drummond from the Scotch Line gave me a sound whipping that put a crimp in my nose I carry to this day. Your Celt is a singular person: Alec Drummond was as nice a fellow as you'd wish to meet and aside from giving me a boxing lesson I roundly deserved never did me a turn of harm in his life. He lost a leg driving the Germans across France and lost a lot of his good, stout heart with it, but I hate him; I hate the sound of his name, and the seed and issue of his generation—all because he licked me fair on and dead centre out behind the dance hall in Foxford. And that's the way it is with them and that's the way it is with me.

Two major events occurred that September of 1939: Bride went away to board in Lindsay where she was enrolled in the collegiate; the Second World War broke out and I was angry because the armed forces of Canada were not yet so hard-pressed for recruits they were accepting boys who were only sixteen. I tried. I went down to the Lindsay Armouries and tried to enlist in an anti-tank battery, but the sergeant told me to go back home and help the old man cut the wheat. I told him, bitterly, where to go, and walked away with the laughter of khaki-clad soldiers jangling in my ears.

As September rotated slowly on its axis, with the occasional splash of scarlet among the green foliage to herald autumn, Nancy set her easel up in the orchard, trying to catch the languid sunlight and the mist-coloured haze that wasn't quite a haze so much as a trick of the light. The row of Canada plum bushes lining the far fence dropped soggy, poorly developed fruit into the thickets of cinquefoil and goldenrod. I sat on the top rail, lazily jabbing the point of my stock-knife into the darkened pine. Nancy fussed with her brushes and swore under her breath.

"I wish you wouldn't hang around and stare at me, Patch. It's impossible to work with someone looking over your shoulder."

"I wasn't looking over your shoulder or anybody else's. I was looking at the ridge, yonder, if you want to know. I was trying to look past it, too."

"What's beyond the ridge for you, Patch?" Her voice softened. She twirled a brush in a container of turpentine.

"Bride, for one thing."

"Do you miss her terribly?"

I nodded. Every time I thought about Bride being away to

school and growing up, a lump stuck itself in my throat causing my voice to break.

"I presume something will have to be done shortly." Nancy looked over her canvas with pursed lips. "This whole thing—my being here, for example—isn't making sense. And there is talk, you know."

"About what?" I knew, but I wanted her to spell it out.

Nancy smiled ruefully. "The current gossip is that I am seducing you—and not just for sexual purposes. Apparently I have my vulturine eye on the ranch and whatever money you and your sister hold in common."

"That's a lot of balls!" I exploded.

"We know that, but does the community? And if not, how can we convince these bucolic minds otherwise?"

"I can't see how it's any of their damn business."

"But, in a sense," Nancy pointed out, "it is: I was appointed by the County Judge in collaboration with the Children's Aid Society to act on your behalf and see to your welfare. Therefore I am committed to the task of pleasing the judge and the CAS and through them the public. And the public is restless with gossip."

"The point is—do you like it here?"

She thought a moment. "I don't know, Patch," she confessed. "I think I would like to do something more with my life than play den mother for two nearly-grown children."

"Then this is your easy way out," I shrugged.

Nancy bit her lip until it whitened.

The following day I hitched a ride into Lindsay on one of the Sigerson Brothers' lumber trucks and went to call on lawyer Slattery.

The gilt was scratched and fading on the door leading upstairs from the street to the lawyer's office. The legend read JAMES PARNELL SLATTERY, BARR. & SOL. I trudged up the uncarpeted stairs, wincing from the manure-coloured walls and the smell of hot grease seeping up from the restaurant kitchen below. At the landing a hall, held together by battleship linoleum, led down to a pair of facing, glass-fronted doors: one belonged to the office of an auctioneer and appraiser; the other was Slattery's.

In the anteroom a thin, getsome streak of a secretary sat behind an old Oliver typewriter. She wore a frock the same colour as the hall linoleum and she appeared to be roughly the same age. Her upper lip, as long as a goat's, was covered with a downy moustache.

"Yes?" she barked.

I admitted to a desire to talk with Mr. Slattery, and provided my name. The secretary gave me a baleful look, sprawled to her large feet and stuck her neck around the open doorway of an inner office.

"He'll see you now," the woman cranked out, as if it wasn't any concern of hers who crawled in off the street with a bagful of woes.

The attorney was slumped in his chair, feet on the desk beside a bottle of whiskey. He held a glass of the liquor in one hand, a cigar in the other. He looked like an unmade bridal bed.

"C'mon in, young Fallon, and draw up a chair. Who have you shot, now?"

I said I hadn't shot anyone, but would surely like to ventilate a couple of dozen.

"An urge that comes to us all at intervals," he said charitably. "The difference between lawyer and client is the lawyer allows himself no such luxury. Save this minor discipline the criminal and lawyer are as one in the sight of God."

I told him that gossip was making rounds; that Nancy Murtaugh was becoming dissatisfied with the situation she'd gotten herself into.

Slattery studied the end of his cigar. "A toothsome woman, your Murtaugh lady. Have you been getting the prod into her?"

"No!"

"Well, don't frighten the horse. I would if I were in your

place. I've never married, but I was on the point of proposing to your Nancy-O. Only the thought of how wounded Miss Dyer would be prevented me," he said, nodding toward the outer office.

"Do you know Miss Dyer? She's been in love with me for years. We have an understanding—she darns my socks. A long time ago we aroused a certain turbulence in each other. Don't laugh—Nellie Dyer was once all fire and speed. A long board for a good teeter, you know. She was in love with me, poor girl. Ah me! a woman's love is like the morning dew—as apt to settle on a horse turd as a rose."

"I didn't come here to learn about your lovelife. What happens to Bride and me if Nancy pulls stakes?"

Slattery poured a glass of whiskey and regarded me benevolently over the rim. "I've taken the precaution to approach old McCabe and get myself appointed *parentus secundus*. Your sister is in town here, pursuing her studies. I keep a check on her through the family with whom she boards, the O'Connors. You are in the north end of the county pursuing the dissolute life. I have my spies."

"Does that mean if Nancy takes it into her head to leave brass-rags Bride and I are in the clear?"

"Not quite. You will have me to contend with. This is going to be a long war and I fully expect you will enlist and be shot or drowned as Ares dictates. I am more concerned with your sister. She is a girl of spirit and determination and will, I believe, be a credit to the Fallon name. You will agree the name could use a few credits. I don't suppose your Uncle Miles . . . ? Mmmmm, I thought not. Miles was wounded, or thought he was, many years ago. He keeps tearing off the bandages; he will eventually die of gangrene. He tried hard, in the First War, to get himself killed. Miles never had any luck."

As I turned to go, the old lawyer added, "Are you coming to the fair next week? I think you might. I think you should take your sister. It will be a change for her; I understand she is studying hard. Kiss Nellie for me on your way out."

The Lindsay Fair was reckoned, at one time, as just about the best county fair in the province, if not in the dominion. The fair normally opened on a Wednesday, running for four days, concluding on Saturday night. The midway was long, raucous, and lively. The harness racing was excellent; the stock show-ing had no equal, and there were rides suitable for sedate grandmaws or for young bucks in snap-brim fedoras with their arms tightly around their squealing girlfriends.

Saturday was a sort of family day. The kids were out of school Saturdays, and most of the up-county people went to the fair on that day. I didn't wish to get mixed up on a family day, so I arranged to pick Bride up after school on Friday and we would visit the fair grounds then. Nancy was in Toronto for the entire week.

The students were released from classes early and Bride came flying down the collegiate steps, hair floating on the wind, her graceful legs pumping, and her unbuttoned coat flapping as she darted through and around the press of pupils streaming toward the sidewalks.

I was "Sunday-dressed": blue woollen suit, belted in back, white shirt with four-in-hand tie–the knot not quite even and pressing too tightly at my throat; polished oxfords and a grey, snap-brimmed fedora that I felt gave me the appearance of be-ing something of a man of the world. The illusion was brief; the young highschool boys were confidently casual in V-necked sweaters and slacks, or leather jackets with sports crests. Bride fitted; she was in place. I wasn't and I was glad when she took my arm and piloted me down the maple-shaded street toward her boarding house.

"You look grand, Patch," Bride said. "You make the town boys seem like third-graders."

I wasn't cheered. "I'm out of place around that joint. I don't know, I guess I got Farmer John written all over me."

Bride introduced me to her landlady, Mrs. O'Connor, and flew upstairs to change. I sat awkwardly in the parlour, wish-ing I could have a smoke, but there was no hint of an ashtray.

A bulky organ took up most of the floor space. There was a vivid chromo of the Blessed Virgin, her sky-blue robe parted as she pointed to an exposed and anatomically-unlikely heart from which rays of purest gold serene radiated. Mrs. O'Connor came into the parlour, wiping red hands on a dish-towel. She was a woman of about forty and bore the thin-lip-ped, eager-to-take-offence-look of many lower-middle-class Irish women. I told her the monthly cheques for Bride's main-tenance would, most likely, be coming from James Slattery's office. She nodded approval.

"Well, that will be a Lord's blessing all round. Oh, we've been getting paid regular, far as that goes, but it don't seem likely, somehow, you two poor children having to depend on some woman that's hardly known. I wonder at Judge McCabe giving her power of attorney. But then he's a dirty Orangeman and not likely to care what happens to poor Catholics like ourselves."

"You haven't got the straight of it," I argued. "Nancy is get-ting the short end of the stick, not Bride and me." I went on to point out that Nancy was acting on our behalf entirely with-out fee and at some disobligement to herself. I made small im-pression.

"I'm afraid I'm going to have to ask for more than six dol-lars a week," Mrs. O'Connor said gloomily, as if it cut her to the bone to do so but business was business. "What with this war starting up over there prices are going sky-high. They just don't know what to ask anymore, it seems." And she sighed over the tribulations involved in providing board and room for one fourteen-year-old highschool girl. She went on to say how she remembered the First War and the time her mother had and how sugar, for instance, had gone hog-wild, and flour right after it. I was greatly relieved when Bride came down in a cute green outfit with a brown cape. We fled to the street with the admonitions of Mrs. O'Connor at our heels to stay away from the midway and if we wanted fun and excitement to go and visit the stands where the pickles were being judged.

"Up hers with the biggest goddamn old pickle ever grew in Mariposa," I snorted. Bride giggled and tucked her hand in my elbow.

"You didn't even notice," she scolded.

"Notice what?"

"My hair, silly. I had it done last night after school."

Bride had beautiful hair. She'd had it fixed in the recent style that was popular: swept high up in front and then falling in waves to her shoulders.

"Why, so you have!" I felt pleased. "Prettiest girl in the whole county."

"Prettier than Lila Kennedy?"

"Mmm . . . Yep."

"How about Laurel Dansinger?"

"I told you—the prettiest in the whole county. And you can throw in Durham and Northumberland along with it."

The fair grounds were all a-crush with people; farm folks mostly, but townies mixed in here and there. Bride tugged at my arm. "I want a big ball of cotton candy on a stick," she cried. "And a big glass of orange-ade, and—"

"Oh, what joy!" The grinning faces of Piper Mulvihille and Niall Sweeney confronted us.

"This is never wee Brigid Fallon." Mulvihille took her hand and bowed theatrically. "What can I get you? Name your heart's desire and it shall be here on the wings of an eagle. Isn't she beautiful, Niall, you bostoon?"

I knew both had been drinking; Niall said nothing, but the smooth smile of an all-mellow world broke his face in half.

"What've you been drinking and where are you off to?" I asked.

"Two bottles of sherry well hidden in Niall's father's car," said Piper, "and we're . . . " He bent his arm at the wrist, sighting along his hand and did a little skip-step.

"Oh, they wear no pants
When they do the hula dance;
And the dance they do . . . "

244

Breaking out of his dance Piper pulled his hat low over his eyes, stuck out his chest and with his thumbs in his vest went into a spiel:

"Step right this way, folks; for one thin dime–the tenth part of a dollar–you may see the hairiest woman in all creation! She's got six feet of hair on her head–measure it if you like; four inches of hair on her chest–see it for yourself; two inches of hair on her belly. . . . And–six inches of hair all over her– Snatch that boy before he gets into the tent for nothing!"

"C'mon over to the car 'n have a drink," Niall urged.

"But I want cotton candy and an orange-ade," Bride wailed.

"Cotton candy and an orange-ade. Did you hear the lady, you up-county lout?" Piper thumped his companion between the shoulder-blades. "At once! her behest–or I'll throw you to the snake charmer. Have you seen the snake charmer? She's got a great damn ol' bull-snake as big as Kavanagh's. . . ."

Mulvihille broke off and broke into another jig:

"Oh, here I come mother,
Me cock in a twist;
It's as long as your arm
And as thick as your wrist–
And a knot in the end
The size o' your fist."

Sweeney was back with an enormous roll of cotton candy and a paper container of an orange drink. Piper danced all around the roll of candy, whooping and flapping his thighs with his hat.

"Did you ever see the like? It's as big as a sheep. It's the size of a ram. Are you going to eat that thing, my child Brigid? The dimensions will strangle you."

The four of us walked in the direction of the parking zone, passing a platform on which stood two black African girls with underlips the size of canoe paddles projecting red and fero-cious-looking above their chestful of bangles and beads.

"Me sacred jasus!" sobbed Mulvihille. "A pair of Ubangi lesbians. You don't get a mouth like that from sipping walnuts through a rye straw."

We found the Sweeney Essex in the car park. Niall groped around in the carry-all box between the rear of the car and the spare tire and fished out a part bottle of Four Aces.

"The fountain of joy, the well-spring of our golden youth," crowed Mulvihille. "Give us the jar and look sharply around for signs of the cobs." For some reason, long forgotten, the police in Victoria County were referred to as "cobs."

Piper unscrewed the top and with a deft bow handed the bottle to Bride. "You'll have to drink from the bottle, me jewel. Niall forgot the glasses."

Bride sipped experimentally, made a face and handed the wine back. "I'd rather my orange-ade."

"To my mother's grey hairs." Piper let the cheap wine roll down his throat. Niall drank and I drank. The wine was warming. I took back the bottle and drained it. The second bottle was brought out and half-emptied.

"Where's your old man?" I asked Niall.

He laughed. "Dead drunk behind the show-barns. He had an early start."

"We rolled him into the high burdock snug from the law," said Mulvihille. "To what palace of delight shall we proceed? The fat lady in the freak tent will allow you to pencil your initials on her butt for fifteen cents.

"Fifteen cents is all I've got—
A dollar's what I crave:
Fifteen cents for to buy me a drink
And a dollar to dig my grave."

"You've a fine tenor, there, me man," Piper told Sweeney. "A pity your face fails to match; we'd have you in the Grand Old Opry. I can see you now. You and Minnie Pearl."

We left the pair where the barker was tub-thumping for the girlie show, and I took Bride on a tour of the rides, feeling myself a little too grown up to be whirled about on wheels, in mock aeroplanes, and being part of a shrieking gang whizzed up, down, around and sideways on a mad trolley car. But Bride enjoyed every screaming minute of it and that was pleasure enough for me. I liked being with her and feeling her body next to mine and the texture of her hand where it caught my sleeve when the ferris wheel began its long climb upward. We rode the rides and went over to the booths and shot at packages of cigarettes to which were fastened twenty-dollar American gold pieces; we threw baseballs at wooden milk bottles and hoops over squares holding glittering prizes. We won a kewpie doll on a slender cane with a bunch of coloured hen feathers stuck around it. We won a terrible thing of plaster that may have been a cluster of fruit or a handful of petrified elephant dung.

We caught up again with Piper and Niall. They were standing near the place where a hidden joker shoots a jet of air from beneath a grating. They were splintered with laughter, their faces glowing with wine, hanging onto each other, and staggering around in circles.

"It was old Missis Turner," stuttered Piper helplessly. "Sure she stepped on the grating—and her with an arse as broad as a barn door. Up went the air and up went her old dress over her head and there she was with her old flour-sack drawers and "The Pride of Canada" printed all over the bottom!" He fell into Niall's arms and they plunged away through the crowd that was thickening as night began to fall and the thousands of coloured lights glowing and glittering like the devil's own necklace across the fair grounds.

We paused near the stand where the derby-hatted barker, hoarse from whiskey and a day's roaring, made lascivious gestures with his cane around the fannies of the strip-teasers who still perfunctorily revolved their navels and flaunted their sad, sweat-stained costumes. The barker pointed his cane at me and closed his eye in a great, lewd wink.

"C'mon, sport. Bring the little lady-friend there inside and she'll learn wiggles and bounces she never found in the hay mow. Folks, we've gathered together here the most renowned kootchy dancers from all parts of the U-Nited States and the Do-Minion of Canady that you'll ever see for a fifty-cent piece and ladies admitted free of charge." He winked again at Bride.

I handed a dollar to a heavy-set man who was taking tickets. He had a fleshy, pock-marked face; earlier, we had seen him grappling in the wrestlers' booth. He didn't offer any change after he tore off two tickets, and I didn't figure it was worth trying his patience for a mere fifty cents. Bride and I pushed inside the tent that was quickly filling up with young fellows and their girls. We sat near a curtained stage on a wooden bench.

"Do they really take everything off, Patch?" Bride whispered.

"I don't know. I bet not. This is Lindsay, not Chicago."

When the benches were crammed, the ticket taker peered inside and high-balled the barker. A hidden phonograph commenced whining some bump-and-grind music and the four girls who had been outside on the platform emerged from behind the grimy curtains and began joggling their fleshy hips and thighs. The oldest of the quartet—a busty dame in her forties—gigged down into the aisle and shook her huge, half-naked boobs in the scarlet face of a whiskered old gent, bringing a roar of amusement from the crowd. As the girls danced the crowd began to howl at them to take more clothing off. The strippers, not ungracefully, removed a flounce here and a truffle there, but without appearing to be any less-dressed than when they started. As the spectators became noisier and more unruly, the barker pranced in, doing a knee-high and stick cake-walk, then he yelled above the noise of the crowd.

"Now for you folks who want some real dancing, the way they do it in Mexico City and Fort Wayne, the girls tell me they're willing to go in back to the rear tent—where the Law don't go—and put on another and a real diller of a show for you. I never miss it, myself. 'Course the girls are getting mighty tired so we're going to have to ask you gents for another four bits, but ladies get in free and you ladies who're married or thinking about getting married, you just come along and learn the secret ways to please your husband so that he ain't about to sneak down the road and set up with the neighbour woman."

Bride's head was heavy against my shoulder. I looked down: she was nearly asleep.

"Let's go, Bridie," I said tenderly.

Her eyes opened, big and dark blue and fringed with long, sooty lashes, and she yawned. "I'm tired, Patch," she murmured, nuzzling her face into my sleeve.

We left the fair grounds, pacing slowly down the wind-littered streets. A sharp night breeze came up, hustling cigarette packages and candy bar wrappers down the cracked sidewalks and along the curbs. When we turned in to the O'Connor's house Bride slipped her arm about my waist. "I miss you, Patch. Oh God, I miss you and I miss Belial and Killylick and the way the sparrows sound in the barn." She leaned forward in my arms and wept softly, but the tiny wrenching of her sobs went through me like silver daggers. I held her tighter and closer and I knew I shouldn't have been feeling what I was feeling. All the time that small, piercing voice inside kept grinding: "She's your sister—she's your sister—she's your sister."

At the door Bride clung to me and kissed me and wouldn't stop until I thought I should go mad. Then the porch light winked on, and the grim, suspicious shadow of Mrs. O'Connor fell across us. I squeezed Bride's hand and fled back toward the fair as the door closed behind her.

I found Piper and Niall among a crowd watching a bellowing argument between Frank Teague and the muscular young operator of one of the phoney gambling concessions. Frank had likely been drinking and got cleaned of his roll; the two youths stood nose to nose and cursed and raved like a pair of

249

strange dogs ill-met on a mountain top. A tall, khaki-clad soldier, wearing the peaked cap, high-hook collar, breeches and puttees of the First World War, somewhat self-consciously stepped between the two and shoved them apart. There was a ripple of approval from the on-lookers, even if they'd been robbed of a first-class fight.

I grabbed Teague's elbow. "Come on, Frank; me'n Piper and Niall's heading north for home. You want to ride along?"

Teague's muscles were still set and tense. "I can beat the can off that fuckin' baboon any goddamn ol' day of the week or month of the year," he raved.

"Sure you can," soothed Piper. "He's a robber and the descendant of thieves, but the cobs are prowling, and devil me dutifully if it's worth a night under the clock just for the punching of some hoolihan running a crooked game."

The three of us set off to locate Niall's father, Charlie Sweeney. He was where he was left earlier in the day–flat on his back in a hip-high stand of burdocks and pig-thistles. He had puked all down the front of what passed for his Sunday suit, and a puddle of vomit cradled his head.

"Isn't he beautiful?" exclaimed Mulvihille. "Look on me works, you mighty, and despair. How," he enquired as Niall played a flashlight on the recumbent man, "are we to get this cargo to the freight yards without the bulls stopping us and running the lot of us through the one-way doors?"

"Never mind the fuckin' bulls," said Teague. "Don't forget my cousin, Tom, is on the Lindsay force. I saw him just before I tangled assholes with that tin-horn carny."

"The hour is saved." Piper scratched his head. "We have relatives among the gendarmes. Niall, you're nearest and sweetest, you take his handsome head; Frank, you and Patcheen are the muscle men; you team up on the mid-section. I, as befits one of me station in life, shall carry the feet–by the boot laces."

I kicked an empty bottle of Seagram's VO off into the weeds, and we bent and picked up the savoury mess that was Charlie

Sweeney. Piper stooped down with a quick exclamation.

"A bottle, lads! Who among you is atheist enough to say there is no God?" He held up a nearly full quart bottle of whiskey, mate and companion to the empty I'd booted away.

"The old man is slipping," Niall said gravely. "Other days he'd've gone through both jars."

"It comes to us all," said Mulvihille, taking, without ceremony, a frightful swallow of whiskey. We all had a drink, then resumed our burden, cursing as we tripped and stumbled through the half-dark toward the parking area. Old Charlie came halfway to, growling and groaning, then lamenting with real tears.

"Yez can't be takin' a poor man to jail and him out only for a bit of fun," he whined, then his voice changed craftily. "I tell yez what, lads, you're cobs and workin' men same's meself. I got a fin tucked away in me fob pocket. Do yez take it and go yer ways and leave me go mine."

"You're going to prison for undecent ass-salt," said Piper sternly. "You jabbed a poor dancing girl in the arse with a length of hay-wire. It's five years for you, me bucko, out on the rock pile making little ones out of big ones."

Charlie shrieked in horror, then squinted at Piper who was delicately hauling him along by the tips of his boot laces. "Assault? Dancing girls? I was drunk, I'll plead insanity, I'll. . . ." and he loosed a great, rolling cloud of bowel gas.

Piper dropped Charlie's feet abruptly. "If you've the strength to fart you've the strength to walk."

Charlie staggered to his feet and lurched forward. "You see," Piper told him cheerfully, "when you're marching you're not fighting."

We gained the Sweeney Essex and shoved the old man roughly into the back seat where he continued to vomit and break wind. Niall took the wheel and we ground out of the fair grounds and headed north.

The wind, driving clouds before, snuffed out the stars and a splatter of rain crinkled down the car windows. We passed the

251

bottle around freely and I began to get dizzy from the mixture of wine, whiskey and the motion of the old car as it thudded into holes and bumped against rotting logs that remained from the days of the corduroy roads when pine logs were placed side by side to traverse bogs and similar low places where the roads were threaded.

Frank Teague jumped out at his darkened house and we drove toward my house. "It's a god's relief not to be riding four to a seat," Piper said. His head was beginning to sag and Niall's hand on the wheel was far from steady. Once the car plunged off the road, made a dive at a telephone pole, missed, and leaped out of the ditch and back on the gravel road.

"You'd of made a grand sailor, Niall darling, but on dry land you're dismal." The near accident snapped Piper's drooping head alert. He began to sing.

"I wish I were in London
Or some old sea-port town;
I'd get aboard a steamboat
And sail the ocean round.
Sailing round the ocean –
Sailing round the sea;
I think of handsome Molly
Wherever she may be."

As we bumped over the Dorgan Crossing we could see the glow of the kitchen lights.

"Someone has placed a lamp in the window for her lost lamb." Piper patted my shoulder.

The five-barred gate was closed. I fumbled in the dark and the rain for the latch, but it seemed to have run away. I climbed the gate, tripped over the top bar and fell face forward in the mud. I cursed, stumbled to my feet and retched. I tried to bring up but I couldn't; the liquor I had drunk and the hamburgers and potato chips I'd eaten remained in the pit of my stomach, a leaden, poisonous mass.

I groped my way to the kitchen door and flung it open.

Nancy was sitting at the table, reading. I stood in the doorway grinning foolishly until another empty retch shuddered up from my tormented stomach.

"I," I said with the judiciousness of the thoroughly soused, "am drunk."

Nancy drew her bathrobe closer together at the throat. "I suspected as much," she said dryly. "Any particular reason?"

I wagged my head and sat down on the edge of the woodbox. "The ould Lindsay Fair, boys," I sang. "Were ye ever there?"

"I've had a letter from Mr. Slattery," Nancy said, not looking at me. I swayed and fell from the woodbox. I remained seated on the floor.

"Then everybody's happy."

"Are they?"

"Aren't they?"

"Perhaps you can tell me better than any other." Her bosom heaved under her dressing-gown.

"Well, look," I argued. "You said . . . "

"I know what I said." Nancy's face was set and taut.

We didn't speak for several minutes. A log in the kitchen range turned a half over, muttered as it fed itself to the blue-yellow flames, then sighed into silence.

"Are you in love, Patch?" Nancy's question was as soft as the hiss of the fire.

I tried to untangle the mindful of knots I was hosting. The heat from the stove was making me dizzier. I moved away from the fire and closer to Nancy, but I stayed on the floor.

I nodded.

I drew closer to her and half-kneeled, sitting back on my legs. Nancy reached out and tousled my hair.

"Who with?"

I stared at her for a long moment. "With my sister. With Bride," I answered blankly.

"Oh no! Oh God—no!"

I looked at her curiously, then an inner spring snapped inside me and I fell sobbing, my face in Nancy's lap. I cried. Tearing, gusting sobs jerked from me, hurting as they fled. I remember the stroking of her hands on my neck, the press of her lips on my shoulders where she had loosened my tie and opened my shirt. Outside the wind wailed, but I don't know if I heard it. I don't know if Nancy heard it. I don't know when we went to bed – together – in the bed of my dead father.

When the last light pinched out, the darkened house settled in on itself and turned a harsh shoulder to the wiles of the weather. The fir trees drew together in gloomy mutuality.

29

Bill Doherty and I sat on a huge, frost-riven granite boulder deposited, stranded from its like and kin by some long-ago glacier, in the southwest corner of the pasture nearest the barn. We sat and looked at the body of Jupiter lying, neck outstretched, teeth a-gape, in death beneath a huge, bottle-shaped basswood now, in this month of November, without the tremble of a leaf, the bare, grey flesh of the twigs stark against the cold autumn sun.

Feeble and nearly blind, the ancient horse pottered about the pasture enclosure, gobbling brown sugar from Bride's hands when she was home, chomping comfortably on the oats I paid good money to the Clancys for him alone. And then on that chill November morning I spied Jupiter down on his side near the granite boulder. I walked over. The horse trembled in every limb; occasionally he would raise his head and peer near-sightedly about, then the head would flop back and the weary, ooze-crusted eyelids close. I went back to the house where I now lived alone and took my carbine from the wall pegs. The shot knocked a handful of late blackbirds out of the basswood tree, sending them checkling across the brown fields in the direction of the Catholic Bush. Bill Doherty, set to winter again in the old Dalton shack, had heard the rifle's crack as he was crossing the pastures on his way home from Kilmore with a slung sack of groceries, and he turned in my direction.

"How old was he? He must have been nigh on to a hundred and six." Doherty pulled a gauze-thin cigarette paper from a red pack of Chanticleer's and rolled a lean quirley.

"Seems to me," I squinted down the empty barrel of the saddle gun, using my thumb nail to reflect light inside, "I heard father and Uncle Miles say he was bought as a colt from the gypsies around 1911."

"By my arithmetic that would make him close to thirty. That's old for a horse; it's old for some men."

"I think a dog's age is reckoned at one year to seven years for a human," I volunteered.

"That being the case I'm getting on to be an eight-year-old dog," Doherty said thoughtfully. The wind sang a low song through the basswood.

Nancy left the day after I returned from the Lindsay Fair. She was about finished packing, strapping her valises with practiced, authoritative movements, when I awoke. A dozen pixies were mining something inside my skull. I struggled to sit up, retched, and clutched my head in agony. Nancy set an old-fashioned china basin, heavily figured with bay leaves, beside the bed.

"Just in case," she said, and continued packing.

"What're you doin'?" I asked through the splits in my head. Shamelessly, I leaned over and brought up a noxious brown substance I judged to be the lining of my stomach.

"Leaving," she said shortly.

I realized I hadn't a stitch of clothing on. I attempted to peer over the opposite edge of the bed to locate my trousers, at least. The effort sent me sprawling back, gasping, on the pillow.

"Did I . . . Were you? . . . Did we. . . .?"

She nodded slowly and without apparent emotion.

"Christ!" I muttered.

After awhile Nancy sat down on the edge of the bed and lit a cigarette, staring out at the orchard where Belial was cropping among the asters.

"You'll be all right here, of course." She smiled enigmatically. "You're a grown man in some ways. But," she blew a puff of smoke toward the orchard window, "I have a life to live. I have my painting; someday I may meet that certain man. And after last night the gossip has a foundation. I don't wish this to sting you, but I hardly care to stay around as the paramour of a sixteen-year-old youth no matter how mature on the surface."

"I don't remember anything," I said honestly. Nancy gave me a dry look.

"Touché!"

I shook my head. I didn't understand her. I looked at her in profile as she sat and smoked. I stared at her strongly featured face, the wide, yet determined, mouth. Her breasts beneath the blouse and rather mannishly-cut suit she wore were full and resonant. I couldn't conceive that I had felt the support of her good, round, woman's thighs hours earlier.

"I was too drunk." My voice sounded limp.

Nancy stubbed out her cigarette with determination. "I must be leaving. Don't try to get up to help carry. I can manage. I've written Bride and will post the letter in Foxford."

She turned and her face became warm and tender again. She held out her hand. "Goodbye, Patch," she said softly. I took her hand and held it, trying to think of something to say.

"So long, Nancy," I said.

After shooting Jupiter I returned slowly to the house; it seemed quieter and lonelier than ever. I had thought of digging a pit and pushing Jupiter's aged carcass in and covering it with clay and sod. But I remembered father telling me about how the Plains Indians had buried their dead—on raised platforms of lodgepole pine or aspen fastened with rawhide. There in the high, dry air of the prairie the bodies of the dead mummified as fats and sinews slowly wasted or until vultures and magpies nibbled the bones clean of every strand of flesh and tissue. It seemed a clean, less putrefying way to go, and I often wish yet that "civilized" people did the like for their deceased instead of wrapping them in vaults of concrete and caskets of oak and walnut, the corpse taking with it the very organisms of rot and decay the expensive vaults were supposed to prevent. So I left Jupiter to the ranging farm dogs and the little dun wolves that were more coyote than wolf, and the ever-wheeling turkey vultures. I thought he'd be happier that way.

Since Nancy left I had not been in her old bedroom; nor had I been in Bride's, although once, after she left to live in Lindsay, I sentimentally gathered some autumn flowers and stuck them in a vase on her dresser. I cleaned the rifle and then wandered aimlessly upstairs. I opened the door to the bedroom Nancy had used. The air was stagnant and chilly. Guiltily, as though I were prying, I jerked open empty bureau drawers and peered into the clothes closet. All I found for my pains was a slip of ruled note-paper bearing in pencil a cryptic telephone number. That and the stubbed cigarette butt in the ashtray on the wide window sill; the cigarette Nancy smoked that last morning.

I turned dispiritedly into Bride's room. There was still much of her there: some of her clothing; a bureau top crammed with knickeries among which was a snapshot of myself, long legs sprawled across my bicycle. The flowers I had so carefully placed in a vase of water were mere brown shrivels. I sniffed them; they gave off a dry, rustly odour. I looked around. Spiders had strung knotted webs along the frilled top edge of the curtain valances, and a pair of dead flies lay legs-up in the dust of the window sill. I turned and closed the door gently behind me.

On a sullen, lowering day I was hashing beans and fried potatoes in an iron skillet, the kitchen range huffily backing up puffs of dry pine smoke through dampers and draughts be-

cause of pipes and chimney long uncleaned. I had been intending for some time–most of the summer as a matter of fact
–to tie together a mess of burlap sacking and weights and go
up on the roof and douse out the chimney. The pipes would
have to be taken down in sections, carted outside and
thumped, banged and scraped until the inner coating of soot
and carbon was rattled out. It was a low job and I put it off as
long as possible. Possible had now arrived, with the cold winter, and the stoves were cranky.

A strange auto pulled up to the front yard gate; an Oldsmobile, perhaps two or three years old. A man in a dingy business
suit got out, unhooked the metal swing gate, threw it open and
then got back in his car and drove on into the yard and up to
the house without closing the gate. That made me sore. The
friendly thing to have done was to have left the auto outside
and walked up through the gate, closing it afterward. That's
what you do on a stock farm. Secondly, the driver, and a
woman he had with him, made for the front door where the
man tried his knuckles out on the weathered two-inch-thick
pine. I let him knock. Sensible people don't go barging up to a
front door where there hasn't been a track or footprint since
the door was hung. Finally, skillet in hand, I went to the door,
pulled back the double bolts and glared out across the fumes
coming from the fry pan. The man tried to appear jaunty and
at home in a badly cut suit he usually saved for funerals or
church socials. His wife wore a hat and had, as far as I could
tell, no face; certainly no figure.

"You the kid owns this place?" The caller tried to get his
head in the door but I kept the smoking skillet level with his
eye-balls.

I nodded, but not giving up a damned inch more.

The stranger grinned, displaying pointed, rat-sharp teeth.
"I heard tell," he gestured with an indefinite swing of a red
hand, "you might be sellin' the log and cordwood rights off a
maple bush you got here."

"You heard wrong. And if I was, what's it to you?"

The man kicked the toe of his shoe at a frost-struck geranium that was keeled over beside the step, its head hanging heavy in death, the stalk turned the sickly clear yellow-green of a water-soaked corpse.

"Well, you see, kid, I deal in a bit of lumber and such now and again. Take a flyer at anythin' these days to turn a wheel, eh. Let me look her over and I'll see you get a fair price. I—"

"You're not getting my smoke signals," I stated. "The maple bush is not for sale. There is nothing for sale here. You turn around and leave the way you came and close the gate behind you. There's livestock around here."

He flushed, made to say something, then closed his trap of a face and set off stiff-legged toward his car.

"Who told you that bush was up for grabs?" I called after him.

"Storekeeper," he flung back without turning his head. "Old geezer in Mavely. Musta thought he was havin' a joke."

I closed and rebolted the door. "Abel Coventry," I mused. "And I don't figure him to be the joking kind. Now I wonder why the old bugger did that . . . I heard father tell him the first year we moved east that bush wasn't for sale. Something to do with the way grandmother felt about it. . . ."

The mess in the skillet left untouched, I rummaged down in the basement among sealers of old preserved crab-apples and Canada plum jelly until I found a bottle of White Horse scotch. For some reason father drank that kind of whiskey at Christmas only. I searched the other shelves, festooned about with cob-webs and thick with the dust of years. I got the crawlies up my back and taking the bottle I lunged for the stairs, barking my shin against one of the unplaned treads. I loaded my saddle gun, and with the whiskey shoved in my mackinaw pocket I swung my legs south toward the Talbert and the shack of Old Man Kavanagh.

A big old pine had been fallen years ago across the river to form a fairly decent bridge. I was halfway over when a voice near startled me into a dive in the cold, roiling water.

"Lookin' fer somebody?"

The voice came from behind me in the direction I had just left. I turned and stepped carefully back to shore. The aged man was sitting on a grey boulder in a copse of blue beech, peering wickedly out at me from behind a screen of thumb-sized, twist-tortured trunks.

"I was on my way to have a visit," I said amiably. "Do you care for a drink?" I dug the bottle out of my coat.

"I've been known to take one." The little ferret eyes never left my face.

I extended the bottle. Kavanagh took it carefully, turning it round and round, holding it at arm's length and squinting at the label. He dragged the cork, tasted a bit with the point of his tongue, then took a long, slow swallow.

"Mighty nice of you," he said blandly, "to walk all the way here just to be givin' poor ould Kavanagh a drink. Can't think of anythin' I might be givin' yez in return. Old man like me ain't got much to give, savin' a lot o' gab . . . " He trailed off in his high, cackling laughter.

He clung to the bottle like an Indian woman to a day-old papoose, cradling it and chuckling over it, taking a mouthful when the spasms of the previous one settled. I realized the old bachelor probably never saw good drinking liquor from one year to the next. Whatever he lived on couldn't much more than provide beans and maybe a fifty-cent bottle of muscatel or catawba.

"Why does old Abel Coventry have an urge to whack down the Fallon maple bush?" I aimed the question at him, keeping my eyes on the ranks of white cedar growing in serried rows on the shelving limestone shale across the river.

"Hah?" Kavanagh let his tongue loll down over his bottom lip. He reminded me of an old thief, of a roving dog surprised at a carcass.

He tilted the bottle to his mouth, never taking his glance away from me. "Fella runs the store at Mavely, y'mean?"

I nodded.

Suddenly the old man whooped with laughter, slapping his thigh. A dribble of whiskey leaked out of the corner of his mouth and got lost in his whiskers. "Both of 'em after Hannah Dorgan like cur dogs after a she-bitch in heat, but Fiddlin' Jack got her in the bush and t'other'n lost out." And he commenced a dirty babble that was perhaps a mixture of the overheated imaginings of lonely, neglected men, and the half-truths of an old reprobate whose time was spent wriggling through patches of brush–a scouting voyeur watching with greedy eyes and hot, shallow breath as couples met and twined in secret coverts away from harsh parents and domineering husbands. When he stopped up the red hole of his mouth with the bottle I raised the rifle barrel. The bottle flew apart, slivers of glass cutting into the grimed, bearded face, raising darts of blood. For a heart-beat I thought the bullet had ricocheted and killed the old bastard.

Kavanagh stared in shock, his right hand still gripping the neck of the shattered bottle. Then he wriggled backward, a greasy bundle of rags snaking furtively away until it dropped out of sight in a small gully where a spring freshet had carved a path to the Talbert.

The next day I walked to Mavely and spoke to Abel Coventry.

"Mr. Coventry. Do we owe you anything? I know some time back my father borrowed money from you. Was that all returned, or wasn't it?"

"Why yes, Patch." The old storekeeper seemed surprised.

"Then I'd take it kindly if you lost interest in our maple bush and whether it's for sale or slaughter." My voice shook a little because I wasn't all that sure of my ground and Abel's steady grey eyes took on a fleeting hurt that was disconcerting.

He nodded slowly. When he spoke his voice came from far away.

"Was that all today, Patch?"

"That's all–today."

The heavy wood and glass door closed behind me and I noticed the faded, artificial holly wreath that was Abel's sole Christmas decoration was already tied in place in the centre of the door. It swung slowly on its cord as the door snicked the latch. As I headed up the road toward home, the storekeeper was standing a few feet away from the window that contained a few pairs of heavy socks, gum rubber boots, and a variety of hand axes. He was an old, gaunt shadow looking back through the misting past at other shadows, seeing me not at all. Neither me nor the oval Esso sign that shrieked a protest with every gust of wind. From inside the closed door of the service station I heard the clink of metal on metal. I heard it until I crossed the wooden bridge that spanned the Perch and the sound was lost in the heavy air.

30

From the vantage of maturity, not necessarily synonymous with wisdom, and the intervention of thirty-five years I believe an element of individual freedom obtained that is absent in our modern day. Bride and I had, to be sure, the semi-bureaucracy of the Children's Aid Society–a blend of upper class "concern" relegated to faceless pomposities with official approval–and the brooding majesty of something at provincial government headquarters at Queen's Park in Toronto called, with sanctity, the Official Guardian. The original idea behind this latter was, as are most humanitarian measures, long on intent and short on effectiveness. The Guardian was a bureau designed to protect juveniles, the insane, and the proven irresponsible, from having their funds, property, or whatever, diddled from them by relatives, business sharks, and others who, in the manner of jackals and dung-beetles, lurk on the fringes of a fresh kill waiting for the corporate lions to become satiated before sneaking in to crack a bone or carry off a fragment of entrail. In interposing a shield between victim and predator, the agency entangled everything in a haze of red tape, crimson seals, and interminable droning letters setting out the relevant sections of that Gibraltar of statutes–The Act –so that in the end property and funds entailed by the Official

Guardian disappeared into a limbo, never to emerge. Our attorney, Slattery, through nimble footwork, kept the sphinx-like paws of the Guardian from clamping down on father's estate so that my sister and I managed to retain a measure of independence and control two youngsters of identical ages would not have today.

I revelled in complete freedom from any form of toil save the mutilating of whatever form of food, mostly canned goods bought at Coventry's, I stoked into my lengthening, broadening frame. The mornings were generally well along before I got out of bed; at night, if I wasn't at home listening to the radio, I was out in the Dodge with Johnny McKelvey, Niall Sweeney, or Piper Mulvihille. We went round to dance halls or village cafes looking for females–an enterprise that in those days was known as "girling." That we were rarely successful hindered us not at all.

Slattery collected the rents from the Clancys, invested the capital from the sale of the stock and machinery following father's death, paid on the mortgage and doled out, not ungenerously, a monthly allowance for Bride and myself. He told me he hadn't paid off the mortgage, which he might have done after the sale, because the mortgage was at 3 per cent and the money invested was fetching 4½ per cent.

"I latch onto the percentage differential for my fee," Slattery told me with the bluff candidness of the man who does not pretend to be wholly honest. "It's sizable, but then this kind of thing is a pain in the ass and there is no salve like money."

Over Slattery's not too-firm objections I learned to drive and bought a second-hand car.

"What kind of a car and who're you buying it from and for how much?" The attorney shot questions at me over the crackling rural telephone wires.

I told him Sib Parker was selling me the car–a 1934 Dodge coupé–and was throwing in driving lessons free.

Slattery swore. "Any time that little oil-stained rat throws anything in for free there has to be a hook in it. What did you say you were paying for that car again?"

I told him.

The lawyer howled. "Where you calling from?"

"Canfield's garage in Kilmore."

"I know where Canfield's garage is; when I want a geography lesson from you I'll ask for it. Is Jack Canfield there? Put him on."

Canfield, a suave man with laughing dark eyes, talked for awhile. When he hung up the receiver he turned to me, his mouth quirking. "Seems as if Sib made a little mistake of $100. Sib isn't too good at figures, sometimes. What Sib meant to say was the Dodge will cost you $350, not $450, and the lessons are still free. This is a private deal between you and Sib; I've nothing to do with it. I wonder why old Slattery called me 'Pontius Pilate'?"

Sib, who had been ear-glued to the door separating the shop from the business part of the garage, came in looking anxious. Canfield gave him the hard news which Sib accepted matter-of-factly as if he'd supposed all along that was the way with the world and all dreams of getting rich overnight.

I didn't know it then, but Jack Canfield, at the age of forty-three, was dying of cancer. He went back to the counter and lay down on it, adjusting his hat over his eyes. "Sib," he asked playfully, "who was Pontius Pilate?"

Sib thought he was a cattle-buyer that used to live over north of Atherley. Canfield nodded, as if satisfied, but his lips twitched as he settled himself under the rim of his hat.

Sib and I went and got the Dodge and started on the first driving lesson.

By the beginning of December I had learned to drive well enough to obtain a licence. What I hadn't counted on were the satellite expenses attending ownership of every automobile ever made: there was gas and oil and the patching of tubes and the replacing of tires, and a mysterious set of metallic infirmities Sib called "points" that were never just right, no matter how new, or how often adjusted.

266

I hit Slattery up for an increase of allowance and was re-fused point-blank and with matching profanity. I was asked if I'd ever thought of working, and if the prospect and the thoughts of the same were too much of a shock for one day I could mull it over for a week; then I could buy an axe and a web saw and go into a tract of low ground and swamp south of the maple bush where grew the more unimportant trees such as black spruce and balm-of-gilead. Such trees, when felled, limbed, and sawed into four-foot lengths, none smaller than four inches in diameter at the smallest end, and the lengths brought out to where a truck could be loaded with them, brought $3.50 a cord on the pulpwood market. Slattery al-lowed there was a current demand for paper so "all the propa-ganda and horseshit about the war could be spread better."

The first day in the woods brought the realization I was, at the age of sixteen, somewhat slack. Not that I was new to an axe and saw; I just hadn't exercised much more than my mouth muscles since father died. Although it was early De-cember and the dark settled quickly and thickly like oyster soup, there was no snow. The wet meadows and leafless tree branches dripped grey in all-day fogs, and people went around, hacking and wheezing and snuffling into red and blue spotted bandanas. "A winter's fog will kill a dog," they said. Or: "A green Christmas makes a full graveyard."

I chopped a kerf in the bole of a foot-thick spruce, sliced a cut through at the rear and slightly above the axed notch with the web saw, and dropped the tree neatly into the top of a swamp maple where it lodged and stuck fast as if it intended to remain there for good and to hell with the pulp business and Allied propaganda. I scrambled up through the needled branches and slashed away at the clinging branches until the tree fell with a whoosh, taking me with it, the law of gravity and Isaac Newton being what they were and are. I like to broke a leg, but didn't, being merely bruised and scratched. A pair of bluejays, watching the fun from a tall balm-of-gilead, and evidently sorry to see me come out alive, flew off south, screaming, "Caaaaat! caaaaaat!" Wearily, I got to my feet, dug spruce needles out of the back of my neck, and set about lopping off the thickly distributed branches. That done, I sawed the trunk into four-foot sections and cleared a space between the stems of a pair of poplars, piling the sawn pieces neatly in a row eight-feet long. Then I quit for the day. I ached that night and went to bed without even opening a can of beans for supper. The old house drew the fog around it after the last light went out and dreamed as I slept of other days and the old wrongs so that unhappiness soaked into the walls like the fog slithered through and into the swamps.

The following day I surprised myself and came near to cutting a whole cord. From then on it was a cord a day. My muscles jumped up and stretched hard along my arms and across my shoulders. My wind returned accordingly. The palms of my hands grew leathery after the first blisters broke and ran stinging water so that I gritted my teeth with every stroke of the axe. Tough, horny callouses an eighth of an inch thick spread over my palms. I could bring the flat of my hand down on my denimed thigh hard enough to make a crack like a gunshot, much annoying the jays who didn't want me there in the first place.

I learned there was, as in most aspects of life, a rhythm to work. If you found the rhythm and kept time, the work went along easily; axe blows struck dead on, sending the fleshy chips flying; the saw bit firmly into bark, sap and heartwood with every stroke, dropping neat trails of wet sawdust on the soggy leaves of the swamp floor.

The cutting site was nearly three quarters of a mile from the house, so I took a lunch: greasy side-pork or bacon sandwiches and maybe a can of beans hacked open with my jack-knife. The chickadees adopted me almost at once, coming in with a flirt of their bits of tail to light on my shoulder or wrist as I ate, and singing their swamp song which is low and gay. They pecked at crusts, attacked spoonsful of beans set on a log, and then zigged triumphantly away as mysteriously as they came, leaving behind fragments of wild song clinging in the damp air.

And sometimes I'd sing, heedless of any kind of a voice I had or hadn't. I'd sing the far-away mournful songs I heard on the console radio on Saturday nights on "The Grand Old Opry" coming all the way from the southland from a radio station in Nashville, Tennessee, with the call letters WSM.

"Tenbrooks was a big bay horse,
He had a shaggy mane;
He ran all 'round old Memphis,
He beat the Memphis train . . .
O Lord!
He beat the Memphis train."

Or maybe it would be "The Hills of Roane Country," or if I happened to be girl-sad, which I was more often than not, I'd sing "Handsome Molly."

The thing about being "girl-sad," at least when one is young, is there is no necessity to have a girl; actually, it works better if one hasn't a particular girl because then you can hum alone in your sorrow, knowing that smarter, better-looking young straps are out with the girls and rumpling up their skirts and drinking wine in parked cars or sashaying to the alle-mande left and the do-si-do music of fiddles at the square-dances. There was no way to win and no easy way out. If a girl let you past her garters, she was "easy," and you talked about her to the other boys in between drinks and cigarette puffs be-hind the dance hall. If she held her skirts down with one hand and you with the other she wasn't much fun and would proba-bly end up marrying a preacher or becoming a Sister of Chari-ty.

There was, too, before the onslaught of age and the erosion of appetite through the knowledge that doesn't inform but merely makes cynical, this aura, this thing some poets refer to as "The Eternal Mystery of Woman." The mystery was there, all right, no matter how many scoffers like Tim Connolly said

269

women were only mysterious because their plumbing was tucked up inside while that of men hung right out in the open for all to see and snicker at until we took to wearing pants. Tim declared that men didn't wear trousers so much for protection as to keep our friends, of both sexes, from finding out that what we had was a short four instead of the long eight we'd bragged upon. The only person who could shut Tim up when he got into one of his scouts and barges against the females was Bill Doherty. While Tim wrathfully proclaimed that all women looked alike if they were stood on their heads, Bill would enquire, "How many women have you stood on their heads, lately, Tim?"

I'd seen but two girls with their clothes off; one was Bride and the other was Lila Kennedy, although Lila had only taken enough off to do what we did and I didn't so much see her, there in the warmth and semi-darkness of the back seat, as I felt her and sensed her. I wondered about Laurel Dansinger, about what she might look like with her pants off and her legs apart. Whether the hair on her pussy would be honey-gold coloured like on her head, or if it would be red the way real blondes were supposed to be according to Thad Whalen.

True, that Lindsay Fair night I must have seen or known that Nancy Murtaugh was naked except for a silk nightgown. But I remembered nothing. I turned Nancy over and around in my mind a great deal. Her flesh, even when hidden by her well-cut clothing, was full-blown and lush. Her green eyes were woman-wise with a touch of iron that could sadden or smoulder. I remember her quick, strong hands as she sketched or painted, and I thought they were hands that could stretch a man out on the sexual rack that hurts without pain, pulling and pushing and twisting until he'd nothing left to give but a sleepy arm-around and a blank body subsiding slowly on the mattress.

At sixteen a youth knows he's missing something, although he's never quite sure what that something is. It is a feeling of one's scrotum being tugged delicately from all points of the body by spider-thin wires. "A stiff prick," grinned the older of the young men, "has no conscience." Tim Connolly said contemptuously that too many men thought with their cocks and not with their brains, although Bill Doherty asked Tim what he thought with, seeing as how he hadn't either. At the same time I never heard Doherty's name coupled with that of a woman—at any time. I wondered what he thought about women and what he did when he needed one—if he ever needed one.

I thought, too, of the time I caught Bride standing upright, impudently holding her nightie in her hand, while I stared, red-eared, at the globes of her breasts and the dark, curling down between her legs that was spreading upward and outward from the soft V of her lower belly. I'd shake my head against these thoughts, shake it like a horse bobs at a bot-fly; it wasn't right; it wasn't like Lila Kennedy. There was something seductively poisonous here. I didn't know of the word incest until later. I didn't know of the taboo that exists and has existed in all races of men, save, possibly, that of the Egyptian dynasties.

The long nights were the worst. I'd lie awake listening to the mocking owls, my mind flittered with fascinations of girls and hips and busts and thighs and saucy patches of pubic hair, until my hand would go down almost automatically and ease the stretching of the taut wires.

Molly, O Molly!
Run, O Molly, run,
Tenbrooks gonna beat you
To the bright shinin' sun,
O Lord!
The bright shinin' sun....

3 1

"Will you go to the liquor store for me and pick me up a bottle of rye?" I asked James Parnell Slattery. He was standing in his office, back toward me, looking moodily out over the Scugog River and its purling, turd-coloured waters.

"I will not!" was his rejoinder. "I won't even go for myself." He turned around and looked at me slyly. "I always send Miss Dyer. It adds mystery and intrigue to an otherwise frightful existence. The clerks at the liquor store are convinced she's a secret lush or else is sleeping with one.

"Have you ever seen her digs? Put light years on you. Nellie lives in an old grey wreck left her by her parents who decided to die on the same day and have a single funeral so's to cut costs. Old Sam and Hetty Dyer–tighter'n bark to a piss-elm stump. Nellie has lived there alone for years. Well, not quite alone: she has a cat the size of a burro. Meanest son of a bitch of a four-footed desperado you'd come across on this continent. Say–what do you want a bottle of whiskey for, and you only sixteen and just beginning to steer a motor car? I hear of you drinking and driving and I'll take my cudgel to you." He dived into a corner and came up with a four-foot knobkerry as thick as my wrist.

"I'll comb you!" he roared. "I'll welt your skull until it looks like a tractor tire!" He leaned his war club against a book case and shook himself with satisfaction.

"Did I ever tell you my old father, Daniel O'Boyle Slattery, could trounce the biggest rogue within the liberties of Dublin? Greatest man with the stick in the nation, was he."

When I was finally able to wedge in a word I told the lawyer why I wanted a bottle. I had driven to Foxford with the excuse of needing a saw file, where I saw Laurel Dansinger. Laurel was going to high school in Lindsay, too, but her father drove her there in the morning and picked her up again after school hours. A talking picture billed as *The Murders At Red Rock Inn* was being shown at the Foxford town hall that coming Friday. I asked Laurel if she would like to go to the movie with me. Her cornflower-blue eyes examined me gravely.

"We'd need to ask my parents." Her voice, although she was born in Canada, contained a slight Germanic accent. I knew she spoke both German and English fluently.

I expected a refusal because when Laurel and I approached her parents neither spoke for several moments. Then her mother looked at Dansinger and spread her hands. He shrugged.

"Vell . . . I t'ink so. Maybe all right. You t'ink it all right, momma?"

Momma thought it would be all right, but Laurel was to come home immediately after the show. Laurel turned and let her eyes smile on me.

I thought it might be good politics if I took her father a jar of whiskey, so on Friday afternoon I drove to Lindsay to sound out Slattery. "I've got my own money," I told him. "I hired one of the Clancys to swamp the pulpwood I cut out to where a truck could run and I sold it for three-fifty a cord like you said. Clancy charged me fifty cents a cord for the swamping, and I had ten cords cut. I got fifteen dollars."

"Where's the other fifteen dollars?" Slattery shot at me.

I said I'd left it at the O'Connors' for Bride. "Half of that wood was hers," I told him.

Slattery drummed his fingers on his desk approvingly. "The Dansinger girl, eh? The one with the yellow hair. Going to pump liquor into the old man and your whang into his daughter. You don't know Dansinger."

He got up and looked out of the window again, humming:

"O, I met her in the lane
And I laid her on a board
And I played a little tune
Called 'Sugar in the Gourd.'

"But not whiskey. We'll buy Rhenish."

"What's that?"

"Wine, you ignorant descendant of bog runners. A light, dry German wine. Did you know Dansinger was an Uhlan in the First War?"

"A Hoolihan? I thought he was German."

"You're just pretending," Slattery said pityingly. "No one could possibly be as ignorant as you let on. Miss Dyer, my plum . . . " He skipped to the door of the outer office. He handed his secretary a scrap of paper on which he'd written something.

"Trot to the vendor's and purchase this. Give her five dollars, Patch. This will rock them over there; they haven't sold a bottle of decent wine since the mayor's wife went mad and purchased a half-dozen of claret."

Although it was only about 300 yards from where the Dansingers lived up over their hardware store to the Foxford town hall I picked Laurel up in my coupé and we drove in splendour to the movie.

Transportation not being as reliable as it later became and with Lindsay laying claim to the only theatre in the county, travelling entrepreneurs with a second-hand batch of equip-

277

ment went from town to town, renting town halls and Orange halls and any other kind of a hall where fifty people could be packed in and shown ten-year-old talking pictures the sound-track of which was disintegrating, the screen images blurring. The war swept them away for good and I don't suppose any-one misses them.

Laurel and I sat on the hard-backed chairs, holding hands in the dusk through which cut the swath of light from the pro-jector. When the movie was over I helped Laurel into the car, and we parked in the driveway at the side of her father's store. We sat and talked for nearly an hour and were not disturbed although from time to time a shadow would come across the light in a room upstairs.

Laurel exerted a powerful attraction for me; her bright blue eyes looking unwaveringly at me, the gentle rise of her small bosoms, the braided corn-yellow hair, and her smooth pink and white skin set up a continuous tugging within me to do other than hold and stroke her hand. But she wouldn't have it, and the watchful shadow at the window would have no more permitted it. We talked about her school, and about Bride.

"She's very popular with the boys," Laurel said without ap-parent envy. "They're always competing to see who can walk her home after school, or take her for coffee at noon."

Laurel laughed softly. "She fights, too. Like a boy. No one cares to make her angry."

The hour went very quickly. When the shadow passed across the light, like a gigantic bat, twice within the space of a minute Laurel smiled at me and slipped out of the car leaving a musical "Goodnight!" hanging between us.

I drove home slowly through the mists clinging to the tops of the tag alders and osier bushes like strands of cotton candy, dodging pot holes filled with gravel-brown water. The woods stood wet and bitter back of the road. Leafless and without snow the countryside seemed hushed and waiting for spring, like a damp day of early April—except this was a mute, de-spairing spring without the rise and fall of the song sparrow's call or the ice-crystal tinkling of tree sparrows or the quiet beeping of woodcock.

I was at once exhilarated and depressed. Laurel's presence was a golden thing and I tested the air with my nostrils for a remembrance of her, but there was nothing. Not even a suggestion of fragrance, real or artificial. I smelled the faintly sterile odour of unknown and arcane chemicals and the peculiar, indefinable scent reluctantly released by automobile upholstery. Sib Parker had been right about one thing: the Dodge had but one previous owner and he a country doctor. In those days doctors had a grey, neutral smell; some of it had transferred to the little coupé.

In later years I was able, through the perspective of time and distance, to reason out the personality, or lack of it, of Laurel Dansinger. At the time I was young, impressed with Laurel's coolness and poise, and quite unable to see that this was all she had. She was intelligent without being intellectual; she was able to be kind because she had no depth of soul large enough to contain anger or any emotion other than mute acceptance of what life washed up on her still, tranquil shores. Long after the end of the war I learned Laurel married a traveller working for a wholesale hardware firm. They married; the traveller became a sales manager; he and Laurel bought a fine home in Etobicoke; they had two children. They lived tranquilly ever afterward. A stranger would have thought Laurel a fine mother and homemaker; he would have thought her husband was happy.

32

The Christmas holidays did not begin for Bride until two days before December 25th. She had several invitations from school friends to have Christmas and the New Year's festival in the Lindsay area, but she wanted to be home for Christmas.

"Let's fix up the old place with colour and decorations," she said brightly. "We'll have lights and big red candles sitting fat in the windows, and real mistletoe in the doorways."

I didn't think mistletoe grew in our part of the country. Too far north, I told Bride.

"We buy it at the florist's, dummeeee!" she shrieked, having picked up some of the flavour of small-town highschool idiom.

A week before Christmas a curt wind from the north drove the damp and fog away. The sun came out, filling the woods and meadows with a weak, saffron light. Then a great blue-black cloud edged across the sun and the lip of the sky. A few flakes spit at the brown earth, then a volley. For twenty-four hours the world was lost in a driving storm of snow.

The next morning I threaded a rope through Belial's nose ring and led the old bull off to the stable to spend a lonely winter in a stall where he snuffled at the blue-green alfalfa I forked in his manger. Twice a day I let him out to walk his rolling, bull-gaited walk down to the Sally Brook for a long, cold drink, while I dunged out his stall and barrowed the manure onto a pile in front of the barn. He was aged and his blood thin. He was happy enough to plod back up the lime-rock path from the brook to the stable, his head down, eyes blinking at the cutting sleet or at the glitter of the sunlight on newly fallen snow. I found him in the mornings, hunkered down in his straw bedding, chewing placidly on his cud, no hint of flame in the jet eyes that were now getting a film of blue that hid the keening backward look of better times when the meadows were green and the heifers fair.

The snow lay nearly a foot deep, weighing down conifer branches and settling in the tops of the various viburnum bushes where the leafless stems grew thickly. On cloudless days the sun shone so fiercely on the breast of the snow tiny crinkles of pain met between one's eyes. I scoured both the Big and Little Swamps, searching out stands of ground yew, runners of princess pine club moss and, on higher ground, the scarlet winter-berry—as beautiful as the cardinal bird that came every day and fed with the barn pigeons on handfuls of mixed grain I bought from the Clancys and stored in the granary inside the barn.

"You're not graining that old bull of yours, are you?" asked Clancy, as I placed a couple of sacks of feed in the trunk of the Dodge.

I said I was feeding the pigeons and some wild birds— starlings and the like.

Clancy scratched underneath his red and black checked winter cap. "It's your money, Patch." But his eye met mine uneasily; to waste perfectly good grain and even better money on a handful of pigeons and starlings was a preliminary leap down the road to the asylum according to county reckoning.

I tacked the dark, black-green yew boughs around the walls; I wreathed club moss behind the picture frames of grandmother and my three dead aunts. I put clumps of winter-berry in vases. I did not decorate Grandfather Matt's photograph frame. It hung alone on the east wall of the parlour. Taken when he was about thirty, the likeness, in the manner of the day, had no visible background and grandfather's face appeared to loom out of a sepia mist. He was, according to Uncle Miles, an admirer of General Ulysses S. Grant and affected a "Sam Grant" set of whiskers. The beard may have been the same, but the eyes were not the slightly puzzled-looking eyes of the Union general. Grandfather's eyes were a-blaze with cold fire with cynicism lurking at the corners. I didn't think grandfather would want a festoon of princess pine around his great oval, oak-framed photograph. I left it severely alone and wished we had a fireplace with andirons and fire dogs and a screen. There was only the enormous, sway-gutted box heater, chased around with iron scroll-work. I humped a great knot of black oak into the parlour stove, setting it on the roaring bed of pine stump splinters I'd used for kindling. That chunk of oak would burn the day along, setting the iron sides to glowing a dark cerise. The stove didn't look like much but no fireplace ever built could beat it at heating a given space.

On a Saturday morning I drove to Lindsay, bought Bride a Christmas gift I couldn't afford, and almost a duplicate for Laurel Dansinger. I bought Uncle Miles a hunting knife with a bone handle and a blade that was heavy and sharp and inclined to murder. Through the offices of Slattery I managed to get sent from the United States a carton of Bull Durham cigarette tobacco for Bill Doherty. I had heard him remarking lovingly on Bull Durham which he had smoked when he worked the lumber camps of Michigan. It was unavailable in Canada.

"Who smokes that horseshit?" Slattery wanted to know when I asked him if he could get me some Bull Durham. "That big aurochs that roams around loose back in Carden? Fighting Bill, they used to call him. Maybe still do. That would be what he'd smoke, all right. I'll see what I can do."

I picked up Bride at the O'Connors'; she had already been

shopping. I carried the parcels, all neatly wrapped and covered with seals and labels, out to the car.

"Are we having anyone for Christmas day?" Bride asked, settling herself beside me as I swung the ram's head that was the radiator cap ornament on the Dodge toward the north and out of town.

"I thought we'd ask Uncle Miles and I think we should have Bill Doherty over the holiday for a couple of days. He's holed up in the Dalton shack again, but I haven't seen him in nearly a month."

"What has Uncle Miles been doing with himself?"

I shrugged. "I don't see him often. I heard he tried to join the army again and they told him he was too old. Which is true: he's nearly fifty. They told me I was too young."

"I don't want you to go off to war some place and get killed," Bride said absently, dabbling a smidge of powder on her nose, peering into a compact mirror.

"It'll all be over before I turn seventeen. The army'll take you at seventeen, but not the navy or the air force. Hey, when did you start wearing make-up?"

"Since I started going to highschool, brother Patch. Say, it's going to be good to get back to that gloomy old house and those gloomy old spruces and all of those gloomy old ghosts that live up in the attic. They'll positively be a relief from the lower-middle-class atmosphere at the O'Connors'."

"What in hell is a 'lower-middle-class' atmosphere?"

Bride wrinkled her nose and batted her long eye-lashes at me. "It's something I learned in social studies. It—well, it's the O'Connors."

"Or the Lynches," I grinned.

"And them, too. I dated Jerry once; he's staying in Lindsay too, going to school. As soon as he graduates next year he's going in the air force. As a flying officer."

"He looks like the kind of flapdoodle the air force likes," I grumbled. I'd seen a few airmen, running mostly to air-frame mechanics, strutting about in grey-blue suits with narrow, stove-pipe pants, kicking their knee-joints sideways in an exaggerated walk copied faithfully from the Royal Air Force, as if they were all stiff from sitting in cockpits and not used to walking on the ground among the common run.

I had a yen to try the navy. I had never forgiven the army for turning me away with a guffaw; now I longed for a sea I never saw, for an ocean I never heard, for a tang of salt air I never smelled.

"Did you hear about Laurel's father?" Bride's question snapped me back from the rolling briny. I swerved the car to avoid a great, loping hare fleeing between the neat rows of snow turned up by the plough.

"No. What about him?"

"He was taken to the county gaol and brought up in front of Magistrate Blake and fined fifty dollars."

"No shit? What for?" I could scarcely think of a more unlikely man to come up rough against the law.

"I heard the kids all talking about it in school. And at O'Connor's. It was in the *Lindsay Post*, too. He was supposed to have said something against the war effort, something about the Allies not going to be in Berlin as quickly as they supposed."

"Well, for Christ's sakes! Was that all?"

"Mmmm hmmm," Bride nodded seriously. "Most of the kids have cut Laurel dead. I didn't, but then she's two grades ahead of me and we never did chum around all that much."

We drove through a long aisle of white cedars flanking a snake rail fence on either side of the road. The road had once been corduroyed and old pine logs stuck up a jagged snag or a rolling hump beneath the crushed limestone gravel. Snow lay on the fence rails and was caught in the spatula-like leaf fronds of the cedar.

To the casual eye looking for exotic scenery such as rugged mountain peaks or palm trees on a coral atoll, the country we were traversing would appear pretty small potatoes and, in an agricultural sense, that's what it was. Tim Connolly claimed that the first Irishmen brought over by Peter Robinson in the 1830's, seeing the watery swamps and thin soil, sent home a plea for "oars and oats," receiving, instead, "whores and rogues." But Tim was off in his locations: the "Peter Robinsons," as they were called with something less than affection by the Orange faction and the Anglo-Saxon elements, were settled in good farming country once the cover of bush was whacked down. The descendants of these immigrants are to be found in the same location to this day, but it is a location east of Lindsay, and not in the cedar bark and niggerhead country to the north. Yet this sour-looking, thin-skinned soil with its sparse covering of cedar and slippery elm had, for me, a beauty of its own, although, as Tim Connolly said, most of that land would "run you fifty bushels of mixed rocks to the acre."

Sour land will more often than not produce sour people. I wondered about the kind of people who would swear half-lies and mixed truths about a man like Dansinger who had got a gutful of war and dead men and trench stench and hated all wars from then out. When the Second World War broke out in September of that year, I remember Dansinger talking excitedly, as many Germans do when the fervour of argument is on them, about the folly of war. And who should be more aware of it than Dansinger, who, as James Parnell Slattery said, was a cavalry man unhorsed and stuck in the trenches when the armies became immobilized and stuck in the mud and chalk of Flanders.

I felt even angrier about Laurel. She was born in Canada. I commenced to have second thoughts about patriotism.

Bride looked completely beautiful and terribly grown-up in a white knitted dress with red accessories. "This outfit is a present," she said, shyly proud, looking down at her crimson leather shoes with half-high heels. "From Nancy Murtaugh."

"Nancy Murtaugh!" I exclaimed.

"Uh huh. She came down to see me last week. She said she'd sold several paintings and was feeling 'spendy.' "

"There's a Christmas card from her at home. First I've heard from her since she left," I grumbled.

Bride stretched her neck and kissed me on the cheek and cuddled beside me, basking in the warm air of the car heater. "Oh Patch, it's wonderful to be going *home!* But I'll have to bake pastries and stuff for Christmas dinner, and then there's New Year's and I got you a tremendous present. Wait 'til you see it, Patch. Oh golly, I don't know how to roast a goose or a turkey."

"Whoa up, mule!" I laughed. "We can buy the pastry stuff at the bakery in Foxford. Shit! Surely to God we can roast a rooster between the two of us. I got some decorations up; winter-berry and stuff like that. And I got you a present, too. So there." I smiled down at her—at her little white knitted hat. I thought she was the most beautiful person I'd ever seen.

"How is old Belial? Does he miss me? You should get a dog, Patch. For company. You shouldn't be all alone in that great gloom of a house. Are you drinking a lot lately?"

I sorted out the questions and answered as best I could. I didn't tell her about the drinking. That I had Sib Parker or Danno Moran buy me whiskey in Lindsay. That I was knocking off nearly a pint a day.

Bride fell asleep before we reached home. I picked her up and carried her—a warm kitten—into the house and placed her gently on the bed in her old room.

About dusk on Christmas Eve Bill Doherty came striding through the snow from his lonely shack a mile through the woods to the north where he was cutting cordwood. He coloured in embarrassment when we gave him his gifts: a box of toiletry items from Bride and the Bull Durham from me. His enormous hands fumbled with the wrapping and seals.

"Oh, don't tear the paper," he protested when Bride went to his assistance, "it's pretty." Later, when he had admired the men's cologne, sniffed the after-shave talcum, and run a finger over the sleek luxuriance of a highly scented bar of hand soap, Doherty rolled a nimble smoke.

"I didn't bring you two anything," he tried to apologize, but we shouted him down. We sat in the parlour with a big bowl of punch sparkling in the light from the gilt chandelier. I noticed that when I twined princess pine in the light fixture I had neglected to clear away the spider webbing. Bride made the punch with cider, a little whiskey, and red wine.

Uncle Miles sent us word on Christmas day he would be unable to come. He sent word by Tim Connolly who was staying with Miles that winter, cutting wood and doing barn chores.

"He said to tell you," Tim blustered, rubbing his hands over the kitchen range, for the weather had turned sharply cold, "he has to watch over a cow that's givin' calf. He can do his own lying. He went off on a drunk three days ago and I don't expect to see him until the middle of January."

"Oh well," I told Bride, later, "he wouldn't have been much fun anyway."

Bride's lip quivered and her eyes grew bright with tears. "We hardly have anyone now," she cried. "Uncle Miles doesn't care! There's just you and I and an old lawyer in Lindsay. Oh Patch, we haven't much left!"

Her hair was like the raven's,
Her eyes were bright as coal,
Her cheeks were like the lilies
Out in the rain and cold.

33

There was a New Year's party at the Kennedys'. Ed had joined the Toronto Irish and was home for his first leave over the holiday. Lila, herself, drove out on St. Stephen's day to invite Bride and me.

She ran into the house smelling sweet and cool, her coat with the fox-fur collar fashionably unbuttoned to show a moss-green dress. She hugged Bride warmly.

"Bridgie O'Fallon! You're getting too lovely for Lindsay High. They don't deserve you. Come to Toronto." Lila was working as a stenographer at the John Inglis factory, a plant that had bitten off some tremendous war contracts.

"And Patch!" She turned to me and let me hold her graceful body just long enough to seduce the old magic I felt for her out of hiding. "Patch, I don't hear anything of you except you keep back here all to yourself and shoot at people you don't like."

"I miss seeing you around," I said, fumbling awkwardly for the words.

"I miss you too, Patch," she said soberly. "It's the war–it's everything. The whole world is changing."

Light streamed from every window in the Kennedy house when Bride and I drove up on the eve of the New Year. The old folks had cleared out, visiting Violet Kennedy's brother, Murt Dolan, and his wife Sadie, in Orillia. Young Ed was home, looking dashing in his uniform with the high green beret pulled over the left ear, and the Irish green kilts with the tightly-tailored khaki jacket. He was surrounded by adoring young girls and he used a lot of new in-service expressions such as "I'll buy that," and "I got news for you." I openly envied him and longed for the day, not far off, when I would reach my seventeenth birthday and could enlist in the navy.

Most of the old Kilmore gang was there, and some from other places I did not know. Johnny Browne and his wife, Edith, Piper Mulvihille, Thad Whalen, Rose Hanley, Frank Teague, Dingo Poole, Johnny McKelvey, and even Len Malloy from Shugan's Swamp, looking slyly vicious. Malloy had brought a girl from over east of Mavely–a thin, rake of a girl in a cheap print dress and with eyes set too closely together under furry brows giving her the look of a knowing musk-rat.

Niall Sweeney came in uniform, too; the khaki of the Midland Regiment. With him was a darkly vivacious girl I recognized as Delia Leger from the French Settlement in east Clifden Township.

Lila was being possessively attended by a navy fellow in the square rig worn by petty officers, but the dark buttons and red flashes on his single-breasted uniform coat showed him to be a naval writer, a kind of clerk pen-pusher. He had wavy hair and a pink and white complexion. Lila introduced him as Kirk Maitland. He talked as if Toronto was the centre of civilization, that once beyond the sacred precincts of Bay and Bloor streets the world ended. I was intensely jealous of the way Lila leaned back in his arms and stroked his milk and water face with her fingers.

Bride wore a dark, hooded cloak over a scarlet dress; her long raven hair bounced about her shoulders. Johnny McKelvey grabbed her immediately and whirled her away as the string band broke into "Over The Waves." I looked around and joined Thad Whalen and Piper Mulvihille in a corner.

"What are we drinking, Patcho?" Piper beat one finger against his palm in tempo with the music. I said I had a bottle of Irish whiskey, John Jameson's, out in the car.

"What'd I tell you!" Piper crowed. "The man's a millionaire. He owns a distillery." He linked his arm with mine. "Patch, me brave lad, leave us drink your health. That was never your own sister? She'd strike the eye from your head. Look at McKelvey glow."

Thad, Piper and I slid out of the side door and walked the half block to where the Dodge was parked. I brought out the dark bottle of whiskey and pronged the cork.

"Mother of Jesus have mercy on me, a thirsty sinner." Piper tilted the bottle and swallowed with joy.

Whalen grabbed the whiskey away. "Come out of that, you sponge-gutted christer, and leave a man have a chance." He raised the bottle, saluting the blear disc of a moon now surrounded by a huge, circular halo hazy with muted rainbow colours. Thad drank heavily, then lifted his voice softly to sing:

"Beautiful, beautiful brown eyes–
I'll never love blue eyes again. . . ."

I caught the edge of melancholy in Thad's lilt. I looked at Piper, my eyebrows forming a question.

Piper shrugged. "Rose Hanley. Got someone else on the string. Didn't you see him inside? Fella from Oshawa workin' at the General Motors."

"I'll kill him! As sure as Christ died of blood-poisoning I'll murder the bastard!"

"Sure, you will that," Piper soothed. "But all in time, Thadd-o, me buck. The night's young and the Lord made time enough to go 'round."

I slugged down a few swallows of whiskey. Irish whiskey is pot-stilled from roasted barley malt, but unlike scotch no smoke from the drying kiln is allowed to mingle with the whiskey and the Irish brands have not that smoky flavour. The whiskey had a strong, exhilarating bite. I drank again and passed the dark bottle over to Mulvihille. He drank and capered comically around the automobile.

"O, young Lochinvar rode out of the west;
No hair on his balls, no hair on his chest;
He stopped not for brake and he paused not for stone—
And jerked off in the village where whores there were none."

Thad had disappeared inside the house. I replaced the whiskey under a cushion on the car seat and Piper and I followed. The band, a blue-grass type of ensemble calling themselves the Gull River Valley Boys, were hammering out a whip-paced break-down, and several couples were whirling through a square dance, Bride among them partnering, this time, with Len Malloy. He winked at me over my sister's shoulder. I glowered back.

When the dance finished, the musicians dipped their flushed faces in mugs of lager and ale. The dancers, perspiring and excited, sought chairs ranged around the parlour, or the girls ran upstairs to the bathroom while the boys stepped out the back door and paid tribute to the lilac bushes against the back fence.

I took Bride's hands and pulled her to her feet as the band swung into a two-step. She moved quickly about the powdered floor, her body hot and strong against mine.

"Well, it was late last night
When poor Willie came home;
I heard his mighty rap on the door. . . ."

sang the banjo-picker.

Bride buried her face in my chest. "Oh Patch, Patch," she cried. "I'm all torn. I'm so happy and so awfully sad at the same time. I feel like the time when you shot the pig. I was so proud of you and so anguished over my poor doll . . . !"

294

I manoeuvred out to the outside circle of the dancers where we could eddy slowly in front of people sitting in chairs. I dropped my face to the warm fragrance of Bride's hair, playfully nuzzling her with my nose. She mewed and held me closer.

"Patch," she murmured. "I feel strange."

"Have you been drinking Johnny McKelvey's home-brew?" I teased.

Bride shook her head. "I guess I'm not much of a drinker. Some Fallon, huh?" Her fingers played accordion rhythms along my back. "I can't explain it, Patch; but it scares me . . . I'm frightened. Patch . . . Do you feel something–something for me?"

The voice of the singer rose high and sweet above the room noises:

"The last I heard from my mama dear–
She was a-doin' well;
Sayin', 'Stop them rowdy ways, my child–
Save your soul from hell.' "

"You're my kid sister, aren't you?" I pretended incomprehension.

"I know, and that's just it! Brothers! Sisters! What are they supposed to feel for each other? Just a peck on the cheek and a squeeze of the hands? Like with a boy from Lindsay High after a Gene Autry movie and a banana split at Wong Lee's? Patch, I cry into my pillow for you at nights. I cry for the romps we used to take along the Sally and across the meadows. And how we used to climb on old Belial's back and punch our heels into his ribs. Do you remember once we lay in the hay-mow. . . .?"

"Oh hell," I said, embarrassed.

"But what is it," Bride cried, shaking me. "Why am I so unhappy? Why do I need you so, Patch?"

I swung my head mutely, feeling my eyes scald over with tears. Niall Sweeney pulled at my arm.

"There's a scrap going on outside. Thad Whalen and somebody. You better come on out."

"They don't need you," Bride protested but I left her and followed the uniformed figure of Niall outside.

A mass of young men were poured onto the street under the frosty bulb shining high under its porcelain reflector on a hydro pole. In the centre, Thad was down on his hands and knees, blood trembling from his nose and sprinkling the tire-packed snow. His face looked raw and pulpy. A heavy-set fellow of about twenty-five stood defensively beyond the fallen youth; his knuckles were cracked and bleeding. Backing him were two strange men of the same age. The three looked warily around at the muttering, cursing Irish who stood around them.

"That's that fucker Rose Hanley's been stepping out with," Niall told me.

Piper Mulvihille pushed through to where we were standing, shivering under the cold starlight after the warmth of the house.

"Old Thad took a mean trimming. That Oshawa bastard's pretty handy."

A struggle broke out in the crowd around the Oshawa men: a knot of tusslers striving and cussing with Jim and Frank Teague in the centre swayed and shoved toward the strangers. I recalled that the Teagues and Whalens were cousins. A handful of local boys—Dingo Poole, Len Grady and Johnny McKelvey—were attempting to prevent the Teagues from getting at the Oshawa men. Thad stayed on his hands and knees, head sagging, mumbling through broken lips. Suddenly the oldest of the brothers, Jim, broke free.

"You cocksucker!" he howled, and the Oshawa man fell back against the hydro pole, blood welling thickly from a deep gash over one eye. His two buddies moved in on Jim and, seeing this, the others let free of Frank who immediately kicked one in the nuts and dropped the other with a straight punch to the mouth. Jim and the burly Oshawa fellow milled and slipped in circles, hitting, sprawling, with the stranger holding his own until Jim ran in, head low, to butt his opponent in the stomach, then grabbing him by the shoulders and driving his head flush into the man's face. He fell forward, his face blotted with blood and his own vomit. Frank crashed his boot against the jaw of the first fellow he'd downed, then aimed a similar blow at the second who was rolling about, clutching his crotch in agony, his face as white as the snow in which he wallowed.

"Fuck that, Frank," I looped an arm around his neck and hauled him backward. He struggled and my feet slipped sending us crashing to the street, Frank on top, but I had him cinched in a deadly elbow-lock.

"Jesus! Jesus! Jesus Christ! Let go of me, you cunt of a Fallon or I'll kill you!" he raved.

Jim Teague, an eye turning puffy, turned toward us. He circled where we lay, trying to get a clear punch at me, but with my neck grip on his brother I kept Frank between us.

"They're licked, Jim," I snarled. "You kick them like that you might finish them. They're not worth a good man spinning rope."

"You takin' up for them?" he panted.

"Don't be a damn fool," Niall Sweeney put in. "Patch ain't turnin' on his own." Johnny McKelvey and Len Grady sided in.

"Turn loose of Frank," Jim ordered. I released Frank's neck and got warily to my feet. Frank rolled over, leaped up and swung hard at me, his fist skinning my ear. I ducked and caught him in my arms and held him. I was surprised to discover how much stronger I was although I doubted I could ever strike as fast and as deadly.

"Cut it out, Frank," his brother said. He gave me a gap-toothed grin and punched me on the arm. "I hear you got some drinkin' whiskey in your car."

"We'd better get some into Thad," I said, soberly. Jim and I went over and, one on either side, lifted him to his feet. His face was a mess. Tears squeezed from under his swollen, discoloured eye-lids.

"I'll kill him, Jim," Thad sobbed.

"We got 'em," Jim growled; his voice sounded as if it was grating carrots. We half carried Thad over to my car and I tried to get whiskey down his throat. He puked, gagged and spit out blood, bits of teeth and phlegm. He wailed like a child. Jim tipped the bottle and let the strong liquor drain into him. I took a couple of good belts, then between the two of us we succeeded in getting some of the fiery stuff into Thad. He slumped on the running board and cried like a baby.

"Fuckin' no-good goddamn wimmen," Frank, who had come up for a drink, spat into the snow. "How come you clamped me, Patch?"

"I felt like a little wrestle. I'm glad you only hit my ear. You got a kick like a fuckin' kangaroo."

Frank looked pleased. "Your bottle's all gone." He heaved it across the street. The out-of-town men groggily and silently shuffled toward an automobile parked far down the street. A handful of cat-calls and threats swirled at them from the victorious Irish group.

"Let 'em go," Johnny McKelvey said quietly.

A knot of girls among whom I could distinguish Bride cluttered at the open front door of the Kennedy house. They parted and Rose Hanley, coated and with her silk scarf about her hair, pushed through, marched, head high, down the steps and up the sidewalk.

"Rose!" Lila Kennedy called, once.

But the girl looked and walked straight ahead. When she came abreast of the Oshawa car, a door opened and she got in. And that was the last the village saw of Rose Hanley. She married the Oshawa fellow, had kids—so I learned in later years—and lived in a brick bungalow and bought a new General Motors car every second year. Once a year she and her children came back to visit Rose's parents. She never spoke a word to anyone in Kilmore; not even Lila Kennedy. A long time after I came back from the war an old Foxford man pointed a teen-aged boy out to me and said his name was Ernest Dzaman and that his mother was Rose Hanley.

"You remember Bob and Eileen Hanley that used to live in that stucco house on the River Road? Bob was at The Crusher for years. Well, Rose was their girl. The old ones is gone now, but you remember Rose?"

I remembered.

Sheepishly, we made our way back into the house, but the musicians had lost their spirit and the dancers circled aimlessly. Bride was dancing with Johnny McKelvey again; they moved tightly together and I was pronged with spears of jealousy. Lila Kennedy, body aflame in a fire-red dress that was bouncy at the knees, swept me into her warm arms and we glided, by her direction, toward the inner parlour. Lila held me tightly so my face was averted from Bride and Johnny. When we were in the parlour, Lila placed her palms on my cheeks, cupping my face. She kissed me long and tenderly and I felt the salt twist of her tears running down both our faces.

"It's all changing, Patch," she cried. "Everything's changing so. And I put out my hands to stop it or slow it and everything runs through my fingers like smoke or sand."

I eased my knee gently between her legs, hearing the soft intake of her breath; her breasts pressed to me until I felt the hard fleck of her nipples.

"Patch," she breathed.

"Let's go. Let's go somewhere."

We were out under the blue bite of the stars and walking toward my car. Len Malloy and a man I didn't know were drinking from a quart wine bottle. As we passed Len bared his dog's teeth in a yellow laugh.

"How about a gang-splash?"

As he raised the bottle to his mouth I struck him full force across the bridge of his nose smashing it in a bloody, splintered mess against his face. He made an ugly, choking sound, then screamed like a woman. I threw my arms around his companion and we fell, grappling, into the road. I curled my legs around his waist, squeezed, rolled him over and drove fist after fist into his face until he threw up his arms and cried out for me to let him alone.

I got to my feet, panting. I knocked the loose snow from my clothing. I caught Lila's elbow and we continued on to the car.

Later, when the heater had warmed the little coupé, and Lila lay snuggled in my arms, naked except for silk stockings and garter-belt, she cruised her fingers slowly and deftly where I'd never been touched before. We mingled slowly and dreamily. Time and time again.

The first waft of dawn sprang up across the ragged edges of the gravel pit cliffs where we were parked; the stars lost their points of fire and a sickly pallor crawled up the eastern horizon. I pulled the car around, after wrapping Lila in her coat over her semi-nudity, and wheeled toward the Kilmore road. As I did so we passed another car that looked like Johnny McKelvey's old Model A. As I looked I thought I saw my sister's face at the window looking out—looking white and frightened and fierce all at the same time.

"What th' hell!" I slammed on the brakes, but Lila's touch on my cheek was cool and steady.

"Nothing ever stays the same, Patch. Bride is growing up."

I drove on and I didn't notice the stark look of the road-side houses against the wrecked dawn or the stricken, sympathetic cry in Lila Kennedy's eyes. I absently kissed her at her gate and left her tucking her clothing about her before she went along the walk that led to her side door—a walk bounded by a chinese elm hedge whose few withered leaves clatted in the bright, bitter wind of New Year's Day.

I drove to Danno Moran's where a sodden party had reached the crawling, puking stage. I bought a bottle of cheap rye whiskey and drank most of it before I got home.

Bride was home and standing in the centre of the kitchen. As I stared wordlessly at her she raised her arms in a half-gesture of hopelessness and explanation. I walked toward her. My feet were encased in concrete. My hard, light eyes stared into her own dark blue ones. I tried to see something there that

300

would make it all right, that would banish the nightmare and her seven ghastly foals back to their horrible pastures. But I saw only a kind of numbness.

I fell at her feet then; fell on my knees, and my arms went round her legs and I buried my head in her thighs and I trembled as fiercely as a man about to mount the gallows. I trembled but I could not cry. On my neck I felt the splash of my sister's tears.

"Why, Bride?" I said, my voice muffled and broken. "Why?"

Her hands were gentle on my shoulders, but her tears continued to fall on my head.

"Because you did first. Because of you."

On my last leave home before being posted to sea aboard a corvette I stood on the wooden platform of the Toronto & Nipissing at Kilmore, smoking a Player's Medium cigarette and laughing down at Bride, who was trying to laugh back but her laughter was full of tear-hooks and she kept choking on them. I had given her an armful of budded red roses and she held them so her raven hair and blue eyes mingled with the crimson buds.

"They're American Beauties," I laughed, "but they look fine on a Canadian beauty."

The whistle gave a short hoot. The conductor swung his hand. "Board!"

I grabbed Bride and held her to me for a long time. The last time I saw her she was racing along the plank platform in her high-heels, waving and waving and clutching her armful of roses, her eyes awash with more than tears.

I never saw Bride alive again. At the time she needed me, I was in the middle of the ocean, and I knew nothing of the anguish of the days before she died.

34

There are days when, filled with dissatisfaction with my bachelor's existence, I jump into my automobile and drive the hundred-odd miles north to the burying-ground where, with I the only exception, all of the Fallons lie. There is Grandfather Matt, and his wife Hannah—who loved Fiddling Jack Doyle. There is the mound of my father; yonder lies Uncle Miles. In a row are my aunts—the three sisters of my father. Nearby are buried some of the Dorgans—kin to ourselves through marriage.

Near the fence under the pines that whisper all day and shiver through the night is the tiny marble cross made from a dark stone native to the County Kilkenny. The cross is made in the Celtic fashion—a circle binding the stem and cross-arms. On that cross, chiseled deep, I read again:

> SACRED TO THE MEMORY OF
> BRIGID MAEVE FALLON,
> BORN IN THE YEAR OF OUR LORD, 1925.
> DIED IN THE YEAR OF OUR LORD, 1942.
> DEARLY BELOVED DAUGHTER OF
> THE LATE WARD FALLON,
> AND MOST DEARLY BELOVED BY
> PADRAIC FALLON, HER ONLY BROTHER.

I look up through the dark green boughs of the pines and the sky is almost as blue as the eyes of my sister—Bride.

Then only say that you'll be mine,
And in no other's arms entwine
Down beside where waters flow . . .
On the banks of the O-hi-o.

I took her by her lily-white hand,
And I led her where the waters wound;
I threw her into the river to drown
And watched her as she floated down.